9/10/16

WINFIELD PUBLIC LIB

P9-CDJ-884

3 7599 00026 6344

THE BAD DECISIONS PLAYLIST

THE BAD DECISIONS PLAYLIST

MICHAEL RUBENS

CLARION BOOKS
Houghton Mifflin Harcourt
Boston New York

Clarion Books
3 Park Avenue, New York, New York 10016

Copyright © 2016 by Michael Rubens

All rights reserved. For information about permission to
reproduce selections from this book, write to Permissions,
Houghton Mifflin Harcourt Publishing Company,
3 Park Avenue, 19th Floor, New York, New York 10016.

Clarion Books is an imprint of
Houghton Mifflin Harcourt Publishing Company.

www.hmhco.com

The text was set in Bembo Std.
Book design by Lisa Vega

Library of Congress Cataloging-in-Publication Data
Names: Rubens, Michael, author.
Title: The bad decisions playlist / Michael Rubens.
Description: Boston ; New York : Clarion Books, an imprint of Houghton Mifflin
Harcourt, [2016] | Summary: "Sixteen-year-old Austin, a self-described screw-up, finds
out that his allegedly dead father happens to be the very-much-alive rock star Shane Tyler.
Austin—a talented musician himself—is sucked into his newfound father's alluring
music-biz orbit, pulling his true love, Josephine, along with him"—Provided by publisher.
Identifiers: LCCN 2015028509 | ISBN 9780544096677 (hardback)
Subjects: | CYAC: Fathers and sons—Fiction. | Musicians—Fiction. | Rock music—
Fiction. | Love—Fiction. | Decision making—Fiction. | BISAC: JUVENILE FICTION /
Performing Arts / Music. | JUVENILE FICTION / Family / Parents. | JUVENILE
FICTION / Social Issues / Drugs, Alcohol, Substance Abuse.
Classification: LCC PZ7.R8295 Bad 2016 | DDC [Fic]—dc23
LC record available at http://lccn.loc.gov/2015028509

Manufactured in the United States of America
DOC 10 9 8 7 6 5 4 3 2 1
4500603361

For my mother, Donna Rubens,
who had a great laugh
1944–2014

CHAPTER 1

I went looking for trouble / and trouble went looking for me /
well me and trouble, we met in the middle /
what a sight for the devil to see

I'm lazy, and I'm a coward, but I'll do pretty much anything if
a girl is watching.

And there're several of them watching right now, really
good-looking ones, maybe the best-looking in school, at least
in that blond cheerleadery sort of way, because that's what they
are — Alison Johnson and Kate Schwartz and Patty Nordstrom
and Marcy Ueland, all of them calling out to me and laughing
and egging me on.

Which is why I'm doing something this dumb-ass stupid,
standing in the canoe like a Venetian gondolier as I wobble
my way across Cedar Lake, paddling an erratic line toward the
beach where they're all stretched out like languid kittens in
bikinis.

"Hold tight, ladies!" I call out. "I'm coming to serenade you!" They cheer and hoot and applaud.

Whoa. Bad wobble. High-wire moment of flailing arms and stuttery teeter-tottering, then I recover. Not sure if the weed is helping or hurting.

"I'm fine! No worries!" I announce, and keep paddling.

How many different flavors of stupid is this? A few. First off because *of course* it's not just the hot cheerleaders on the beach, it's the hot cheerleaders and the four massive scowling guys from the varsity hockey team, and even from fifty yards away I can tell that they're a lot less amused by my impending visit than the girls are. I can make out a torn-open case of Miller High Life and lots of empties on the beach, and each hockey player has a can in his hand. Just what they need to make them less aggro: beer.

As I was climbing into the canoe, preparing to set off from the little willow-protected cove where Devon and Alex and I were smoking the world's worst pot, Devon said, "Dude, Todd Malloy is over there."

Todd Malloy, legendary bully and scourge of the Edina public school system. Not nearly the biggest of them all, but by far the meanest. The sort of person who would push a kid with cerebral palsy. Which he's done, because I saw him. And then punch the kid who makes a halfhearted attempt to intervene. Which he's also done, because I saw that, too. Up close, because that intervener was me. I got a black eye for my efforts, and there wasn't even a girl watching.

Just before I pushed off, Devon said, "What are you doing? You think you're going to add those girls to your playlist?"

His term, not mine, for the girls I've been with.

"What you're going to do," he said, "is get your ass kicked."

"Where's your sense of romance and adventure?" I asked him.

"Where's your sense of not getting your ass kicked?"

"It's all right," said Alex, who I'd thought was asleep, his spiky bleached punk-rock hair crunched into the damp sand. "He won't even make it over there."

Which is probably accurate. That's part two of the stupid. Everyone knows you shouldn't really stand up in a canoe, especially when you're a wee bit altered, but of course being a wee bit altered tends to make you forget those sorts of facts. I'm pretty likely to do a header into the lake, and I'm not a great swimmer, so there's a good chance I'll drown and get eaten by carp.

Which might actually be a blessing, considering I've got the mandolin slung over my shoulder—stupid part three—and it won't survive a dunk in the murky gray-green water any better than me. And it's not just any old mandolin. It's an *actual* old mandolin, a beautiful bluegrass mandolin. Vintage. Antique.

Also . . . it's not exactly *my* mandolin.

Strictly speaking, it belongs to Rick the Lawyer, my mom's boyfriend. He bought it to demonstrate to her that she's rubbing off on him, that he's learning to be like her, to be *fun! Yayyy!* A grateful lab rat in her grand project, Extracting the Stick from Rick's Rectum: *C'mon, Rick! Let's take swing-dance lessons! C'mon, Rick! Let's go to the circus! C'mon! Let's go on a hot-air-balloon ride! C'mon! You should get a hobby! Wheee!*

3

So he surprised her by getting the mandolin. Except you know how often he plays it? NEVER. And you know what it sounded like the few times that he has? ASS. It's just another expensive thing for him to collect, like the way he *has* to have the most expensive watch and *has* to have the Audi TT, and the carbon-fiber bike that I think he's ridden, like, once, and the frigging seventy-two-inch flat-screen TV in his downtown Minneapolis apartment. Which, yes, is the penthouse.

He brought the mandolin over to our house about six months ago during one of their "sleepovers"—that's what my mom calls it when they both need to get some—and then he left it there. I think he was sort of showing off—*Look at my new toy!*—because he knows I like to play instruments and write songs and whatnot, and other than a twenty-five-dollar keyboard and a garage-sale ukulele, all I have is the crappy guitar my mystery dad left behind when he died, which was before I was even born.

Sleepovers. Just call them humpy-humpy time. I'm sixteen. I get it.

I always used to ask my mom about my real dad—Who was he? What did he do? What was he like? She'd deflect and deflect and deflect, until finally one evening at dinner she blew up and slammed down her fork and said, "He was an *asshole,* okay?"

I was six. That's the last time I asked.

Anyways, the mandolin. Rick leaves the mandolin at my mom's, but he also tells me not to touch it. Like he's taunting me. Actually, he tells *my mom* to tell me: "Honey, Richard would prefer that you only handle the mandolin when he's there to supervise."

I need you to understand how beautiful this mandolin sounds. Not plinky-plinky and annoying, but rich and warm and lovely, tobacco and honey and brilliant stars in the summer night sky.

It seemed a shame to keep that loveliness trapped and voiceless in a hard-shell case, so I started pulling out the mandolin and researching stuff on the Web and practicing a lot while my mom earned her twelve dollars an hour at the salon doing the nails of rich Edina ladies. I'm pretty much crap at, let's see . . . everything. Life in general, really. But I can sing, and I can play things. I can play guitar and ukulele really well, I can play keyboards not too horribly, and I'm no Chris Thile, but now I can play this beautiful mandolin.

So earlier today, when Devon came rattling over in his dying Subaru and asked if I wanted to head to the lake and rent a canoe, I said, Hold on, let me grab something.

Let the stupid commence.

* * *

What other stupid things have I done for girls?

In third grade I walked across the top of the monkey bars in the school playground because Martha Meinke was watching. I entertained her with the little dance I did in the middle of the bars, and then by breaking my arm when I fell.

I lost a tooth and gained a concussion for Danica Morgan, something involving a steep hill and a sled and a jump and an oak tree.

I gave Kelly Harmon a ride around the block in my mom's

car, which resulted in exactly zero injuries to either car or occupants, but I still got in trouble, seeing as how I was thirteen at the time. Grounded for two weeks, no TV, no sweet cereal, no comic books, no Internet, but worth it for the kiss I earned.

Later on, things got more complex.

I started running for Samantha Wu. That lasted three days and one puke.

I took Spanish because Annie Narcisse idly mentioned that she wanted to know what the Clash were singing in the background of "Should I Stay or Should I Go." That lasted one semester and a D minus.

There was a brief and really weird episode I'd rather not go into where I joined an evangelical church group because of Jennifer Vikmanis.

I started smoking for Gretchen Olson. I tried to stop smoking for Abby Winter. There was trail hiking for Jessica Clift, PETA stuff for Elizabeth Conner, astronomy for Lara Denton (late nights; lots of naughtiness under the stars). I have a messy blotch of an abandoned homemade tattoo on my forearm which I started for Erin Baltimore.

What else?

Oh, right, the only thing I'm *really* ashamed of: For Hayley Benson I pretended for several months to like EDM.

And now today's adventure.

"Are you ladies ready for awesomeness?"

"We're ready!"

"Totally!"

More cheers and hooting. More dark scowls from non-females. I'm about twenty yards from the beach.

Did I mention that, amid all the other stupid, I shouldn't be here at all? Because I shouldn't be here at all. Where I should be is at the first day of summer school. Math. I have particular issues with math. I need to overcome those issues, or I'll be repeating eleventh grade. So Monday mornings are reserved for summer school. But the weather is so nice this morning, and I'm sure I can just show up next week, and *carpe* YOLO . . .

Ten yards. Todd Malloy is sitting up now and glaring at me, his irritation further evidenced by the complex rhythm he's tapping out on his thigh with one hand, and on Alison's incredible behind with the other. Weird fact about Todd Malloy: talented drummer. Or was. He used to play in the school band, and even when he was thirteen the upper school would ask him to play the drum set during school concerts. You'd think we'd be kindred spirits, united by music. But no. At some point Todd went to the dark side and became a jock, and jocks at my school don't play instruments, they beat up people who play instruments.

My voyage is coming to an end in unexpected safety. I hop out into knee-deep water and drag the canoe onto the sand.

"Greetings, ladies!" Bows and little curlicue hand gestures, like a French aristocrat, the girls applauding. "I have arrived to entertain you! And you gentlemen, too!"

Alison, the loveliest of them all, says, "Hi, Austin!"

Todd Malloy says, "Hey, nutsack, get the hell out of here."

"Todd!" says Alison, swatting at him. "Go ahead, play us something. Strum a tune!" She claps her hands grandly.

7

"'Strum a tune'?" says Todd. "He's going to run away and pee himself."

"Okay," I say, "just to set the record straight? I did *not* pee myself. Any requests?"

"Yeah, but you sure pussied out, didn't you?"

"There were extenuating circumstances."

"Yeah, like you're an extenuated pussy."

I will explain this exchange later, okay? It's excruciatingly embarrassing, and at the moment I'm pleasantly buzzed and there are girls and let's just leave it for now. Thank you.

"Well, at that time I didn't have such a lovely audience," I say. Really, I'll explain soon. "So who's got a request?"

"How about go screw yourself?" suggests Todd.

"A great song, but not for mixed company!" I say jauntily. Then, in cheesy lounge-singer voice, looking right at Alison: "How about a special tune for a special lady?" She smiles back at me. "Here's an oldie but goodie by Elvis Costello. Anyone? Elvis Costello? No? Okay. The song is called"—dramatic pause, smoky slow-mo wink at Alison—"'Alison.'"

"Awwwww!" say all the girls.

"Dude, you don't get out of here and I'm gonna smash your friggin' ukulele over your friggin' head," says Todd.

"No you won't," I say in the same jolly tone. "Because it's not a ukulele. It's a mandolin!" The girls are giggling. I play a chord. "Isn't that a gorgeous sound?"

Todd gets to his feet. I don't think he appreciates the subtle acoustic overtones this mandolin produces.

"I'm warning you," he says.

Todd is wearing a shirt that says FIGHTING SOLVES EVERY-THING.

"Todd!" says Alison. "Go ahead—play!" she says to me.

"Thank you."

I start playing, singing the opening verse.

"Awww!" say all the girls again.

GLERRRK!! That's the sound the mandolin makes when Todd lunges at me and clamps a hand on the neck of the instrument, strangling the sound.

"Whoa whoa whoa! I haven't even gotten to the chorus, the part where I go, *'Aaaaaaalison. . . .'"*

"Todd, stop it!" says Alison.

Todd yanks violently on the instrument, pulling it out of my hands, the strap popping off from the bottom peg. "Um . . . could I have that back?"

"I warned you!" says Todd.

The intelligent reaction here would be terror. But no. I'm stoned, I'm pissed off at Todd, the girls are all watching, and I can feel my pulse rising and my grin getting manic.

"I'll tell you what," I say. "You just go ahead and hold on to that, and I'll finish the song a cappella."

"Do you think I'm bluffing?"

"Oh, Aaaaaaalisooo—"

WHANGCRUNCH!

This is going to be a really bad conversation with Rick.

CHAPTER 2

I didn't crash and burn / I was on fire before the impact /
finished the third before the first act /
made sure to lose / before they attacked me

I have all this music in my head.

I hear it most often at night. Not like I'm writing it. Like I'm hearing it, fully realized. I lie there, listening to it, enraptured. Sounds and sweet airs, that give delight and hurt not. The thousand twangling instruments humming in Caliban's ears, that when he wakes he cries to dream again. I want to capture it, but when I try it's like embracing a cloud.

Sometimes it happens during the day, and when I was younger I'd freeze in place, my eyes distant, face slack, as it played. My mom took me to a specialist to see if I might have a seizure disorder, but they didn't find anything.

I have words, too.

Lots of words, lyrics that materialize from nowhere. A

nonstop conveyor belt of words, words tumbling out of me, scribbled on random scraps of paper and thumbed desperately into my phone, each new snippet of song fighting for attention before I can complete the one that preceded it.

Devon calls me Half-Song Austin.

Maybe you should focus on finishing *one* of them, he suggests.

Or put a bunch together, says Alex, and you'll have, like, ten great songs to perform.

Perform? He can't even get up on a stage, counters Devon.

True story.

I have some sort of mental block. Once there're more than, say, a dozen people in front of me, they become an Audience, and I can't. I just *can't*. There're always just . . . *problems*. Things happen. I've somehow managed to screw up or flake out on every opportunity I've ever had to perform in front of a real audience:

* The big party in Jean Salita's backyard: Got a little too stoned beforehand.
* The open mic at Calhoun Coffee: Got lost.
* The second open mic at Calhoun Coffee: Got the date wrong.
* The third open mic: Weed again.
* The fourth open mic: Don't be foolish. There was no fourth. Three-strike rule, friends.

They were all honest mistakes, I say to Devon.

Uh-huh, he says.

Honest or not, they pale in comparison with my real masterpiece. Which brings me to that explanation I promised earlier.

Jennifer Donaldson was in choir, and I wanted to impress her. You would too, if you saw her. So I auditioned for choir. Then dropped the class after a week, because really? *Carmina Burana?* But Mr. Peterson, the choir teacher, was always trying to lure me back. "Open-door policy, Austin!"

So, a few weeks ago: It's late in the afternoon on the day of the year-end choir concert. The kid who was supposed to sing the solo on Leonard Cohen's "Hallelujah" gets stomach flu. A panicked call from Mr. Peterson: "Austin! I have a situation! Do you know the song? You do?! Listen, I'm going off the reservation here, because you're not a member of the choir, but . . ."

I decline. He counters with promises of extra credit. Mother gets involved, applies pressure. I retreat to my room to consume illegal substances. Judgment altered. Bad decision made.

The concert is practically starting when I arrive. No time for rehearsal, just a rapid set of instructions, Mr. Peterson grabbing me by both shoulders and saying, "Austin, *thank you.*"

Five songs in and it's time. The band is vamping. The choir is on the risers, *hmmm*-ing and *oo*-ing. The sold-out auditorium is silent and expectant. It is now the moment for Austin Methune to stroll from the wings to the spotlight-illuminated microphone and break everyone's hearts with the purity of his singing.

Except Austin Methune never materializes. He is otherwise occupied, being at that moment in the prop room with a certain senior named Emily Sanderson and having lost track of time.

Which in the perverse high school scoring system you'd think might launch me into hero status. Except I couldn't even get any cred for it: Emily made it clear that if I told anybody (a) she'd deny it, making me look like a pathetic liar, and (b) her boyfriend would adjust my life span to however long it would take for his fist to travel to my face. I couldn't even tell Devon or Alex, because any vow of eternal silence from them would be good for about an hour. So the conventional wisdom became that I simply chickened out, and it was humiliating and agonizing and *argh argh argh* I can't bear to even think of it. And I can tell myself that there were extenuating circumstances, that I didn't pussy out, as Todd so crudely puts it, but . . .

I pussied out.

Sheer self-sabotage.

So when I say I'll do anything if a girl is watching, I will.

Except the one thing I really, really want to be able to do.

"Maybe," Alex told me once, "maybe you just need the right girl watching."

Devon says, "Half-Song, you can't finish anything, and you can't perform. You won't put anything online—"

"Have you *seen* the comments people put on there?"

"Fine. Whatever. So how's your Big Secret Plan going to work?"

The Big Secret Plan: The second I graduate high school, I'm heading to New York. I'm going to be a singer-songwriter like Jeff Tweedy or Rhett Miller or Shane Tyler. And I'm going to write songs that make people think and feel, and I'm going to be successful and famous. I'm going to be successful and famous and inhabit the distant orbit that people like that do, free from gravity's smothering pull, the pull that drags everyone down into sameness and sadness and defeat. Free in a way almost no one gets to be.

I have yet to present this plan to my mom.

I love her, and she's awesome, but holy *fuuuuh* can she be moody. Like, she enjoys it when I sing old songs to her or make up silly verses and play them, then abruptly she'll get sad and say, okay, that's enough. The one time I floated the idea of me not going to college, because what's the point, she reached over, took the guitar from me, and said, "If you ever say that to me again, I will slap the crap out of you."

I believe her. Three weeks ago, I was listening to Shane Tyler's *Good Fun from a Safe Distance* on CD, something dusty and untouched from her collection. She yelled at me to turn it off. I didn't. She stomped downstairs, ripped the CD out of the tray, disappeared. Then there was a horrific ten-car pileup of a noise, an explosion of grinding and popping and whining gears, the sound a garbage disposal makes when it's force-fed a CD.

Moody.

A seizure disorder. Christ. I just want to listen to the music. You understand, right?

* * *

The music.

When Todd hits me with the mandolin, the music explodes in my head, a cacophonous burst like a cosmic orchestra and choir tuning up, fireworks erupting behind my eyelids.

Somewhere behind the noise, I can hear everyone say, "Ooh!" and I stagger, stunned, my hand coming up. The orchestra and choir are fading, my vision returning as I unscramble my brain and reconstruct what just happened—did he really just hit me?—and that's when I spot the crushed mandolin lying in the sand, so deeply wrong, like a swan with a broken back. I whisper, "Oh, crap."

I drop to my knees and stare dully at the mandolin, dimly aware of everyone else repeating *Oh, crap!* too—in surprise and dismay in the case of the cheerleaders, pure joy for the hockey players. They're laughing gleefully and high-fiving each other. Alison is saying, "Todd! *Todd!*" and swatting at him.

"I friggin' warned him!" he keeps saying. "I warned you!" Like that somehow makes it reasonable that he has clubbed me over the head. I pick up the wrecked mandolin, gently brushing the sand off of it, and all I can think to say is "Dude, that's so uncool, that's *so* uncool," over and over, and I think a majority of rational people would agree. Not the hockey players, though—they clearly think it's so *very* cool, about the coolest, funniest thing they've ever seen.

On the plus side, the cheerleaders respond by gathering around me in a cooing, protective cocoon, mothering me, making sure I'm okay, pausing now and then to direct a high-pitched rebuke at the jocks. Alison is particularly solicitous, which, awesome:

"Austin, are you sure you're okay? You poor thing. *TODD, YOU ARE SUCH AN ASSHOLE!* Oh, you poor thing, you're bleeding!"

Her attention, of course, just makes Todd even more pissed off. "Methune, you better take your goddamn banjo the hell out of here or I'm going to hit you again."

"*TODD SHUT UP YOU ASSHOLE! DON'T TOUCH HIM!* Let me see your head, you poor thing."

I play up my injuries and indulge in the coddling and, yes, probably push things a bit too far, especially when I do my best Cumberbatch and tell Alison, "My God, you're absolutely *gorgeous*," and profess my love (all the girls: *Aww!* again). It's also possible that I tell her my phone number and ask her several times to call me. Which leads to more pushing and shoving, with me on the receiving end, which leads to Alison shrieking at Todd, "We are *SO BROKEN UP!*"

Boom. Dramatic, stunned silence. Open-mouthed wide-eyed oh-my-God looks between the cheerleaders. Todd's turn to stagger, like *he's* been clubbed. Total reality-show highlight-reel moment.

Then everyone turns to me as it dawns on them that Alison's abrupt dumping of Todd means she no longer has any sort of leverage over him or his behavior. Meaning *I* have no leverage over him either. Meaning time to go. Now.

I sprint to the canoe and launch it with the ruined mandolin in one hand, then toss the instrument into the half inch of water at the bottom of the boat and sprawl into it myself, all clumsy awkwardness and banged limbs and digits as I struggle to get upright and wrestle with the oar and start desperately paddling, Todd and his buddies pelting me with clods of wet sand and sticks and at least one half-filled beer can that comes within an inch of cracking me on my already-injured skull.

When I'm far enough offshore, I shout back at Alison, "Call me! I love you!" and duck another Miller High Life.

*　*　*

Devon and Alex are waiting for me when I get back to the cove, wading out to help pull the canoe to shore, holy crap—ing about the busted-up mandolin and the blood trickling down my face from the wound near my hairline.

"Dude, what the hell!" says Devon. "I *told* you—"

I cut him off, a hand held up for silence.

"Oh, great," says Alex. "He's got another song."

Indeed I do. I sing them the snippet I'd been working on as I canoed my way back to them: "I crossed the night-black waters / the dark and angry sea / to tell you that I loved you / and ask if you loved me"

"Yeah," says Devon, "and then you got your ass kicked."

*　*　*

I ride back home in Devon's car, Devon telling me he's just about had it with my crap and berating me for ruining the afternoon and never paying for the weed and for getting blood on his seats. He adds, "Half-Song, here's what I don't get. You go over to serenade those girls, even though you *know* you're gonna get mauled. But you can't just get up onstage and perform? You're frigging useless."

"That's okay," I say, "you don't have to try to cheer me up."

Next: What do I do about the mandolin?

Get rid of it, Devon says. If and when they figure out it's gone, act dumb, say maybe it got stolen. They can't prove anything.

Fake an accident, says Alex. Fall down the stairs with it, pretend you're hurt. Get their pity.

"I could just fess up," I suggest.

"True."

"You could. You could fess up."

Pause while we all consider that.

"Fake accident?" I ask.

"Fake accident," they agree.

Rick will be over at some point next week, I figure, and I'll offer to fetch the mandolin, and then — *crash thump bam* — I'm falling down the stairs, and *Oh, no! What have I done!*

It's going to work.

I drop the mandolin at home and ride my not-at-all trusty motorcycle to the market to do my shift as a grocery packaging technician — *Paper or plastic?* — and conjure up some texture and detail for the narrative as I work. I'm still adding finishing touches on the way home and walking up the front path to enter the house, and —

My mom and Rick are sitting on the brown sofa in the living room, the mandolin on the table in front of them.

"Austin," says Rick, "may I speak with you?"

Like I said, this is going to be a really bad conversation.

*   *   *

"If I were still a prosecutor for the District Attorney's office, I would address the court and say, 'Considering the value of the instrument, one could easily make an argument that these actions constitute felony theft.'"

"Oh my God, Rick," says my mom.

It's a far worse conversation than I'd even imagined.

We're sitting in the living room, my mom and Rick next to each other on the sofa, me in the chair. On the low coffee table in front of us is exhibit A, a vintage Gibson mandolin with its delicate arching back staved in and ruined, the curvature of the splintered wound conforming more or less to the shape of my skull. Corroborating evidence: the large Band-Aid on my forehead.

"Rick," says my mom, "Austin is going to replace the mandolin." She sights down an index finger at me. "You are going to pay Rick back, mister!"

Rick waves a hand, dismissing the idea.

"No, he is going to pay you back!" insists my mom.

"I'll pay you back," I say feebly, already dreading the weeks I'll have to work bagging groceries to earn the . . . what? Several hundred dollars?

"I doubt he'll be able to do that," says Rick, "unless he has approximately four thousand dollars lying around."

Holy *shyuuuuuuuh* . . .

"Oh my God," says my mom again.

* * *

What can I do? The mandolin is still moist and covered with sand, so I tell them the truth as to borrowing it to play songs in a pastoral setting. I absolutely do *not* tell them about Todd playing whack-a-mole with my head. I tripped, I fell, there was a rock, end of story. You think I'm going to squeal on Todd? And have that get around school? No way. I'm in enough trouble as it is.

"Austin," says Rick, shifting to the slow, deliberate speaking style he uses when he's signaling that something is important, "I would feel. Remiss. If I didn't. Express. My . . . deep disappointment."

He doesn't look at me as he says it, instead delivering his disapproval to a fixed spot somewhere on the tabletop in front of him. His fingers are steepled together, and he does a little dip with his hands to emphasize each major syllable. It's only after he says "disappointment" that he shifts his gaze to lock onto mine so I can feel the full weight of his reproach.

I drop my gaze. I hate him at this moment. Just hate him. I hate him and his blond hair and designer glasses and golf shirts and Prada shoes and forty-two years, eight years older than my mom. I hate him even more so because I've provided him with yet another opportunity to play parent, a creeping and creepy pattern that's been growing in frequency since he appeared on the scene a year ago. Rick offering to take me to museums or movies or to see music. Rick buying me presents on my birthday. Rick wanting to hear my songs. Rick giving me life advice. Rick really thinks you're special, says my mom. He thinks you're great. He truly loves you. Well, guess what? I hate him.

I know what I'm supposed to say but can't.

My mom kicks me in the right shin.

"Um srry," I mumble.

"What?" says my mom.

"I'm *sorry*," I repeat.

No one moves. Then she says, "Rick, could we . . . ?"

I don't look up to see what she means, but I hear him rise out of his chair and I watch his feet and legs stride out of the frame of my field of vision. I listen to him pass me to my left and step out the door to the front porch.

"Austin," says my mother. "Austin, look at me."

I look up and feel my face flush, my heart beating.

"Austin, they told me you weren't at summer school today."

"Yes," I whisper hoarsely. "I'm sorry."

She nods. Then she reaches over to the oversize book sitting on the coffee table in front of her, lifts one side of it, and pulls out a glossy brochure from underneath. She wordlessly positions it on the table so that it's facing me.

MARYMOUNT ACADEMY it says.

The cover photo is of a line of boys my age in uniform, standing at rigid attention against a Photoshopped background of the Stars and Stripes.

I look at her, mouth open.

"I've already contacted them," says my mom. "They have scholarships. You remember cousin Eddie?"

Legendary cousin Eddie, famed in our two-member family lore for sticking up a Tulsa convenience store at fifteen. I continue to gape.

"He went there. He was being even more of a little turd than you — although you're giving him a run for his money — and it straightened him right out."

"Mom," I finally stutter, "you can't do that."

"Yes I can," she says. "I can and I will. I swear it. Austin," she says, her voice dropping to a whisper, "I love you, but you're scaring me. You have to complete your summer school. You have to graduate. You have to grow up. You *have* to. And now you do this. Austin, I just can't . . . I don't . . . I really . . ."

I see it coming and I'm cringing, steeling myself, and now

it's here, the point where she breaks down, where the tears well up and her sentences fracture into disorder and incoherence: " . . . might lose my job . . . don't want to ruin things with Richard . . . can't deal . . . can't deal . . ."

You understand it, right? How a mom can be your best bud, and fun and funny and full of life and want to take you hot-air ballooning or polka dancing and attract someone like Rick to her because of that spirit, and still be like this—so fragile.

It destroys me when she acts this way. It's far worse than the threat to send me to military school. She can yell at me or ignore me or grind CDs in the garbage disposal or throw a bowl of cereal at my head, which she did once. But this, I have no defense against it. All I want is to make it stop, to make it better.

"I'm sorry, Mom, I'm sorry," I say over and over. I feel her dread that she'll be abandoned, that Richard will go, and I realize that even though I can't stand him, I don't want him to leave my mother. And I *really* don't want to join the proud ranks of Marymount Academy. Right now, I'll do anything to fix it all. It's the new Austin from now on, hard-working, no screwing around, no stress for my mom. "I'll fix it, Mom. I'll fix it," I say, hugging her, and she garbles something at me that I think indicates she wants me to go say as much to Rick. So I do.

He cocks his head expectantly when I step out onto the front porch—*Well, young man, what have you got for me?*—and I have to fight the urge to scream. Instead I say, "Rick, I'm sorry. Really. It was dumb. I'll pay you back. I don't make very much money at my job, but I'll figure something out. I promise."

He nods sagely. "I appreciate your taking responsibility. I've discussed the matter with your mother, and also the matter of your grades and summer school. Which is equally important, if not more so. And actually, Austin, I think we can address both issues, and I'd like to propose a solution."

CHAPTER 3

I'll throw stones at you / until you notice / break your heart /
so you'll fix mine / drive you off / so you'll come closer /
I'll be your anti-Valentine

School smells different during the summer. It sounds different
too: empty and echoey and hollow. A barely detectable airy
whooooosh of the HVAC system. I sort of like it, the sense of
unrippled serenity, the interior cool and quiet and deserted,
and I feel self-conscious about the squeaking of my high-tops
on the polished granite of the corridors.

There were a few cars in the parking lot when I arrived
on my motorcycle, but so far I haven't seen or heard another
soul—I just went in door five, surprised that it was open, and
made my way through the near silence toward the classroom
where I'm supposed to meet my math tutor.

Rick has arranged for me to have a math tutor.

This is part one of the penance I shall be paying to expiate

24

my mandolin-related sins: each Wednesday I shall attend tutoring sessions to supplement my Monday-morning summer school class.

Which is annoying, but it pales in comparison with part two. Part two is indicated by the shirt I'm wearing as I *squeak squeak squeak* my way through the halls. It's a blue-collared polo shirt. On the left breast it says RICK'S LAWN CARE SER-VICE.

Did you think Lawyer Rick is just a lawyer? Oh, no.

Lawyer Rick is also Entrepreneur Rick, investor in and part owner of several fascinating businesses. One being a restaurant. One being some sort of cloud-data computery thing. The third being the creatively named Rick's Lawn Care Service.

So almost every day, with half days for summer school and tutoring sessions, I'll be an indentured Lawn Care Servant, tending the grounds of the retirement homes and industrial parks of suburban Minneapolis. It offers more money and more hours than bagging groceries. By the end of the summer I'll have enough to pay off about half of the cost of the mandolin.

The remaining debt will be forgiven if, and only if, I faithfully attend all my summer school and tutoring sessions and pass algebra.

I have signed an actual contract to this effect.

The contract being my mother's suggestion. "Great idea!" said Rick, and he lawyered one up in about twenty minutes, and then I swear to God we went to a bank in downtown Edina *and got the contract notarized*. I signed it in the presence of Rick and my mom and a smirking bald guy in a bad suit, Rick countersigned, and my fate was sealed with an embossing stamper.

Afterward, my mom stood there smiling while Rick shook my hand and patted my back with his other hand—I *hate* when he touches me—and said, "Congratulations, Austin. To a new beginning." I wanted to emboss his nuts.

But you know what? It's all good. I actually feel optimistic today. Healthy. That presatisfied feeling you get when you're being responsible and doing something that you'd rather avoid. Granted, that's not a sensation I'm all that familiar with. And granted, it's all contractually obligated.

But this morning, I'm on the right track. This morning, I'll sit with my tutor, I'll apply myself to bettering my knowledge of mathematics—it's the key to the universe, really— and after I've improved myself intellectually, I'll go and begin my first day of work and improve myself physically and fiscally. *Physically and fiscally,* I repeat to myself as I march along. *Fiscally and physically.*

I pass the room where I did English last year. I liked the teacher, Mrs. Jensen, who is one of those who's about sixty years old but will still drop an *F*-bomb and barely bother to apologize.

"You know what you are?" she said to me once, after I'd failed to complete another assignment.

"Um . . . I bet you're going to tell me."

"Yes, I am. What you are is a SmartTard."

"SmartTard. Smart and . . ."

"You know what I mean."

"Are you supposed to say stuff like that?"

"Hell no. But I can't think of a better description for you. You're smarter than lots of these other kids, but you won't get off your ass and get stuff done. I see you with books all the time. I mean, you're reading that, correct?" Pointing to the copy of *Infinite Jest* I'd been lugging around lately, admittedly a bit ostentatiously. "Or is that just some sort of affectation?"

"I'm reading it," which was true in that I'd reread the first half chapter several times.

"Good. I was beginning to wonder if you were functionally illiterate. What else have you read?" she said, so we played checklist: Hemingway, Vonnegut, Steinbeck, Kerouac, Pynchon—

"Oh, c'mon."

"No, seriously. Or I tried."

"So why can't you turn in a goddamn assignment? What's wrong with you? They not giving you the right mix of meds?"

I explained the complicated varieties of meds and therapies I had received over the years with somewhat dubious results.

"Also," I added, "we're trying this new thing now where I get more healthy male guidance in my life. Which apparently is important."

"Male guidance," she said.

"Right."

This was just after my mom broke up with Loser Tom, who followed Total Loser Phil (preceded by Absolute Disaster Chris), and right before she started dating Lawyer Rick. She signed me up for a Big Brothers thing where a guy came by once a week, a guy who decided that the ideal shared activity would be basketball. Which I think is called misreading your audience.

"Male guidance," repeated Mrs. Jensen.

"Yes."

"Maybe you just need to pull your head out of your ass."

Tough but fair, that Mrs. Jensen.

She ended our conversation by saying, "Someday, you'll figure out what your problem is, and *maaaaybe* you'll achieve something. For now, do yourself a favor and try to focus more on the smart part, and less on the 'tard, okay?"

Less on the 'tard. Copy that.

Today, and going forward, is all about smart, and not about 'tard. *Smart not 'tard. Physically and fiscally. Smart not 'tard.*

I get to the classroom. I pause outside the open doorway, making sure I'm clear of the sightlines of anyone in the room, reshoulder my backpack, rehearse my excuse/apology for missing the Monday session of summer school, and go in.

And stop.

There's a girl in the room. A girl my age, blondish hair. She's standing on the other side of the conference table that dominates the space, focused on putting books into her own backpack.

There's a shallow part of my brain—okay, it's mostly shallow parts—but a specific part whose job it is to alert me to the presence of attractive girls. And that part says, *Oh, hey.*

And then another part immediately says, *Really?* Because she's not at all the type of girl I'd usually notice. Not that she's *bad*-looking or anything, and from what I can tell she does have a pretty good body, particularly her—

Which is precisely when she chooses to sense my presence and look up. *Erp.*

Our eyes lock. We're both motionless. She has the book

halfway into the backpack. There's something about her gaze—I feel pinned by it, a thief in the spotlight, guilty—and I'm waylaid by a sudden and nearly overpowering urge to start babbling an apology.

Then she returns her focus to her book, shoving it the rest of the way into the bag, and the moment is over. "I was just leaving," she mutters. She zips the zipper.

"Oh," I say. I recognize her now: She's in my grade, one of the Smart Kids, student government and debate team and math club and all that. I feel like I've seen her somewhere else, too. Jessica? Geraldine?

She fixes me with that X-ray gaze again. "That's it?" she says. "'Oh'?"

"Um . . ." I say. *Oh, you're really weird?* "You don't have to leave . . . ?" I venture.

"You're over thirty minutes late."

Now I'm *really* confused.

"I'm here for a tutoring session at nine thirty," I say.

"No, it was scheduled for nine."

"How do you know? Are you here for a tutoring session also?"

"Uh, yeah, I suppose you could say that."

The force of sarcasm is strong with this one.

"Okay, well, even if it was supposed to be nine o'clock, the tutor's not even here."

"*I'm* your tutor!" she practically shouts.

I probably should have read the email more carefully. It probably specified the correct time, and also that my tutor is a *peer* tutor. Then I remember that Devon had made some joke about it, because he did the same program last summer.

It's called Peers Helping Peers, which Devon shortened to "PHaP," as in, I gotta go do some phapping.

So here I am, late for my first phapping session, and my peer doesn't look at all eager to help out her peer.

"I'm really sorry I'm late," I say.

She shakes her head and sighs, making a big deal out of unzipping her backpack and pulling out the textbook, dropping it onto the tabletop with a *thump*. Then she sits with another dramatic sigh, just in case I don't know that she's pissed off.

"I'm Austin," I say.

"I know," she says, opening up the textbook.

I'm still standing. "What's your name?" I ask.

"Josephine."

"Josey?"

"Josephine."

"Sorry. Got it. That's a nice na—"

"Can we start? We only have twenty-four minutes left, and then I have to go to work."

This is going great.

I sit. She flips through her notes and textbook as I get myself prepared, feeling flustered and off balance. *Do not,* I remind myself, *start running your mouth.*

Just then she looks up sharply and says, "Did you just smoke a cigarette?"

"Yes?" I say.

"Can you please not do that?" she says.

"Um, yeah," I say, and scratch at my ear. *Oh, God, Austin, do* not *start running your—* "The thing is, they totally trick you and put this nicotine stuff in there?" *AUSTIN, STOP*

30

RUNNING YOUR— "So, one day you're like, I'm gonna try one of those burning-stick things, because they look so cool and all that, and the next thing you know you're this pathetic object lesson in the dangers of marketing and peer pressure and you're getting lectures from people you just met."

Wonderful. Great job. I'll just step out now and let you handle things from here (footsteps; door slams).

"Fine," she says. "Could you skip the burning-stick things right before we meet? I'm allergic to it. It makes me throw up."

"Throw up? From smelling it? Who throws up from smelling tobacco?"

"I do. Do you want me to prove it to you? Happy to do so."

"No, I'll take your word for it. Any other allergies I should know about?"

"Yes, gluten," she says, then mutters so quietly that I barely hear her, "and jerks."

"You should say 'assholes,'" I suggest.

"What?"

"Instead of 'jerks.' 'Assholes' is funnier."

"I wasn't going for funny. But fine. Assholes."

"Excellent. Well done."

Tiny eye roll from her. Any optimism I felt earlier is long gone. I drum on the table. *Doot doo doo.*

"So," I say, "what kind of music do you like?"

She looks at me.

"Kidding," I say. "Isn't that what people always ask to break the tension? 'Hey, what kind of music do you . . .'"

Arched eyebrow.

31

"Never mind," I add.

"Okay," she says. "So—"

"What about Wilco? Feist? The National? No? Tegan and Sara?"

Unchanged expression.

"Shane Tyler? Do you like him?"

"I don't know him. Should we maybe—"

"Really? He's my current fave. You should check him out."

"I'll make sure to do that."

"Shane Tyler. S-H-A—"

"Got it."

"I can make you a playlist, if you want."

Her eyes narrow.

"What?" I say.

"Nothing. Can we—"

"So where do you work?"

"Can we begin?"

"I'm just asking. Now, me? I work in the burgeoning field of lawn care," I say, stretching the shirt with two hands to better display the logo. "I mean, I'm just getting my start, but I gotta say, I'm pretty optimistic. Big things coming for me. *Big* things."

"I bet. Now we have about twenty-two minutes left."

"Honestly, I'm sorry about being late. I thought it was at nine thirty."

"Okay. But even if it was at nine thirty, you were still late."

"Point taken. Agreed. I also had some trouble getting my bike started, so that slowed me down a few minutes."

"Fine. What did you go over in class?"

"Uh . . . Right. Class. I have to be honest. I sort of didn't make it."

That penetrating stare again, making me squirm inwardly. She says, very deliberately, "What."

"I didn't make it."

"You blew it off."

"Yes. True. You've never blown off a class?"

I might as well have asked her if she'd ever killed and eaten a hobo.

"I'm gonna take that as a no," I say. "And you've never been late."

"I try not to be."

"I really *am* sorry about that, okay? You've never screwed up or broken a rule?"

Stare.

"No," I say, "of course not."

"Twenty-one minutes."

"Right. Sorry. Let's start."

"Fine. So—"

"Okay: The light is red, but there's not a single car in sight. No cars at all. Do you cross?"

"*Argh!* Look, I get it, okay? You're a rebel who rides a motorcycle and is too cool to do math because you're going to ride off on your motorcycle and do rebel motorcycle things and you won't need math."

"Whoa. Hold up. It's only a 175 CC, so it barely qualifies as a motorcycle. The 'CC' in this case referring to—"

"The cubic displacement. I *know.*"

"Oh, do you know motorcycles?"

"No, I know *math,* which is what we're supposed to be working on."

"I bet Jack White or Ryan Adams or Conor Oberst isn't that good at math."

"Fantastic. Let's see, are any of them here? Oops! Nope! Looks like it's just us."

"Well, I'm going to be like them."

"What about your great career in lawn care?"

"Well, yeah, of course. I figure after a few months of mowing lawns I should have several million bucks socked away. But honestly? Can I tell you a secret?"

"Um . . . no?"

"My plan—which is a secret—is I'm going to be a singer-songwriter."

"A singer—"

"Songwriter. Yes."

"You're going to be a performer."

"Yep."

"Onstage."

"Yep."

"In front of people."

"Yes!"

She looks at me evenly. Then shifts her gaze, mouth open slightly like she's trying to figure out how to word something or whether to say it at all. She shakes her head and says, "Good luck with that."

I realize how I recognize her.

Choir.

She's in the choir. She was one of the people left standing

there on risers, humming and *oo*-ing endlessly while I was otherwise involved.

My face is prickly hot.

"So. What chapter did they cover in class?" she says. "You don't know."

"No," I mutter.

"Didn't think so. What do you want to work on? Quadratic equations? Factoring polynomials?"

"I don't know. Whatever. It's all good. Let's go. Boom."

"Right. Well."

She claps the book shut and stands up.

"This," she says, "is not going to work."

* * *

She doesn't say another word as she crams the books into her backpack and walks out of the room, ignoring my *Aw, c'mon*s and *Look, let's just start again*s. No, that's inaccurate. She says one thing, to herself: "I'm such a fool."

"I signed a contract!" I say. "You don't understand! I have to do this! You can't leave me like this!"

She leaves me like that.

I listen to the squeaking of her shoes receding down the hallway. Then I clap my hands together and announce to the empty room, "Fantastic! Okay! Let's go repay Rick!"

Except I'm not going to repay Rick. Instead what I'm going to do is screw up again and die.

CHAPTER 4

I'm gonna be smiling when they find me /
because I've left it all behind me

I'm going to—am *about* to—die, a gruesome, spectacular splatterfest of a death. A death caused by a commercial-grade lawnmower and my own stupidity.

And Josephine. She deserves at least some of the blame.

Sccrrrttcch goes the gravelly soil under my sneakers as I skid another few inches toward perdition.

"Help," I squeak, but I'm straining and out of breath and can't get any volume behind it. Not that it matters—I doubt anyone else on the lawn crew could hear me over the roar of the machine, even if they weren't wearing the big rifle-range ear protectors we've all got.

I am on a very steep slope.

Directly downhill from me is the narrow top of a retaining wall.

Directly downhill from the retaining wall is lots of air to fall through.

Directly *up*hill from me, and pushing me inexorably downhill toward the retaining wall and the air and death, is a four-hundred-pound walk-behind mower, its knobbly wheels churning uselessly as it slides slowly in the wrong direction.

Sccrrtch. Now the balls of my feet are on the retaining wall and skidding backwards. When I run out of wall, the machine and I are going over the precipice. And if the fall doesn't kill me, the weight and vicious twin blades of the mower will.

I think it qualifies as ironic that the job Rick got me so that I can pay Rick back is going to instead cost Rick more money, because cleaning up my remains is going to require hiring a white-suited HAZMAT team equipped with wet-vacs. Sorry, Rick.

"Okay—important item: Don't use a big mower on the steep sloping areas. Use the smaller push mower. You copy?"

Those were Kent's instructions, which I should have listened to. Kent being the REALLY HEALTHY-LOOKING pre-law college student who manages the crew and has FANTASTIC TEETH and INCREDIBLE HAIR and a REALLY POSITIVE DEMEANOR and CHARISMA and is basically the purified essence of every church youth group leader ever, the sort who is going to just friendly-enthusiasm you into a life of RIGHTEOUSNESS and JESUS. Exactly the guy Rick would hire. When I arrived, he approached me with a big smile, used his God-salesman grip to crush the bones in my right hand while squeezing my shoulder muscle with his other hand—the alpha-bro handshake, you know it?—and said, "*Hola, amigo!* Boss-man Rick tells me I need to keep a special eye on you. So first thing, a little tough love: You're late."

"What? I thought—"

"It's eleven twenty-six now," he said, showing me his watch. "You're supposed to be here at eleven."

"Sorry, got a little lost, and—"

"No explanations necessary. Tomorrow you're here at eight thirty for the team meeting, right?"

"Team meeting."

"You bet. Every morning. Go over the goals for the day, get the team spirit up. But, Austin? If you're late again tomorrow, don't come back." Pat-pat on my cheek. "All right, *vamos*—the others have already started."

He gestured out toward the vast hinterlands. I spotted a few distant figures mowing, the grounds of the retirement community so extensive that I was pretty certain you could see the curvature of the earth.

He introduced me to the walk-behind mower that will soon be killing me, showed me how to fuel it, start it, and operate it.

"Austin, you know how to walk in a straight line, go back and forth?"

"Yes I do, Kent."

"Outstanding, Austin. Go do that over there," he said. "But what are we not going to do?"

"We're not going to use a big mower on the slopes."

"Exactly. What are we going to use?"

"We're going to use the small push mower."

"Outstanding. Get going."

I started off on the field he had indicated and went back and forth, back and forth, each trip taking several centuries. It was intensely boring. I don't know why the residents need acreage like this—I guess to gaze at and recall their youth during the Civil War while they ponder the peaceful hectares of lawn and trees and landscaping, all of which needs mowing and tending and will presently become the scene of a grisly accident.

While I worked, I argued with Josephine.

Out loud, my own words inaudible to me. Crazy guy, walking back and forth, quarreling with thin air.

It started with me replaying the things she had said to me, and I'd think of new ways to respond. *Oh, yeah?*

Pretty soon, though, fantasy Josephine had taken control, saying entirely *new* things that real Josephine hadn't. Criticizing me, my life, my Big Secret Plan, my everything, telling me I'm lost and rudderless. *And even if you did have a rudder, it wouldn't help, because, let's be honest, you don't have a map, or even an engine.*

Okay, Josey—

Josephine.

Fine. I didn't ask you.

Why did she get to me so much? Who was *she*, anyway?

You, *Josey*, are just some girl who is never late and has never blown off a class and would give someone that disapproving grownup frown if they crossed against a red light. I don't give a crap what you think of me, *Josey*.

I really don't. I don't care what she thinks.

Is what I kept saying. But the squabble kept going, me doing my best to parry and counterattack, and even though I was conducting both sides of the argument, she was winning, slicing me to ribbons.

It was that way she looked at me. Like I couldn't fool her at all.

Your usual nonsense will not work on me, Austin Methune.

Around the time the argument was really heating up, I was mowing along the wooded edge of the slope on which I was supposed to use the small push mower.

Somehow that rule turned into all the other obstacles in my life—the mandolin, Rick, the contract, Kent, everything, and I was thinking, *Screw it, I'll show you all,* and just then Josephine's lecturey voice popped into my head: *Don't be stupid!*

"Would you just SHUT UP!" I bellowed, and did a hard left-hand turn down the slope.

The mower immediately started sliding.

Panic.

Turn nose uphill. Sliding continues. Sudden terrible clarity regarding Kent's instructions.

I told you so.

"Shut up, Josey!"

Josephine.

"Argh!"

Now my body is one straight line, my arms extended over my head, hands in a death grip on the mower. I'm leaning so far forward that my nose is only about two feet from the twenty-degree slope, my quivering body at an acute angle to the ground. Or is it an obtuse angle? Which is pointier and narrower?

This is why you're in summer school!

"Yes, got it, thank you!"

Stuck on a ledge, wheels spinning helplessly.

Which, you realize, is a pretty accurate metaphor for your life.

"Zip it!"

My feet are slick with grass juice. I'm sliding backwards, six inches from the edge of the retaining wall. Five. Four.

Then I spot him. Right at the top of the ridge that I shouldn't have descended. Another member of the lawn crew, silhouetted against the blue summer sky, armed with a gas-powered weed whip, concentrating on trimming the fringe around a nearby tree. Salvation!

"Help!" I shout. "HELP!"

I don't know if it's because he heard me or sheer chance, but he turns his head and looks down the slope and spots me. I don't get a good look at him because the sky behind him is so bright. He takes a few steps down the slope toward me, which brings him into the dappled shade of the trees. He pulls off his yellow eye-protection goggles and stares at me and my predicament, and in that moment Todd Malloy and I recognize each other.

"Help," I say. "Help!"

A big smile spreads across Todd's face.

Then my foot slips and I go over the edge.

* * *

Things you think about as you're tumbling violently downhill with a twin-blade lawn mower hurtling just inches behind you: *GAHOHMYGODI'MGONNADIE!!!*

Which I *am* thinking, plus *GAHOHMYGODTODD-MALLOYISONMYLAWNCREW!!!*

So, no, I'm not dead, but it's still early.

A few milliseconds ago: My foot slipped.

I bailed, jumping backwards off the retaining wall, which turned out to be somewhat less than a hundred feet tall and maybe more like five.

The ground where my feet hit was mossy and even more steeply sloped than that above the retaining wall, meaning it threw me directly into a brutal backward somersault and kept me rolling downhill—which is what saved my life for the time being, because the mower came crashing down an instant later right on the spot I had just vacated.

Now it's all straight-up action movie, an action movie featuring a murderous lawn mower and a stoner idiot.

Tumbling, head-over-assing, mower right behind and now somehow upright on its wheels. Get my feet under me, stumble desperately forward and down, death machine on my heels, the two of us doing a fifty-yard dash down a leaf-covered, wooded, double-black-diamond slope. *Root! Hole! Low branch! Rock! TODD MALLOY IS ON MY LAWN CREW!*

Shallow creek just ahead at the bottom. Hurl myself into it—Aaaaah!—*splash*, turn just in time to see the mower barreling toward me and then *FWOOOM* hit a hidden bump that alters its course and then *CRASH* it front-ends into a tree trunk and *clunk* the engine cuts out.

Everything is suddenly very quiet. I can hear birds chirping and the breeze in the branches above me and the soothing gurgle of the stream. And from far above me, the sound of Todd Malloy's hysterical laughter.

Better, perhaps, that I had died.

Then things get worse.

CHAPTER 5

I'm not waving / and I'm not drowning /
and I'm not feeling no fear / 'cause I'm not even here . . .

"Austin, we're glad you're home. We'd like to speak with you."

!!!

Oh, God. They know. They know about Josephine and
the lawn mower and Kent, and they know that I've already
violated the contract and that Further Steps will have to be
taken, Further Steps that might mean me wearing a uniform.

It's even worse because they're not angry. They're smiling—no, *beaming*—at me, arms around each other. They
were both standing there, my mother and Rick, just inside
the front door when I opened it—I went, "Eep!"—and it's
almost like the situation is reversed, like I'm the one who had
opened the door from the inside and found two eerily jovial
people on the front porch, there to share some life-changing
literature with me. Or to announce, *Hello, we'll now be cheer-*

*fully escorting you to the van that will take you to rehab and please
don't resist we have stun guns.*

"Glabble blabble gotta take a shower florble!" I say, or
something like that, and they both chuckle and say, "Of
course!" And then part like swinging doors to let me pass,
Rick giving me a thump on the shoulder as I go by.

I stumble up the stairs as fast as I can, even the air resistance
a source of pain to my battered carcass. I get to the bathroom,
close the door, and lean against it, panting. *Think. Think!*
When you get in trouble and they're smiling, you know you're
really in trouble. Because whatever they have planned as punishment is so insidious and awful that it's actually giving them
pleasure.

Damage control. What do I do? Tutor! Fix the tutor thing!

I turn on the shower to help block out the sound and call
Josephine.

"Nope" is the first thing she says.

"Josey—"

"Josephine."

"Josephine, please, I'm really sorry about what happened
today. I was a total jerk. I was hoping you'd—"

"Austin, I can't be your tutor. I made a mistake. It's not
you, it's me."

"You know, I hear that from girls a lot."

"Fine. It's *not* me, it's *you*. I don't want to be *your* tutor.
You specifically."

"Josephine, I just—"

"Sorry, I have to go."

She cuts off the call.

I cry in the shower. I cry partly because most of my body is either a bruise or an abrasion and it hurts so much. But mostly I cry because of *everything*. It's actually just a follow-up to lots of earlier weeping, the first occurrence being a few hours ago when I was at the bottom of a ravine, soaking wet, bruised, bleeding, and draped over a commercial-grade lawn mower that was refusing to start. This after an hour of yanking fruitlessly on the starter cord, until my hands were blistered and my arms so weak I had to stop. If that's not a low point in one's life, I'm not sure what is.

Which is an even better metaphor.

Yes, Josephine. Thank you.

I kicked the thing. I hugged and stroked the engine and murmured pathetically like it was a wounded animal. I sang it several songs.

And, yes, if anyone asks, I can say I've kissed a lawn mower, because following the tears and stroking and singing it finally roared to life after a single feeble pull, and then it was one long mow of shame up a side path to continue my work.

Then, when I was done, Kent fired me.

He was waiting for me by his pickup truck, checking his watch. Nearby, Todd Malloy and Brad Zohlner were leaning against a car, grinning in anticipation. Brad being the third member of the close-knit and harmonious crew of Rick's Lawn Care. My strongest memory of Brad is that he likes heavy-metal T-shirts and that he was good at using a spot welder to fuse two triangular pieces of sheet metal into throwing stars in eighth grade shop class, which was about the limit of his achievements.

"Austin!" said Kent. "I told you. We have to finish by six. It's nearly six twenty. That means you're fired."

I instantly burst into tears again, babbling through sobs and snot about contracts and losing my tutor and begging him not to fire me, while Todd and Brad fell all over each other, the hilarity too much for them to handle.

"Please," I said to him. "Please, please, please."

Kent stood there, arms crossed, not saying anything.

"Please," I repeated. *Bloop,* said a snot bubble as it burst after ballooning from my right nostril.

Silence. Then Kent nodded.

"Congratulations," he said. "You passed."

"I w-w-what?" I blubbered.

"Austin," said Kent, "I will take this passion that you're showing right now as evidence of your commitment to this team." WHERE DO PEOPLE LEARN TO TALK LIKE THIS? "Are you truly committed?"

"Yes."

"You're committed to this team?"

"Yes, I am truly committed to this team."

"Can you apologize to your team members for letting them down and making them late?"

Arrraaarrrraarrrr. . . .

"I'm really sorry, team members, for letting you down and making you late."

"Excellent. All right, Austin, if you are truly committed to this team, I will give you one more chance. One more."

Okay, I exaggerated. Kent didn't fire me. He fake-fired me as a humiliating loyalty test.

46

I was still sniffling while I loaded the push mower onto the flatbed trailer hitched to Kent's pickup, and was just stepping off when a convertible Mercedes eased past and stopped, its top down.

"Austin! Hey!"

Holy crap. It was Alison. Of course—Todd famously lost his license after only three months, DUI. She must have come by to pick him up.

"How *are* you?" she said.

"Uh, I'm *OOOF!*"

Shoulder check from Todd as he passed by. He turned and walked backwards a moment. "You're not gonna last," he said, and winked. Then he pivoted and sauntered the rest of the way to Alison's car, jumped over the door into the passenger seat, and looked straight at me as he turned Alison's head with his paw so they could kiss, going at it for *juuust* a bit too long. *Yeah, I get it. You're back together.*

* * *

When I finish my shower, I stay up in my room as long as I dare, taking a few drags from a pinch hitter and blowing the smoke out my window as I review this shipwreck of a day and the larger shipwreck of my life.

Here's the real secret of my Big Secret Plan: The secret is that even *I* know it's a joke. *I'm* a joke. I won't be going to New York. I won't be writing songs that will make people think and feel and performing those songs onstage. I won't be going anywhere. I'm stuck at the bottom of a ravine, totally alone, useless, unable to get the lawn mower of my life started. And it's never going to change.

My mom and Rick are already seated at the dinner table when I get downstairs, and they turn in unison to smile creepily at me.

"C'mon, the food's getting cold," says my mom.

I sit, easing myself cautiously into my chair. There's a fresh salad, bread, and a big bowl of linguine with clam sauce that Rick made, my mom's favorite food. I do a quick scan to make sure there's no sharp knife within easy reach.

"Linguine?" she says.

"Sure," I say, and she serves me.

Salad?

Sure.

Bread?

Sure.

She and Rick serve themselves, trading little glances. I catch a whiff of exotic herbs from the infusion my mom is drinking out of her big Renaissance festival earthenware mug, a calming potion prescribed to her by her wicca/Reiki/ovary-magic psychic, Terry. It must be effective, because she's so uncannily relaxed right now.

"So," Rick says, "how was work?"

I stare at him.

"Really good," I say. "Really"—I make a little rah-rah punching gesture—"good."

Rick smiles and nods, apparently pleased that I'm gathering precious life lessons by virtue of manual labor.

"And the tutor?" asks my mom.

They're toying with me.

"So great," I say. "So, so great."

"Fantastic," says my mom. "Austin, we—"

"Mom, I know. I *know*. It's just that I—"

The doorbell rings.

We all look at each other.

"I'll get it!" I say, and practically leap out of my chair.

Save me save me save me.

It's a UPS guy. I dart past him and sprint across the lawn and dive into his truck and roar away to a new life in Yuma, Arizona.

It's a cult recruiter. I say, *Yes, yes to all of it, where do I sign, let's go now, now, now!*

It's a Girl Scout selling cookies. *Quick! Let's swap clothes! You go inside!*

But when I open the door, it's none of those.

It's the least likely option of all, an option that drives every thought out of my head other than *I must stop smoking weed,* which is clearly damaging my brain and causing hallucinations.

Because facing me is Shane Tyler.

* * *

As in Shane Tyler the singer-songwriter Shane Tyler. *Blue Limbo Blues* Shane Tyler, *Good Fun from a Safe Distance* Shane Tyler. CD in the garbage disposal Shane Tyler. That Shane Tyler. Standing at my door.

I goggle at him, no words coming out.

He's got his hands in the pockets of his faded and torn-up jeans, shoulders a bit hunched, his face squinted into the kind of half grimace you make when you're prepping yourself to get stung by bad news.

He clears his throat diffidently. "Uh . . . hi," he says.

"Guuh," I say, goggling at him some more.

"Um . . ." he says, like he's weighing whether to ask the question he came to ask. He fidgets, looks away for a second, then back at me. I'm aware of how loud the evening crickets are.

"Uh . . ." he says again, then scratches his head and takes a deep breath, evidently having decided to be a man and tear off whatever the internal Band-Aid is. "Sorry to bother you," he says. "Um . . . does Katie Methune live here?"

"Katie? No," I say automatically, thrown by how close his question slices to real life while just missing the mark.

"Oh," he says. Relieved, I think.

Sudden inspiration as I realize the obvious. "Wait," I say. "Did you say Kay-Dee? Like, Kelly Dean Methune?"

"What? Yeah. Yeah, Kelly," he says, perking up. "I'm a . . . friend of hers. I'm just in town a bit for this thing, and I thought—"

"Austin, who's at the door?"

My mother's voice, coming from inside. When Shane hears her, his expression changes, like he just got a big mainline shot of adrenaline.

"Austin," repeats my mom as she approaches behind me. "Who's at the—"

She cuts herself off. Shane is looking past me at her, his face a mixture of hope and uncertainty, like he's got a gift to offer and isn't sure how it's going to be received. And then he smiles.

"Hey, KD. How have you OW, CRAP! OW OW OW! WHAT'D YOU DO THAT FOR?" he shrieks, frantically shaking his head and wiping at his face, because she's just dashed her scalding-hot herbal infusion right at him, *splat* on

50

his shirt and neck and right cheek. I can't even get a word out I'm so astonished, staring at him wide-eyed as he dances on the front porch, swearing, pulling his steaming black T-shirt away from his chest to escape the burning. "KD! Are you out of your fricking—" Which is as far as he gets before *BONK* her heavy mug rebounds off his forehead, snapping his head back. The rest of his body follows that momentum, his rear foot missing the edge of the porch and finding air, and he flails his way backwards to land ass first in the hedge, moaning.

"Mom!" I say, finally able to force some words out. "Do you know who that is?!"

"Of course I know who it is!" she says. "It's your friggin' father!"

Winfield Public Library

CHAPTER 6

I got off at the wrong station of the holy cross /
and I was lost / the light too bright to see my way

"You told me he was dead!"

"I never said that!"

"What?! Mom, you told me—it was my fourth birthday, we were at the frigging nature preserve—and you told me that he died in a car wreck!"

"Oh my God, Austin, I can't believe this. You know, Terry was completely right. She predicted this month would be full of drama. She said, 'The coming month will—'"

"Mom, are you going to explain—"

"Do you have any weed?"

"Mom!"

It's twelve thirty at night and we're in the kitchen, and I swear we've been arguing like this since MY DAD showed up on the front porch earlier NOT BEING DEAD. My mom has her elbows on the tiny kitchen table, her face in her hands.

"I know you have weed somewhere, Austin."

"I want you to explain to me how you could tell me all these years that—"

"I need. Some. Weed."

"Mom, you're not supposed to—"

"I'm not supposed to *drink,* Austin. And right now it's either drinking or *smoking some goddamn weed.* Get me some weed."

* * *

You ever hear someone shriek at someone else with such rage and volume that you're worried their vocal cords will rupture and explode out of their mouth? And the shrieker happens to be your mom? And have that barely coherent uber-shrieking happen on your front yard, so that all the neighborhood can enjoy it? That's what I got to see tonight as my mom assaulted my still-alive dad with the contents of her mug and then the mug itself, followed by her fists and feet and then nearly one of the logs from the front porch woodpile as he scrabbled backwards on the lawn, trying to shield himself.

She had the log raised up, ready to do to my nondeceased father what Todd had done to me, except I finally shook off my paralysis and ran up behind her and grabbed her arm so that my continuing-to-be-alive father could continue to be alive. Up until that point, I had just watched in stunned silence as she assaulted him physically and verbally, screaming a mixture of really bad words and "Get out! Go! Never come back!"

While I was tussling with my mom and trying to get the log out of her hand, Rick came running out of the house, saying, "What's going on? What's going on?"

"Go back inside!" screamed my mom, either at me or Rick or both, and jerked the log out of my grasp and went after Shane, who was still crab-scuttling backwards, apparently aiming for the relative safety of a blue vintage Range Rover that was parked at the curb.

Rick, meanwhile, was following after my mom, saying "Honey . . . honey . . .", and tentatively reaching for her shoulder, and she was violently shrugging him off. Shane had made it to his feet and was yanking at the passenger door, then dove in and slammed it just as my mom took a home-run swing at him, batting the sideview mirror clean off the car and sending it in a fifty-foot arc into the Elofsons' front yard. When he finally got the car started up and screeched away down the block, my mother turned her ire on everyone else, trailer-park style, screaming, "What're y'all looking at!"

* * *

"Your father," says my mom now, pausing to exhale some blue-tinged smoke, "is not dead."

"No kidding," I say, and hold out a hand for the joint.

We're both seated at the kitchen table. Things are a little calmer now. Rick is staying at his penthouse apartment tonight, sent home by my mother. All other issues—including the tutor crisis—have been eclipsed.

"My dad is Shane Tyler. *The* Shane Tyler."

"Yeah, so what. Big deal. And he's your dad in that, yes, you know, we—"

"I get it." *Yech.*

"But he's not your *dad* dad, like a dad should be."

She takes the joint and puffs on it. "A dad is supposed to

54

be there. You know? That's what a dad is. Jesus, this stuff is terrible."

I give her the what'd-you-expect expression, shrugging, hands palm up to the ceiling.

"It's bad for you, you know," she says.

"Being lied to by your mom?"

"No. Well, yes, I'm *sorry,* I already told you I'm sorry. *Weed* is bad for you."

She emphasizes that point by taking another drag. You see why I might have some issues?

"So how did you," I say, trying to figure out exactly how to angle into this, "I mean, what . . . ?"

"What happened? I was seventeen. He was, what, twenty-one, maybe?"

"This was down—"

"In Austin, yes. When I lived with my dad. Then you were born, and when my dad died I moved up here with you to live with my mom. You were two."

This house once belonged to my grandmother, and my mom inherited it when my grandmother died. You think we could afford to live in richy-rich Edina, Minnesota, otherwise? No way. My mom had me and never went to college.

"My dad's the one who named you," she says. "You know that?"

"Yeah, I believe you've mentioned that several times. And also that he liked barbecue and vintage cars and took you skeet shooting. Good ol' grandpa. It's that other thing you somehow forgot to mention, that thing about—what was it? Oh, right, my dad still being alive."

"How many times you want me to apologize?"

"But why even do that? Why lie to me?"

"Sorry. I shouldn't have."

I have a whole warehouse full of *why*s for her, but I know my mom and know I'm not going to get any answers. I have a lot of other questions, too, all of them jumping up and down and waving their hands, and I'm not sure who to call on first.

"When's the last time you talked to him?" I say, because that seems a reasonable place to start.

"Since before you were ever in this world. He ran out, I shut that door, I've never taken a dime from him, I didn't want it, I don't want it, I'm not interested, I don't want him back in my life, or your life, thank you, good night. Nothing."

"That's it, isn't it. Him being who he is, that's why you don't like me playing music."

"What I *like* is the idea of you going to college and having some options in your life. That's why it makes me happy that the tutor is working out. He's helping you?"

She doesn't know. *She doesn't know!*

"She. Yes. She is. She's helping. A lot."

"Good. Will you promise me you'll study and work hard and pass that class?"

"Yes."

"And you promise me that you'll work hard at your job?"

"Yes."

"Pinky promise?"

Holds her pinky up. What choice do I have? We hook pinkies and she smiles, pleased. Then she stands and says, "C'mere, buddy," and I stand up so she can hug me. *Buddy,* like we used to call each other. And for just a moment I'm

56

five again and feel safe and warm and want to stay that way. Go back to when it was me and my mom, buddies against the world.

"I love you, you know," she says.

"I know. I love you too."

When we both sit down, we're quiet until I say, "What if Shane comes back?"

She takes another drag on the joint.

"He comes back? He's leaving in a pine box, that's what. I don't want you talking to him. He's a bad influence." Punctuating the sentence by gesturing with the hand holding the joint.

There's a beat. Then we both do a little giggling at that one.

"Austin, seriously," she says, "that guy is all sweet words and BS. He's an awful, lying, treacherous bastard."

"Aren't I, by definition, sort of a bastard?"

"You know what I mean. And you, Austin, you are not going to go looking for him. Do you hear me? *You are not going to go looking for him.*"

*   *   *

"Of *course* I'm going to look for him!"

"Mmmph," says Devon on the phone.

"I mean, are you crazy? Shane Tyler is my father!"

"Mmmph," he says again.

I started blowing up Devon's phone immediately after the conversation with my mom, text after text:

Shane Tyler is my dad!

He came over today.

My mom beat the crap out of him.

SHANE TYLER IS MY DAD!!!

Until he wrote back,

Dude it's two a.m. WTF are you talking about

I called him, hanging up twice when I got voicemail and calling right back, until he answered.

"Austin, it's two a.m.!"

"This is two a.m. news!"

So I recount the whole thing, everything: Shane's sudden appearance, my mom, the mug, the attempted murder with the log, Rick, all of it, barely pausing to breathe.

"Whoa," he says.

"Right?"

"That kind of explains it," he says.

"Explains what?"

"You."

Now he says, "Austin, this is the most amazing thing I have ever heard. It's, like, mind-blowing. Really."

"I know!"

"Can I go back to sleep now?"

* * *

I stay up for another hour finding everything possible about Shane on the Internet—songs, videos, lyrics. His Wikipedia page is bare bones: a short description; his date of birth, putting him at thirty-seven years old; a discography that indicates his last album was recorded a decade ago. No update on what he'd been doing since then or is doing now, no truly personal information. Certainly nothing about a sixteen-year-old son named Austin Methune.

There are reviews of his music, a really good one from ten years ago in *Rolling Stone*, favorable comparisons to Jeff

Tweedy and Jeff Buckley and Rhett Miller. People calling him a musician's musician. An ancient fan page. Some mentions on discussion forums, people asking what happened to him, is he dead, no, he's in Atlanta working as an audio engineer, no, he's in Nashville, no, Los Angeles, he's given up music entirely. Then I change the search to find mentions in the past few months and something pops up: a mention on Pitchfork, then one on Stereogum, both mentioning rumors that Shane Tyler, now more myth than man, is back in the recording studio after a decade of mysterious nonactivity, legendary producer Barry Perlman backing the effort. No details on where he's recording, but there are reports that he's in Minneapolis.

I have a mission! I have a goal, something to focus on!

I do a search for local recording studios, inputting numbers into my phone, a strategy forming, then get in bed.

Then get out again and do a search for Josephine Lindahl.

No Facebook page, but she's tagged in a few photos, one for Edina High School student government. Debate team, holding a trophy. Oh, look, there she is posing with the staff at a nursing home where she volunteered, because of course. I find a paper she wrote about the Plantagenets. Not much else. I go back and click through the photos of this girl I don't like but can't stop thinking about.

I get back in bed and lie there, trying to focus on the reappearance of my father and my new mission. As I'm drifting off, I hear the music. Shy at first, the instruments gently announcing their arrival as they join, intertwine, soothing me, lulling me deeper—then they abruptly scatter like frightened deer and I'm fully awake again. Pulled out of sleep by the ragged sound of my mother weeping.

Know that sound? It says that everything is not okay, won't be okay.

It terrifies me.

The last time I remember her crying with this intensity was when I was thirteen and she had to go away, and I had to stay with Devon's family for three weeks.

I see my mom like the game where you pile the sticks atop each other, the structure going higher and higher and more wobbly with each new addition. Then finally there're too many sticks and everything collapses. I'm guessing that the appearance of Shane Tyler is a big stick. I have to make sure I'm not adding another one. Plus, there's a spot waiting for me in the incoming class at Marymount Academy.

That means my mom can't know I'm looking for Shane. And it means I have to either get another tutor or convince Josephine to take me back. And it means I can't just up and quit the job, even though Todd's working on the crew. Actually, screw him—I'm determined to keep the job exactly *because* he's on the crew, and there's no way he's going to make me quit. Seriously—what could he possibly do to me?

CHAPTER 7

Come here and say that / I dare you, I dare you /
you find out how little I care / and it might scare you

"I'm gonna cut your balls off," says Todd.

Todd snaps shut the massive hedge shears to add some color to his threat. I believe him.

"Todd, I'm just trying to mow the frigging lawn."

Todd and I and the hedge shears are at the far border of a big hilly lawn, beyond a rise that hides the buildings of the office park and hides us from Kent. My walk-behind mower is sitting patiently on the grass near me, the engine running, the mower unaware that Todd intends to do some topiary work on my nether regions.

"What's wrong, Methune? You afraid?" says Brad, standing behind Todd. "You look like you're sweating."

"Uh, Todd here is threatening to cut my balls off with hedge shears," I say. "So, yeah, I'm a little nervous."

Brad sniggers. This is definitely his kind of scene.

What happened is this: It was getting near lunch. I was minding my business, head down, mowing mowing mowing along the pedestrian pathway by the parking lot, thinking about how I was going to use my day off tomorrow to find Shane Tyler. I look up, and who's there? Alison, standing right in front of me, smiling and waving at me. I can't hear her over the noise, but I can see her lips forming my name — "Austin! Austin!"

There's her car, parked by the pathway. She's holding a brown paper bag. Todd's lunch. *She brought Todd his lunch,* like she's his mom. I stopped the forward motion of the mower and walked around it to go greet her.

"Hi!" she said, or shouted, speaking over the racket from the engine.

"Hi," I said, or shouted.

"How *are* you!" she says, all bright and cheery, and gives me a great big hug. And holds on. Right as Todd comes into my field of view. Looking not at all bright and cheery.

There was a brief flash when I thought of going out in a blaze of glory, of pulling Alison into a ballroom dip and kissing her on the mouth. Instead I decided to keep living, and separated myself from her as quickly as possible.

"I'mfinegoodtoseeyouIgottakeepgoing!" I said, and turned and quick-stepped it back to the mower, wrestled it in the other direction, and made my getaway at three miles an hour, not even glancing back.

Cut to about a minute ago. I'm mowing near the edge of the trees, and suddenly, *boom,* I'm shoved down on the grass, and when I scramble to my feet *SNAP SNAP SNAP* Todd starts chasing me around with a giant set of scissors.

Now he's advancing toward me, shears at the ready.

"Todd," I say, "why don't you put those down, and we can settle this like real men?"

"Okay," he says. He drops the shears.

"Actually," I say, "can I borrow those?"

Brad sniggers again.

"I don't like you, Methune," says Todd.

"Really? Things seem to be going so well between us."

"Why are you here?"

"Why am I . . . ? I love the land. I love the smell of grass and gasoline. What do you mean, why am I here? I need a job, Todd. And you know what? It's actually your fault that I'm here, so, yeah, there's a little poetic justice for you."

Confused rottweiler expression from him.

"I want you off this crew," he says.

"Off the crew? Listen, Top Gun, it's a lawn-care service, not a team of fighter pilots. Other than our stupid team meeting, we don't even have to talk or deal with each other ever."

The Kent meeting, which of course ends in one of those hands-in-the-middle pregame-style "GO TEAM!" things.

"You know what, Methune? Just seeing you makes me sick. So you're gonna quit."

"No, I'm not. I'm not gonna quit. You can beat me up if you want to."

"Okay."

"No! I'm just saying that! You can't actually beat me up! You understand that, right? You hit me again and I'll tell Kent, and I'll go to the cops, and I'll frigging tell my mommy if I have to. And if you come another step closer to me, I swear I'll poop in my hand and start throwing it at you."

He hesitates. More brow furrowing that suggests there's some basic cave-bear-level cognition going on.

"Oh, just beat his ass already," says Brad.

"Right," Todd says, and starts stalking toward me again.

"Hey!"

A new voice, commanding and authoritative, freezes Todd in his tracks. Cue dramatic trumpet sound. Cue my savior, Kent, his golden mane backlit by the sun as he crests the rise on his trusty steed, a Simplicity Cobalt 32 hp riding mower.

"What are you doing!" he shouts down to us. "Get back to work!"

Todd goes to retrieve the shears. Brad fires up his weed whip. I head back to my mower, which requires me to walk right past Todd.

"You're gonna quit," he says.

I point to my headphones and Brad's weed whip.

"What?" I say. "Can't hear you."

* * *

"Can I help you?"

"Uh . . . I think I must have the wrong house."

It's the next morning. I'm standing at the front entrance of a massive mansion in west Edina. I think—thought—it's Josephine's house, but the person who answered the door and is standing here judging me is an insanely beautiful girl. I recognize her now—she was a senior and on the cheerleading squad when I was a freshman, and we all harbored impure thoughts

64

about her. What was her name . . . ? Jacqueline. Jacqueline . . . Lindahl. Holy smokes, goddess-level hot Jacqueline Lindahl might be Josephine Lindahl's older sister.

"Okay, well, bye," she says, and starts to close the door.

"Wait," I say. "Is this Josephine Lindahl's house?"

She pauses, then reappraises me with amused curiosity, a literal head-to-foot, foot-to-head sweep—with special attention given to what I'm holding in my hands—and in that moment I think I understand something about Josephine.

"Are you a *friend* of hers?" she says, and there it is again, that amused disdain. *A boy,* she's thinking. There's an actual *boy* here to see my uggo sister.

"Yes," I say. And then add, "I'm her boyfriend."

You know how girls make that little disgusted OMG sound, a short exhalation like a cough, packaged together with raised eyebrows and an open-mouthed sneer? I earn one of those, plus a repeat of the full-length sweep.

"Is she home?"

"Hold on."

I fidget on their front porch, waiting. It's probably a waste of time coming here, but I figured it was worth one last-ditch in-person effort.

I should not have said the boyfriend thing. It was just going to piss Josephine off, torpedoing my efforts to convince her to tutor me. I don't know why I did it. No, not true. I did it because of the way Jacqueline was looking at me, because of what her expression revealed about her and her sister.

I look around. There's a shiny new Ford pickup truck parked in the driveway, I guess for all the hauling they have to do on the back forty. On the side of the truck is a vinyl campaign sign with a photo of a handsome, smiling, silver-haired gent, the sort who looks like an actor who would play a handsome, smiling, silver-haired politician in a TV series. GERALD LINDAHL FOR STATE SENATE says the sign. Aha. Mental note added.

It's taking too long for Josephine to appear. I've screwed myself with my unclever cleverness. Then, from somewhere inside the house: "He's *not* my boyfriend!"

So I *did* piss her off, but at least the sound of her voice is getting louder, meaning she's coming toward me. And then, yes, a few seconds later she jerks open the door.

"Why did you tell her that?" she demands.

"Tell her what?" Pure innocence. Am I lying here? No.

"That you're my b—" She cuts herself off, unwilling to even repeat it. She looks back over her shoulder, annoyed. She must think her sister made it up to tease her.

She turns back to me. Then, not even in the ballpark of delight: "Oh, God. What is *that?*"

That being the bouquet in my hands, a special assortment chosen with great care from one of the decorative planters at a retirement home.

"Um, I think these are irises, and these are snapdragons, and I'm not sure what—"

"Austin—"

"Josephine, I'm sorry. I'm *sorry*. I was late, and an asshole, and I'm sorry, and I'm here to say I'm sorry and ask you—*beg* you, be*seech* you—to please be my tutor again."

"Austin, I don't think we're a good match," says Josephine.

"I think you should contact the school and get a different tutor."

"There's no one available. And we're a *great* match! You're smart, I'm stupid—it's perfect!"

"You see? Everything is a joke to you."

"I'll be serious! I'll be the best tutor subject, tutoree, whatever, in the world, ever. I swear. Here. Smell this."

I pull my shirt collar toward her. She looks at me funny.

"I haven't had a single cigarette today, Josephine. It's killing me. I gave up nicotine *for several hours* just for you."

"I appreciate it. I have to get ready for work."

Starts to close the door.

"Hold on. Where *do* you work? You never told me."

"Someplace mind-numbingly boring. Where I have to go. Now."

Door starts to close again.

"Wait!"

She waits. I try to think of something. "Uh . . . that was your sister, huh?"

"Wow. You figured that right out."

"All by myself. See? There's hope for me. I have to say, your sister, she's—"

Josephine scowls.

"Hot," she says, exactly as I say, *"Awful."*

"I *get* it," she rolls on. "I *know* she's hot, everyone *knows*— What?"

"I said, she's *awful*. She's terrifying. I mean, yes, she's hot, but *yeeesh*. It must be like five nightmares at once to live with her."

There's two seconds when she softens, like I might get a smile out of her.

"I don't know about five, but it's at least three," she says.

"I bet. So . . ." I say, "wanna be my tutor again?"

This time she does smile, just a suggestion of one, shaking her head.

"Never mind," I say. Then, before she can disconnect, I gesture at the truck with its garish sign. "Your dad's running for the state senate, huh?"

She glances at it, makes a face, does a bad job of hiding it. "You figured that one out too."

"Amazing, right? My mom's psychic says I'm very intuitive."

"Her psychic. Your mom has a psychic."

"Well, strictly speaking she calls herself a shaman. Lots of herbs, turquoise, that sort of thing. You know."

"Not so experienced with shamans, but I get the idea."

"I could probably hook you up with a dream catcher, if you want."

"I think I'm good."

"Sure. How many can one person have, right?"

"Yeah, my room is pretty full."

I indicate the truck again. "The pickup truck's a nice touch. Jes' folks. Man of the people. Proletariat."

She looks mildly surprised.

"What? 'Proletariat'? I'm not good at *math*. I like to read. I read Pynchon," I say. "That's supposed to impress you."

"I'm impressed. I didn't mean—"

"It's fine. You're right to think I'm dumb. I told you so myself."

I'm not sure why I'm working to keep her here, not giving up. Maybe just to overwrite our first two conversations, the real one in the classroom and the virtual one while I was mowing.

"I suppose the pickup's probably useful for all the hauling you have to do on this here farm, milk the chickens and whatnot."

"I'm pretty certain you don't milk chickens."

"Pigs?"

"That sounds closer. Look, you think it was *my* choice to get the truck? Or live in this house?"

"I didn't say it was. And let's be honest—this is really more of a mansion, right?"

"It's got six bathrooms, so yeah, I think that's fair." Now she checks her watch again.

"What's it like?" I say quickly.

"Having six bathrooms? There's never a line."

I laugh. I have a flash of her deadpanning jokes in that manner at the family dinner table, dry as dust, offhanding them for no one's entertainment but her own. "I mean," I say, "your dad running for senate and all. Is it . . . fun?"

She regards me for a moment, then twists around, double-checking to make sure no one is listening. Then steps out onto the front porch and lets the door close behind her.

"Is it 'fun'? You mean, being a prop in campaign appearances? That? Standing next to my parents and my sister and smiling and pretending that I'm happy to be there, when I'd rather someone just lit me on fire? Yeah, I adore it. That's what I am to them, a prop so that my dad can get his prize, because he got rich firing people and that means he deserves to be a senator."

"So . . . pretty fun."

"Yeah, it's great. And you wanted to know where I work? I'm going to campaign headquarters to spend all day calling really unpleasant people to ask them for money. For him."

"I'm guessing candidate Lindahl shouldn't depend on your vote."

"If I were old enough, I'd vote against him twice." Then she says, "I don't know why I'm telling you this."

"Do you love him?"

She looks at me oddly.

"What kind of question is that?"

"I don't know. A bad one. I forgot we're not really friends. You might have noticed that stuff just comes out of my mouth now and then."

She leaves that one alone.

"So . . . do you?"

"Love him?" She shrugs. "He's my dad. Can it be the thing where I love him without liking him?"

"Yeah, sure. That counts."

"Do you love *your* dad?"

"I don't know. I love my mom. I like her too, 'cept when she's moody. Which is usually my fault, so . . . But my dad, he was dead when I was born."

"Oh. I'm sorry."

"It's okay—he got better," I say, and start to laugh again. She watches me. "You going to expand on that?"

70

"Ah, it's complicated."

"Sounds like it."

There's another space where neither of us says anything, and she doesn't seem to be trying to flee. Like we are, sort of, friends.

"I find it hard to believe this is your family," I say.

"You and me both," she breathes. "I'm sort of counting the days until I can go to college."

"Where do you want to go?"

"Columbia. That's my top choice."

"That's New York, right? That's where I'll be. We should hang out. I mean," I add, "if we were actually friends."

"Right."

One more glance at her watch.

"I really do have to go," she says.

"Okay. You want the flowers at least?" I say.

"Um . . ."

"Don't tell me. You're allergic."

"I forgot to mention that one."

"Of course," I say. "So, tobacco, gluten . . . and flowers."

"Flowers. Yes."

"And assholes."

"That too."

"Right. Never mind, then."

I toss the flowers over my shoulder, hear the soft sound as they land scattered on the grass behind me. This earns a sort of weary sigh from her. But also another ghost of a smile.

"Don't worry. I'll clean them up. Lawn-care professional."

"Great."

"I guess I'll see you at school. Or New York."

"Why are you going to New York?"

"You know." I mime playing a guitar and singing.

"Oh. Right. Your big music career."

Another pause, this one very different.

"What?" she says.

"You know, you were right the other day," I say. "This would never work."

I turn and take the three steps down to the pathway that leads from her door to the street where my motorcycle is parked, not bothering with the scattered flowers, not bothering to look and see if she's still watching me.

CHAPTER 8

*I said goodbye before you ever said hello /
so now I'll never have to watch you go*

Your big music career.

Just a reminder about what this girl really thinks of me.

A reminder of who I really am.

What was I playing at there? Even if I *was* attracted to her, she'd never lower herself to be with someone like me.

Forget about all of it. Forget about the contract, forget about mowing lawns, forget about tutors and math and Todd. Forget Josephine forever. Because I have a Mission, and my Mission is giving me something I haven't had in a long time. Hope.

I'm downtown. I came here on my motorcycle, right after my futile attempts with Josephine. No lawn mowing this afternoon, which leaves me free to complete my mission. I'm going to find Shane.

I'm going to find my father.

I don't know downtown Minneapolis very well, and I don't know the warehouse district at all, so I get a bit confused by the numbered avenues and streets, some of which start and stop and get interrupted by railroad tracks. I finally locate the building, then search the exterior for several minutes before I notice a door with a small acid-treated metal sign no larger than a hardcover book, letters cut through the steel announcing the name of the studio. The door is beat up and industrial and locked. There's an intercom button, so I push it, and after the second push I hear a faint buzzing and the door clicks.

There aren't that many recording studios in the city. I started calling them. "Hey, the label is sending a package to Shane Tyler—he going to be there tomorrow?"

Twice I got a "Who?"; another two times I got a "Shane Tyler? He's not recording here," and on the fifth call I got a bored "Yep." That's the studio I'm at now.

The hallway is exposed brick and wide-plank wood floors, warehouse-y. It leads to a modern-looking reception desk, plopped incongruously in the midst of what looks like an unfinished renovation project. It doesn't appear that there's anyone behind the desk, until I get a little closer and see a rocker dude leaning way back in a chair, his legs stretched out in front of him. He goes more with the warehouse look than with the clean lines of the desk. He's got long hair and a scruffy beard and is wearing a vintage Thin Lizzy tour shirt. He's reading a copy of *Guitar Player* and keeps reading when I reach the desk and stand across from him.

"Hi," I say.

He glances up at me. After a moment, he gives me the

universal eyebrow raise and head movement that signifies, *Yeah? Spit it out already.*

"I'm supposed to meet Shane," I say.

I'd thought about what would be the best approach. I could have said, "Is Shane here?" but that would likely have inspired suspicion. "I'm here to see Shane" could also have raised questions. "I'm *supposed* to meet Shane" indicates that someone else made the decision, that I'm only here to carry out my assignment. At least that's how I hoped it would be perceived.

Rocker Dude stares at me. I'm guessing he was the bored voice who answered the phone before. I hold my breath. Then he makes another exasperated eyebrow raise/head movement that's the universal gesture for *So why are you just standing here and distracting me from my "Five Yngwie Malmsteen Solos You HAVE to Know" article?* and goes back to reading.

"Thanks," I say, and walk past him down the hall. I'm not sure exactly where I'm going, but I don't want to pause, in case Rocker Dude finishes his research and decides maybe he should actually do his job. The hall is sloppy drywall, lined with framed articles and band posters and the occasional gold record. I get to the end and take a left. The hallway extends another twenty feet or so and then dead-ends into a closed unpainted metal door. When I get to it, I pause, unsure what to do, and then hear voices. Loud voices. Loud, angry, shouting voices. Getting louder.

I step back from the door, and it's lucky I do, because in that instant the door bursts open toward me like it's been kicked and slams into the doorstop, rebounding halfway closed, and gets kicked open again. Then I have to flatten myself against the wall to avoid being speared in the stomach by a hard-shell bass guitar case, carried by a guy who is talking over his shoulder as he storms directly at me.

"Yeah, well, guess what?" he's saying at someone behind him, "*I* don't need this crap either!" Then he marches past me without as much as a glance in my direction.

"Rob! Rob, c'mon!" says a woman, and she emerges from the doorway in pursuit. She's maybe in her early twenties, and very pretty, sandy brown hair, in jeans and a T-shirt. Rob stops and turns to her.

"Amy, I'm sorry, I can't. I love you to death, but I just can't," he says.

"Rob, c'mon, we can work through this."

"No, I don't think we can."

"We *can*."

"No, we *can't*," says a new voice, and then there's Shane, who has tromped out of the doorway and planted himself right in front of me, not registering my presence. "We *can't* work through it, because you don't know how, because you don't know how to be a professional!" he says, jabbing a finger at Rob.

"Oh, *I* don't know how to be a professional?" says Rob, putting down his bass and stalking back toward Shane, ignoring Amy as she pulls at him and says, "Rob, c'mon, just leave it!"

"Let me tell you about being a professional!" says Rob, reaching Shane, and then the two of them do that thing where you stand too close to each other and point fingers in each other's faces and shout angry sentences simultaneously with barely a pause to breathe, while Amy does her best to interject and split them apart. I'm right there. I'm so close, I could put a hand on each of the disputants' shoulders without straightening my arm, but I'm invisible.

This is a totally different Shane from the one the day before, the cautious, needy supplicant. I note that he has a bandage similar to mine on his forehead, which I'm assuming covers a wound caused by a Renaissance festival mug.

"I can get another bass player in an hour!" Shane is shouting.

"Yeah? And, what, your third drummer? Your fifth guitarist? It's been *weeks* of this crap!"

Amy is facing me directly across the hallway at handshake distance. As she tries to keep the confrontation from escalating past words to fists, her eyes fall on me like I'd just materialized that moment. I look back at her helplessly, apologetically. The shift in her attention makes the other two glance at me, and that breaks the momentum of the argument.

"Ah, screw this," says Rob, and he turns away, and marches down the hall, picks up his bass, and disappears around the corner.

"Yeah, that's right, just quit!" shouts Shane after him. "You suck, Rob! You *suck!*"

Then he looks at me again, and I can see the process as he recognizes me.

"Oh, great," he says, and stomps off through the door and slams it shut behind him.

"Shane!" says Amy, but she doesn't follow him. "Oh,

crap." She closes her eyes and leans against the wall, sighing. Then she opens them and looks at me, seemingly surprised that I'm still there.

"Hi," she says. "Can I help you with something?"

"Um," I say, and point toward the closed door, "I think that's my dad."

* * *

About fifteen minutes pass before she reemerges from the door, fifteen minutes that I spend rocking back and forth on my feet, then pacing, then leaning against the wall and lightly drumming on it with my knuckles and palms, then finally just sitting on the floor. When she comes out, I clamber to my feet, but I can immediately tell from her expression—pained, embarrassed—that she's not the bearer of glad tidings.

"I should probably take off," I say before she speaks, saving her the trouble.

"I'm sorry," she says. "It's just . . . It's not a great time."

"Sure. Sure, yeah, no worries."

"I'm Amy, by the way," she says, and holds out her hand.

"Yeah, I gathered that during all the excitement," I say. "I'm Austin." We shake hands.

"Sorry about all this," she says.

"No worries."

"Still, sorry."

She pauses.

"Are you really, you know . . . ?"

"I don't know. I think so. Or my mom thinks so. I'm kind of new to the whole thing."

She nods. "Wow."

"Yeah. So . . . you working on the new album?" I know

78

I should leave, but I'm stretching it out, hoping Shane will change his mind.

"Yeah, moral support, that sort of thing."

She's very attractive, and I can't help wondering exactly what sort of moral support she's providing.

"How's the recording going?"

She gives me a *What do you think?* look.

"Right," I say. I do a bit more foot shuffling. "Maybe if I came back some other time," I say.

She hesitates, looks embarrassed and pained again.

"Uh . . ."

"Or maybe not," I add quickly. "Okay. Well. Nice to meet you."

"You too," she says, and we shake hands again and I turn to go. After a few steps, I stop.

"Hey, Amy?"

She pauses, her hand on the half-open door.

"Can you give him a message from me?"

"Sure."

"Could you tell him to go screw himself?"

She smiles sadly. "Sure."

"Thanks."

Then I leave.

CHAPTER 9

It's pretty clear / this beauty here / is gonna turn to ugly/
I'm pretty sure / this pretty girl / will pretty damn near ruin me

"You know something? It's actually kind of comfortable lying here," I say.

"Austin," says Alex, "seriously, there's one coming. Get up."

He's about five yards to my right, straightening up after resting his ear on the track. He doesn't need to tell me a train is coming—I can feel the vibrations growing stronger through the back of my skull, which is resting on the polished steel surface of the rail, my body parallel with the oil-soaked ties, the opposite rail cool and hard under my calves.

"No, I think this is a perfectly reasonable course of action," says Devon, who's sitting on the opposite rail. "He failed his math test, Alex. *His math test.* What else can he do?"

It's Monday. Let's summarize the past few days.

Thursday: The narrowly avoided gelding via hedge shears.

Friday: Both Josephine and Shane rejected me.

Saturday: Lawn mowing. During which time *someone* let the air out of both of the tires on my motorcycle. I had to wheel it about a mile to a gas station to fill them up.

Sunday: More lawns. *Someone* decorated the seat and handle-bars of my motorcycle with smears of dog crap.

Sunday evening: I tried to study for my math test. I lasted for approximately ten minutes and one polynomial. I could have asked Rick for help, but, vomit. Then I went to sleep, the music in my head, and dreamed Josephine was telling me I was late for class and I was going to fail my test.

Monday, today: I woke from that dream and realized I had slept through my alarm, was late to summer school, and failed my test.

I have to hand it to Terry the Shaman: she really nailed it regarding this month.

So when I staggered out of my summer school session, with no lawn crew duties today, I called Devon and said, let's go to Mr. Whitmore's house.

Which is where we are now, except there is no house — nor is there a Mr. Whitmore. It's what we call this wooded area where the train tracks pass over a creek, because when you like to smoke pot with your friends, you invent clever and hilarious code names for your little meet-up areas. *Want to go to Whitmore's after school today? Sure. Tee hee!* I'm not sure why we settled on that name. But when we want to do some serious weed ingesting—which, after the events of the past few days, I really wanted to do—we go to Whitmore's, where we like to sit leaning against trees near the creek and smoke and watch the trains go by a few yards away, trying to count the cars as they blur past.

Several hazy minutes ago, I decided that it would be interesting to see what it's like to lie down on train tracks, like in Rhett Miller's song "Fireflies," or like a damsel in distress.

"You're a friggin' idiot in distress," said Devon.

Once I was lying down, I started pondering my problems, which seem to be mounting up at an alarming rate, and then started thinking that maybe I could let a train solve those problems.

"Why don't you guys go?" I say. "I'm good here."

Beneath my skull, the vibrations are getting stronger, and I think I can hear the sound of the train in the distance.

"Dude, get up," says Alex.

"No. I'm happy here," I say, my eyes closed.

"You're gonna be dead there."

"That will make me happier."

"STFU," says Devon. "I swear I'm going to placekick your nuts."

My teeth are starting to rattle from the train. I hear Alex say something to Devon.

I've been friends with Alex since, what, seventh grade? He's easygoing. We both like weed and music and talking about girls. We hang. It's not a very complicated relationship.

"No!" says Devon. "He just wants attention! Let him get run over!"

Devon and I have a complicated relationship.

We're sort of like brothers. I stayed with him and his family several times when my mother had to sort things out in rehab, and also when I had to sort things out on my own. We touched winkies when we were six. We've had three fist-fights. We lovehate each other. He knows me better than any-one, and vice versa. Periodically he'll inform me that he's sick of my crap, and we don't talk for weeks.

Alex is speaking now. *Something something* "he's pretty stoned."

"Do it yourself. I'm tired of his drama," says Devon.

There's a pause, and then I feel someone grabbing my ankles and lifting them off the ground. I open my eyes. It's Alex. *Thud.* My head drops off the rail as he starts dragging me off the tracks.

"Ow."

The stones and gravel grind underneath me. I reach up and grab at the rail, holding on.

"Austin, stop being an idiot," says Alex. "I can see the train."

"I'm fine."

"Idiot."

More pulling. I hold fast.

"Dude, you're pissing me off," says Alex. "The train's coming!"

I can feel it through my hands, but you don't have to be touching the rail—you can hear it for real, and I turn my head to the right, and yes, there it is, maybe twenty seconds off, the whistle blowing. At that moment I seriously think, I could. I could just lie here. Because who cares?

"Austin!" yells Alex, the roar of the train growing louder. "Get up! Devon, a little help here?"

I hear Devon swearing and the sound of what I'm guessing

is a half-full beer can hurled in anger at a tree trunk. Then the whistle blotting it out, blowing even louder, the noise deafening.

"Pick him up! Pull him!"

I hold fast.

"What are you friggin' laughing at, Austin!" screams Devon. He gives a mighty yank, and the rail above my head is torn from my grip and they drag me violently across the rail bed and over the other rail, *scratch grind clunk thud*, down the embankment and into the grass as the train thunders by, Devon leaning over into my face to scream more angry insults at me that are inaudible. Then he disappears from my view. Then reappears to give me the finger with both hands. I can't hear him, but it's hard to misread someone's lips when they're screaming, "I'm sick of your crap!" See?

Then he exits the frame again. I observe the featureless blue sky, listening to the noise of the train dying away in the distance.

I prop myself up on my elbows. Devon is nowhere to be seen. Alex is lifting his bicycle up, preparing to leave.

"Thanks," I say to him. "You guys are the best."

Alex glances at me, shakes his head, and starts wheeling his bike down the long dirt path that will eventually take him to the street.

"Thanks!" I say again. Then, "You guys are really great!" and "Thank you!" and "Thanks, Alex!" None of which he responds to as he recedes into the shade of the woods.

Add one more item to the list of my accomplishments for these past few days: Wore out the very last of my friends' patience.

I lie there some more. Time passes. The sky maintains its blueness. I listen to grasshoppers. My brain starts to meander its way back from Fuzzy-Wuzzy World toward a more normal state, whatever that is for me.

I get up and look around. Neither Devon nor Alex has returned to tell me that it's all good and we're still friends. I go to pee against a tree, evidence suggesting that it's the same tree Devon targeted with his Beer Can of Anger. I'm midstream, drawing decorations, when I get a text. Alison.

Meet me at the lake. I'm alone.

Well, as long as I'm on a streak of really bad decisions . . .

* * *

"Austin! Austin, over here!"

Alison, calling to me as I approach from the parking lot, waving both hands above her head as she hops up and down like a game show contestant who has just won a washer-dryer. She's at the outer periphery of the crowd gathered at the Lake Harriet band shell, standing with Kate and Patty and Marcy, all in cutoff jeans and bikini tops. A few of the dudes near them turn to see who the ridiculously hot girl is shouting and waving to. *That guy? Really?* I have the urge to tell them I agree.

"I'm so glad you came!" she says when I get close, and then I get the big hug again. More hugs from the other cheerleaders; inquiries about my general health and well-being. Onstage, the band is sound-checking and tuning up, amps squawking and sending feedback into the summer afternoon.

"Let me see your head!" says Alison, and so I lean forward to show her and the other girls the wound, and I earn the requisite *awww*s and *OhMyGod*s and feel a bit sleazy for exploiting the opportunity to check out all the boobage I'm being presented with. Then I forgive myself and decide I should just do my best to enjoy the situation.

"Here, I'll kiss it," says Alison, and she plants a kiss on the Band-Aid while the other girls trade mischievous smiles, like we're doing something daring and naughty. "Better?" she asks.

"Not sure. Maybe I need one right here," I say, and point to my lips. Giggles from the other girls.

"Okay," says Alison, and she does it, she kisses me on the lips—a real kiss too, one that lingers softly for a moment longer than I expect. She steps back and looks at me, smiling, triumphant. Enjoying being bad. Enjoying playing with her toy. Her toy is sort of enjoying it too. Gleeful shock from the other girls.

"Better?" she says.

"Better. I have some other ideas . . ."

"I bet you do," she says, and then the band starts into a passable cover of a Bob Marley song.

The girls dance and sing along, Alison sometimes linking her arm with mine or giving me hip checks. I cast furtive, nervous glances around for bulky hockey players. We pass several songs like this, chatting briefly between songs, Alison poking me in the ribs with her finger if I'm not paying enough attention to her, and once biting me on the ear. It's boner inducing.

"Why are you doing this?" I shout over the music.

"I like you!"

"You have a large boyfriend!"

"We broke up again!"

86

I'm doing some internal forecasting of how that breakup might affect Todd's mood, and hence my continued well-being, when the band finishes up. The general female consensus is that more music is desired, and they're a hard crew to say no to, so we all end up sitting on the grassy hill that overlooks the band shell and the lake, and I play some songs on the ukulele, singing whatever the girls request.

After a bit, Alison grabs my arm and says, "Let's go get ice cream," and the two of us walk down the hill and stand in the concession line.

As we shuffle along toward the order window we talk. Or not really talk. Banter. She says something flirty or suggestive, and I say something that I hope is clever, and so on back and forth, her hand sometimes resting on my shoulder like she needs to support herself because she's laughing JUST SO HARD at my brilliance. And let's face it, it's intoxicating and really erotic, because *damn*. Look at her. My head is spinning.

It's also . . . boring.

I'm deadly bored. I'm simultaneously fighting two urges: an almost overwhelming one to hump her leg, and another to just keel over, fast asleep. She might as well be speaking R2-D2 language to me right now. That would be about as meaningful.

What is wrong with me? She's any straight boy's fantasy, and instead—goddammit—I'm thinking about Josephine. Her intelligence, her quiet confidence, the way she seems to know exactly who she is. Thinking about those eyes.

I'm wishing I could just swap out Alison for Josephine right now, even though that conversation would be a big tangled bundle of spikes and thorns.

We get to the window and we order and Alison flirts with the guy and he gives her a cone for free. That's what life is like for girls like Alison: one free ice cream after another.

We stand just apart from the concession stand, Alison chattering.

"Austin, are you even paying attention?" she says, giving me a little backhand whack in the stomach.

"What? Yes!" I say.

"What was I talking about?"

"You were holding forth about David Foster Wallace," I say. "It was mesmerizing!"

"You are such a jerk!" says Alison, but it's all in the same flirty-silly voice, and she laughs and hangs on to my arm.

"No, what were you saying? About the party?"

"I said, are you going to that party at . . ." and her voice once again fades to R2-D2 blerps and blorps in my mind and then to total silence.

"Austin?" she says. "Austin, you really aren't listening at all, are you? What are you looking at?"

"I'm really sorry," I say. "I gotta go."

I hear her calling after me, and I turn once to wave and mouth *Sorry,* and I keep going, walking toward the parking lot, toward where Shane Tyler is leaning against the rear bumper of his blue vintage Range Rover, hands in his pockets, waiting for me.

CHAPTER 10

*I wonder if you hear me / if you're still near me /
or were you ever really there /
or just a trick of the light in the air*

It takes me what feels like an hour to walk across the parking lot. I'm not sure where to put my gaze as I go, so I look at the ever-changing patch of black asphalt just ahead of my feet as I stride, glancing up at Shane now and then to make sure I'm on course, pausing to let cars pass in front of me.

I stop a few yards away from him, the distance you use when you don't know someone so well and you're not quite sure how either of you feels about the interaction you're about to have. He's examining me, that same cautious, slightly apprehensive expression on his face as when he was standing on my front porch, mixed with a hint of something else. Amusement, maybe. The look of someone laughing at himself. Sad-amused. Bitter-amused.

Neither of us says anything for a moment. Then he leans a

bit to the side, looks past me, straightens up again. "She looks like a big scoop of fun, and three big scoops of trouble," he says.

"Yeah, I think you're probably right about the trouble," I say.

He nods, smiles. Again the melancholy amusement.

Then, "I followed you," he says. "Saw you leaving your house and I followed you." I had gone home briefly after my visit to Whitmore's to fetch the ukulele and change my clothes, which had railroad tar on them.

"I felt real bad about what happened at the studio," he says. I can hear the southern in his voice, stronger than my mom's accent. "Stuff is just . . ." He waves a hand, annoyed. "Anyway, I was up all night thinking about it. I didn't know how to find you other than going to your house, and I saw you riding off on your bike, and I followed you."

I nod. More mutual examination.

"I'm Shane," he says, finally, sticking out his hand.

"I know who you are."

I don't move. His hand is still extended, one beat, two, and then he looks down at it like he's noticing it for the first time. Then he lets it drop to his side.

He takes a breath, sighs it out. He looks at me some more. "Amy couldn't remember it, so I don't know your name," he says.

I don't know why I pause as long as I do before answering. Like something is hanging in the balance. Even as I'm opening my mouth to speak, I'm not sure what I'm going to say.

It turns out to be "I'm Austin. My name's Austin."

Then I stick out my hand to him. He pushes himself off the truck and takes the step forward to shake my hand, his grip firm.

"Austin. Great name. Nice to meet you, Austin."

"You too."

He releases my hand and we stand there.

"You have a really nice voice," he says. "I heard you earlier, singing to the girls up there. I didn't want to intru—"

"Are you my dad?"

He blinks at me, taken aback.

"Sorry," I say.

"No, it's—"

"But are you? Are you my dad?"

He rubs his head, pulls at an ear.

"Honestly?" he says. "I don't know. KD is your mom, right?"

"Yeah, of course."

"Right. Does she say—"

"She says you're my dad."

"Yeah."

He gives a little snort of laughter, shaking his head, sighs. *Ain't that a thing,* he's saying.

"I guess it's possible," he says. "When were you born?"

I tell him.

He thinks about it.

"Yeah, I guess that makes sense."

"But what do you *think?*" I say.

"You do look a lot like me. And you got a voice on you . . ."

I wait.

"Yeah, I think . . . it's . . . possible."

"Possible."

"Yeah."

I wait some more.

"Okay . . . *probable*," he says. "I mean, I think . . ." He doesn't finish the sentence. He looks off, shaking his head again. *Ain't that a thing.* Then looks at me again, gaze level. "Yeah, Austin," he says, "I'd wager I am."

I let go of the breath I didn't know I'd been holding. "Yeah," I say, nodding. "So . . ."

"Yeah," he says, "So."

Ever had this conversation? I bet you haven't. There's some awkwardness. The silence stretches out. There are a lot of important questions you should ask your dad who disappeared before you were born. Right at this moment I can't think of a single one of them.

"That's a cool truck," I say instead. He seems relieved.

"Not poseur-y? I feel poseur-y."

"No, I think you can rock it," I say. "You look cool."

"Thanks."

Part of me is taking notes, because he *does* look cool. I've never met a grownup who looks so cool, not a bit of effort to it. He even somehow looked cool when he was trying to avoid getting his skull bashed in.

"How's your head?" I say.

"Hurts," he says. "Should have seen that coming, I suppose. KD always was, uh . . ."

"Moody," we say at the same time, then look at each other, both of us grinning shyly.

"Her work?" he says, gesturing toward my head.

"This? No, someone hit me with a mandolin. Smashed a Gibson A3 over my head."

"What? That's a crime!"

"Yeah."

"I mean to do that to an instrument like that. I hope it's okay."

I laugh. "Totaled."

"Girl involved?"

"Yeah, that one," I say, twisting to point at Alison. She's standing by the concession stand, watching us.

"Probably worth it," says Shane.

I laugh again.

"Hey, you know what?" I say. "I think I might have your old guitar."

"Really?"

"Johnny Cash sticker on it?" I indicate where the sticker would be.

"Holy crap! Yes! Johnny Cash sticker! Man! I wondered where that got to!"

"You can have it back, you want."

"No, you keep it."

"Thanks."

"Yeah, jeez, that old guitar. No kidding. No kidding."

Then we're quiet, both of us shifting around a bit. I'm hoping he wasn't listening the whole time when I was singing to the girls, didn't hear me wreck the title song from his second album.

"How is KD?" says Shane, serious again.

"She's all right."

"I'd say tell her I said hi, but . . ."

"Yeah. She says she'll kill you if you come back."

"Yeah, I suspect she would. She with someone?"

I stare at him.

"I'm just asking. I just want to know that she's okay."

"She's with a guy named Rick. He's a lawyer."

"That the guy who came out when I was there?"

"Yes."

"What's he like?"

"He's a douche. But mostly he's just boring."

He nods.

"Yeah, well, sometimes boring is okay. They married?"

"That why you're here? You gonna rekindle the romance?"

He grimaces, looks away.

"Sorry," I say.

"Curious, is all. I haven't seen her for sixteen years," says Shane.

"You're the one ran out."

"I didn't know about you," he says. "Okay? I was twenty-one. I wasn't much older than you, and probably half as smart. This is as big a surprise to me as it is to you."

We both shift around a bit.

"You really upset her, showing up like that," I say.

"Uh . . . no kidding?" he says, touching his forehead.

"I want you to leave her alone."

"Sure," he says.

"I mean it."

"I understand." Then, "I can leave *you* alone too, you want."

I think about it. While I'm doing that, he glances at his

watch. "Crap," he says. "I have to get going. Look, I'm only in town a few weeks. I understand if you don't want to hang out or—"

"I want to. I mean, we should talk, right?"

"Absolutely. I'd like that."

"Okay."

He nods. I nod. We nod.

"So . . ." I say.

"What happens next?" he says.

"Yeah."

"Depends. You busy tonight?"

"No."

"Can you get away for a bit without getting in trouble?"

"Yeah, sure."

"Good. What happens next is you come to my show."

CHAPTER 11

When we met each other on the street /
I said it's funny, I was just thinking of you /
and it's true, 'cause that's all I do /
I just think of you

Amy is waiting for me outside the venue in cowboy boots and a skirt and seems genuinely happy to see me—"So glad you could make it!"—pulling me in for a hug and a kiss like we're old friends.

She escorts me into the club, a medium-size downtown place with a real light grid, some folksy-hipster band finishing their set and thanking the audience just as we enter.

"Shane here?" I say over the applause.

"He's getting ready. Come on."

Amy leads me by the hand through the crowd, recorded music coming on as the folksy hipsters start packing up. I catch a brief glimpse of Shane and wave at him, but he's conversing with someone from the club and seems focused on getting ready.

First show in ten years, he told me before we parted at Lake Harriet. What have you been doing? I asked him. Been here and there, some studio work, audio mixing, that sort of thing. Some hard living along the way, he said, and chuckled. "But that's all behind me now."

The other thing he said, leaning out the window of the Rover before pulling away: "You sang it better than me." Then smiled and waved and drove off.

Amy brings me to a circle of grownups who are chatting at the back of the club and says, "Everyone, this is Austin. He's awesome."

Handshakes and fist bumps and high fives, people telling me their names, which I instantly forget, and then they all go back to talking. Which is fine, because I feel shy and intimidated, surrounded by all these strangers who are all cool and worldly and, you know, cool and worldly, everyone talking about gigs and recording sessions and SXSW and Coachella and video shoots. There's lots of beardage and tattooage. *Did you do that gig at the Troubador in LA? How was the show at Brooklyn Bowl? When you headed to Nashville?* I've never met grownups like this. I stand there feeling like an infant, reminding myself not to pick my nose or wet my pants.

Out of nowhere, Ed, a balding nervous-looking guy who I gather is Shane's producer and audio engineer, says, "How do you know Shane?"

"From being awesome," says Amy quickly, and I look at her with gratitude.

The audience is doing the changeover thing as we wait for Shane, people who were there for the first band departing, new people coming in. It's getting more and more crowded, and I hear snippets of conversations, people saying how psyched they are to see Shane Tyler play — first show in, what, a decade? WTF ever happened to him?

I catch another glimpse of Shane, who's paused halfway up the five steps to the backstage area and bends and kisses Amy on the lips, which sort of answers the whole "moral support" thing. I'm left to mill about with everyone else, and end up drifting over to the wall and parking myself there.

"Yo, dude," says somebody next to me, and when I turn there's a huge guy with a red Mohawk and black spiked leather looming over me, pure punk-rock mayhem, and he says, "You're with Shane, right?"

"Uh, yes. I guess. Yes."

"Cool! Here!" and he shoves a pint glass of beer at me.

"Thanks," I say, and then *zzzhooop!* Amy swooshes in and intercepts the glass before it reaches my hand. "Patrick!" she says to punk-rock dude. "He's sixteen!"

She gets me a Coke and rescues me from the side wall.

"Who is that guy?" I say.

"That's just Patrick," she says, as if that explains things.

"Doesn't seem like his scene."

"Yeah, Patrick's full of surprises. Come on — come stand with me." She leads me by the arm to the platform where the audio board is, and we squeeze up there next to the sound guy, who nods to us gruffly once but otherwise doesn't take any notice of us.

The recorded music cuts off, and people start to whistle

and applaud, and then Shane comes out onstage and the place erupts, Shane waving shyly to everyone and doing little mini-bows with his head. Then he steps up to the microphone, adjusts it, and says, "Uh . . . hi. I'm Shane Tyler," and the place explodes again, and he just starts playing.

Wow.

His voice sounds different than on the recordings. Not bad, just different, weathered, miles on the highway and tobacco and Scotch. On the recordings he sends his voice soaring up into the tenor range, and its purity catches at your heart, pulls you along with it, but he leaves some of those highest notes alone now. I watch his eyes as he sings those passages, and maybe I'm projecting, but I see something there, that wry self-amusement, like a man squinting up at steep mountain passes he was once able to climb with ease and sighing at how age has started to catch up to him.

The room is hushed as he sings, no one yammering away in the back or at the bar like they always do when someone's performing. This is special. Shane Tyler, minor legend for those in the know, has returned. They're getting to see him play, and they'll get to say, *You know, I saw him when he was just starting his comeback tour, before he was selling out the big auditoriums.*

My father. I'm watching him and I'm thinking, that's my father, that's my father onstage. *Feel that,* I'm telling myself. *Feel something about that.* But all I notice is the absence of feeling. I'm watching a man perform onstage. He is my father. Nothing. So instead I try to just enjoy watching Shane Tyler play.

His voice has aged, but his guitar technique is drop-dead

dazzling. He strums and flat-picks and fingerpicks, surprising you with little fills and unexpected side trips between the verses, or dancing a complicated choreography with his voice as he sings.

I alternate between watching him and watching the audience. In the crowd I see smiles, solemn expressions, eyes closed in concentration, bodies swaying. Something shared and sacred about it, even if Shane is singing about love and lust and drinking and death.

Then, as I'm scanning the crowd, my gaze jerks to a stop. Like it got snagged on a face. I get a burst of that same hallucinatory *no-way* moment I had when I first saw Shane on the front porch of our house. Across the room from me, facing the stage, is Josephine.

She's watching him, nodding her head to the music like everyone else. From what I can see she's dressed way too formal for the room, her hair up, a black dress with straps, like she escaped from the prom and ended up at this club. I can't believe she's here, can't believe it from twelve different directions.

I suffer through a quick spasm of paranoia, wondering if she's somehow in cahoots with my mother or checking up on me, but just as I'm thinking that the song ends. As everyone is clapping she glances randomly in my direction and spots me, and you can't fake her expression: *BOINK!* Straight-up shock and surprise, comical, like she opened the fridge and found a raccoon in there waving at her.

I look away reflexively, but I'm sure she knows I saw her. I fake it anyway for a few seconds, doing a bad job of pretending that I'm unaware she's there.

"Man, it's so good to have all you folks here tonight," Shane is saying, and there's the requisite hoots and *yeahs!* and applause, and I join in, darting a look over at her—just as she looks at me. She doesn't smile or wave. She just tilts her head a bit, the gesture saying, *Well?*

I give her the bro nod—a little tilt up and then down of the chin. *I see you, you see me, we're both here.*

"Okay," Shane is saying, "I got time for one last song tonight. Here's one I think you might know." He strums the opening chords to "Good Fun." The song I sang for the girls at the lake. Everyone starts applauding again, a shared *ahhh,* like an old friend has finally arrived at the party. I turn my eyes back to the stage, and I can feel Josephine watching me.

Shane is vamping, playing the opening chord progression, like he wants to stretch the moment out longer and knows we want it too.

"I love you, Shane!" someone shouts, and everyone laughs, Shane with them, and he says, "I love you too!"

A glance at Josephine. She's still watching me.

Josephine is watching me.

Maybe you just need the right girl watching you, says Alex.

It propels me, that gaze, gets me moving, stepping off the riser.

The gaze moves me through the crowd—not toward Josephine, but to the stage, slipping past and around people effortlessly, like they're clearing the way for me, and then I'm at the edge of the stage itself, then I'm hoisting myself up onto it, the surface pitted and scuffed under my hands. The crowd murmuring. Shane has been playing with his eyes closed but opens them just then and notices me, and it's almost like he was waiting for me to do this—the faintest moment of puzzlement, instantly replaced by a smile that spreads, says, *Welcome. What took you so long?* Then a quick shake of his head at the black-clad roadie who is moving onto the stage to cut me off.

Shane keeps the chord progression looping as I pick up his mandolin from the stand behind him, put the strap over my shoulder. He keeps playing as he moves himself a step to his right, an invitation to join him at the microphone. I'm aware of the sense of anticipation and mystery in the room, everyone silent, leaning forward, waiting, breath held, and then Shane gives me a nod and we start to sing and play together.

It's like a dream where you're flying.

Where you can do it because you've forgotten that it's impossible. The delight, the freedom, the nonsensical joy. While a small part of you wonders, *But how? But how?* And then just shrugs its shoulders and watches.

The glare from the stage lights renders everything but the first few rows invisible. Is Josephine smiling, I wonder, or shocked or impressed or even still there? But I try not to think about it too much, because I'm afraid that I'll become too self-aware and remember that gravity exists and then *ahhhhhh!* the dream will end.

We get through the first verse and to the chorus, and I'm the one who sends my voice up to soar, Shane on the lower harmony, and I hear the calls of surprise and pleasure, people clapping.

It ends too soon, the applause exploding as we finish. All those faces looking up at us, eyes shining, the blurred flutter of all those hands. Shane reaches out to shake my hand, his other hand resting on my shoulder. As the cheers and applause crest he leans forward to his microphone and says, "This talented young man right here is Austin Methune. He's my son."

CHAPTER 12

The one you see up there, that's me /
the one in the bright blue sky / the one that's free

I float from the stage. Hands patting me on the shoulders and mussing my hair, drunk people shouting to me from six inches away that it was awesome, *I* was awesome. I'm so high I want to hug them all, to take everyone in the room in my arms and squeeze them and share the warm heaven I'm feeling inside.

And I want to find Josephine.

But she's gone.

I'm searching for her, attempting to move through a crowd that's reaching for me, murmuring at me, while I'm standing on tiptoes and jumping up to get a better view over the sea of heads. *There!*

I move in the direction where I think I spotted her, but then—"DUUUUUDE!"—Mohawk Patrick is in my path, engulfing me in a bear hug so intense that there're popping and cracking noises and I fear my internal substructure is going to give way. When he releases me, I realize his face is wet with tears. "Duuude!" he repeats. "That was incredible! Incredible! You friggin' made me friggin' cry! That's the power of music, straight up, yo!" He grabs me again and crushes whatever is left uncrushed inside me, and by the time I've escaped and reinflated my lungs Josephine is nowhere to be seen. Then Amy snags my arm and gives me a hug—"What a fantastic surprise!"—and there are more hands to shake and people to meet and I give up on Josephine.

We spill out onto the sidewalk, everyone milling about and talking and laughing and smoking, then Shane emerges with his guitar and ignores everyone else and comes straight up to me and grabs me in his own huge bear hug, his voice warm in my ear as he says, "Great job, kid. Great job. Great job." And it's euphoria on top of euphoria. There are more hands patting us, people pulling Shane's attention away, and I'm still twisting and turning around and searching for Josephine, even though I know she's long gone.

Then I see her.

First I see the people in formalwear who are streaming slowly out of the fancy restaurant a few doors down, stopping to chat on the sidewalk, a parallel-universe version of our group, older and wealthier than ours. Then, wait, is that her sister? It is! It's Jacqueline! Then an instant later a woman emerges who just *has* to be their mother: a senior version of Jacqueline, blond and tan, a woman who'd be introduced as the wife of senatorial candidate Gerald Lindahl, and you'd say, *Ah, yes, of* course *she is.*

Mother Lindahl is pretty, or could be pretty, but right now her face is deformed into an angry snarl. She's in snippy-hissed-lecture mode, and her target is Josephine. Josephine is walking a step or two behind her mother with the pinch-lipped, eyes-front glare of any kid on the receiving end of that sort of talking-to. I see her make a few attempts to say something, each of which her mom shuts right down. Father Lindahl is unaware of or ignoring the whole thing, focused on glad-handing and schmoozing with the other formalweared folks. Jacqueline, though, might as well have a bag of popcorn, enjoying the fireworks with the sort of venomous, satisfied grin that makes you yearn for a voodoo doll.

They've all paused on the sidewalk so Gerald can continue his handshaking. Josephine has her arms crossed, jaw set, while her mother repeatedly performs an amazing feat: alternating between sniping at Josephine and then turning to deliver a dazzling smile to whichever VIP has wandered within reach — handshake, hug, kiss-kiss — then right back to vicious sniping with about as much transition as a light blinking on and off.

Other people are talking around me, maybe to me, but I'm oblivious to it all, watching Josephine. Then she sees me.

It happens during one of the more extended hug-hug kiss-kiss interludes. Jacqueline is taking the opportunity to talk to her sister now, or talk *at* her. Josephine doesn't answer or even glance at her, she just pivots a quarter turn away, which leaves her facing me. She still has her arms crossed, her face locked in the same expression, but I know she sees me. She's looking right at me, not moving.

Her sister is still yip yip yipping into her left ear from close range. Now her mother is turning from the elderly couple she was talking to, her smile instantly extinguished, and she says something sharp to shut Jacqueline up so *she* can resume *her* tirade.

So now Josephine is flanked by her mother and sister, like a boxer getting an angry between-round lecture from the trainers. Jacqueline keeps trying to insert her own bits of wisdom, Mom Lindahl cutting her off. Josephine is still gazing right at me, stony-faced.

Her arms uncross and lower to her sides.

We stare at each other.

I raise a hand, cautious, hesitating, and hold it up in greeting.

She doesn't wave back. She doesn't move. Until she starts walking toward me.

Again the feeling that I'm dreaming. The way she separates herself from her mother and sister and glides away from them, wordless, still focused on me.

I can't hear her mother, but I can see her hissing through clenched teeth, "Josephine. *Josephine!*" Then some woman is touching her on the shoulder and there's a flash of murderous annoyance at the interruption, instantly replaced with that smile, and Mother Lindahl is forced to turn for the hug-hug kiss-kiss while her daughter escapes, crossing the no-man's land between their group and ours, Jacqueline staring after her open-mouthed.

When Josephine reaches me, she stops.

"Hi," I say.

"Hi."

Behind her, I can see her mother and her sister conferring, her sister pointing toward us. Josephine notes the shift in my gaze but doesn't turn around. "It's a fundraiser for my dad," she says. "I just had to get out of there, and then I randomly wandered over and saw the name posted outside and remembered you mentioned it . . ."

I nod.

"Anyways, that's why all this," she says, and sort of indicates her dress.

"You look nice," I say, because she does.

She shrugs, and I wonder if I've somehow insulted her.

"The singer," she says. "He's . . . ?"

"Yes. My dad."

"I had no idea."

"Yeah, me neither, until a couple of days ago."

"Ah. The one who was dead, and then got better."

"Exactly."

"Sounds like an interesting story."

"Maybe I'll tell you about it sometime."

Her father has now joined her mother and sister, and a family confab is going on, still interrupted by handshakes and hugs. This time Josephine twists to glance at them for a moment.

She sighs.

"You're in trouble," I say.

"Little bit, yeah."

"I'm not unfamiliar with that feeling," I say.

She almost smiles.

Behind her, I can see that a family decision has been made, that Jacqueline is being prepped to go retrieve her wayward sister. Josephine seems to sense it without looking.

"I should go," she says.

"Okay."

She doesn't, though. Instead she examines me, brow furrowed. Like she's revisiting a complicated math problem and is finding a different answer than she first expected.

"Austin," she says finally, "you were really good."

"Aw . . . thanks. Whatever. You know."

"No," she says firmly, shaking her head, rejecting my deflection. "You were *really good*."

I drop my gaze. "Thanks," I say again, quietly. I don't want it to feel this gratifying to have her compliment me.

She looks to be about to say something else, then seems to change her mind.

"What?"

She shakes her head.

"Nothing."

"Austin, you ready? We're heading over."

It's Shane, starting to move down the sidewalk in the opposite direction with a herd of people.

"I'm coming," I say. Then to Josephine, "Everyone's headed to some bar."

She nods. Jacqueline has broken off from the other group and is stalking purposefully toward us. Josephine glances back, sees her, turns back to me.

"Time's up," says Josephine.

"Austin, come on!" Shane again.

"I'm coming!" I shout over my shoulder.

Amy shouts, "Bring your friend!"

I look at Josephine. This time she does smile, just a bit. She says, "We're not actually friends."

While I'm opening my mouth to answer, she says, "I have to go," and turns and walks away, brushing past Jacqueline without a glance.

* * *

"Cheers. To a great musician, a great show, and many more of them."

"Hear, hear!"

We clink glasses and beer cans.

"And to Austin Methune!" says Shane. More cheers.

We're at a bar, squashed into a booth and extra chairs, me and Shane and Amy and Justin and Ed the engineer and some label rep named Drew, and Patrick the giant punk rock miscreant.

We've been sitting and talking for an hour, reviewing the show, discussing music, toasting, the grownups referencing people and places I don't know, but I still feel part of it all. Shane is the center, full of stories and life and joy, keeping everyone laughing, clapping his hands on people's shoulders, high-fiving, half standing to give hugs. The bonfire around which we're all gathered, everyone focused on and nourished by his energy and warmth, everyone delighted.

At one point I catch Ed observing me, nodding to himself.

"What?" I say.

He shakes his head, and I think he's not going to answer. Then he leans in and says, "You have something, okay?" Then he rejoins the flow of conversation.

Now Shane is finishing a story about a disastrous gig at a farm festival, the livestock outnumbering the audience five to one, all of us laughing. There's a moment of contented silence, the point that signals a new chapter in the night. Then Ed says, "Well, I'm heading home. Shane, we're getting back in the studio, right?"

"Yes, yes."

"I'm serious, Shane. Lots of good stuff, but lots of work to do."

"I know."

"Amy, you make sure he stays on the straight and narrow," says Ed.

"Can't promise that," says Amy. "But I'll make sure to get his ass in the studio."

More laughter. Ed hugs Shane, gives a salute, and departs. The others drop away one by one, Patrick grabbing my head between his hands and kissing me on the forehead before he leaves. Finally it's just me and Shane and Amy, and Amy says, "Babe, I'm taking the truck home. You get to cab it."

They kiss, she gives me a big hug—"You star!" she whispers in my ear—and she walks out, pausing to blow another kiss at us.

We watch her go. Now it's just the two of us in the booth. It's one a.m. Shane is sitting across from me in late-night bar pose: one elbow planted on the table, propping up his head with the palm of that hand; the other forearm resting on the scarred, sticky surface, fingers curled lightly around a can of beer. I'm going with my own variant of the bar pose, slumped back into the corner of the booth, hands clasped on my lap.

Shane just looks at me, idly pivoting the beer can back and forth a few degrees, *shish shush. Shish shush.* Joe Henry's "Trampoline" is playing on the jukebox. I return Shane's gaze.

"Cheers," he says finally, and slides his hand forward across the table, knocking his beer can against my can of Coke.

"Cheers," I say, and pick up my Coke, and we drink.

"You did great," he says.

"Thanks. It was really fun."

He nods.

"Amy's really nice," I say.

"Yeah, Amy's the best. And you should hear her sing. There's a talent, I tell you. Gonna be big."

"You ever record with her?"

He laughs.

"Naw. I'd prefer we stay on good terms."

He sips his beer.

"So who was that you were talking to after the show?" he says.

"Her? Just some girl."

"Huh," he says, and scratches at the stubble on his jaw.

"What?"

He shrugs. "Dunno. Some girls are just some girl, like some guys are just some guy. But she seems like she's more. The kind of girl who knows who she is."

I look at him sharply.

"What?" he says.

"Why do you say that?"

"Which part of it?"

"That she knows who she is."

He shrugs again. "You look at her and you know it. You like her?"

It doesn't sound exactly like a question.

"No."

"Okay."

"I don't."

"Okay. She like you?"

"No."

"Okay."

We're quiet a bit longer. Then he takes a deep breath and says, "Austin . . . I'm sorry."

I look at him, confused. Or maybe knowing what he's saying and not wanting to acknowledge it.

"What do you mean?"

"I mean I'm sorry," he says.

"For what?"

He snorts. "Where to start. For being me. For being a mess. For not being there."

I shrug, take another sip.

"No biggie," I say. He doesn't answer for a moment and I sit there, looking at the top of my soda can, squeezing the aluminum so that it makes crunching noises.

"Nah," he says, "it is a biggie. It's about as big a biggie as you get."

I shrug again. "Whatever. It never bothered me that much."

"Okay," he says. "I guess I'm glad to hear that. But it bugs *me*. It bugs me a lot. I can't go back and change anything, but it's important for me to tell you how sorry I am. That's all."

"No worries," I say, dismissive, wanting to move on to the next topic. I'm still looking down at my drink, plucking at the pull tab with my index finger. *Boing. Boing. Boing.* He's silent long enough that I finally look up. He's watching me in that way he does, intense, that mix of longing and pain and grim humor.

"Well," he says, "I'm glad we got to meet."

113

"Yeah, yeah, me too," I say in the same light tone, and then goddammit out of nowhere something inside me gets knocked loose and I give a sound like a hiccup and start bawling.

Sobs. Wrenching. Wracked by them.

Ambushed by sixteen years of sadness and need in the booth of that bar, sadness that I didn't even know existed. I'm crunched over in my seat, hands clapped tightly over my face like that will somehow keep it all inside, my palms wet with tears and snot. I don't want to be crying, so of course that makes it worse, each exhalation a cramped *hhnnnhhh* that clenches me into a tighter ball, followed by that explosive hiccupy gasp as I suck air in again.

I feel Shane's hand on my shoulder from across the table and *boom,* I'm ambushed by another unexpected explosion of emotion. Rage.

"Don't!" I say, and whack his hand away. "You don't friggin' know me!" I say, or as close to that as I can muster through the sobs. He's sitting back in his seat, hands up at chest height like I've got a gun pointed at him. I wipe my nose with my forearm, like a little kid, try to control my voice. "You don't get to do that!" I say again, and jab a finger at him. "You don't. You don't friggin' know me!"

I don't know what's happening. I don't know where this came from, all that joy converted to this ugliness. I clumsily work my way out of the booth and to a standing position, tears still streaming down my cheeks.

"Austin," he says.

"Shut up," I say, and let out another honking sob. "I wish

you'd never come back." I turn and push my way through the bar to the exit, aware that the remaining late-night drinkers are all gawking at me.

"Austin!" Shane calls, but I'm already out the door and kick-starting my bike.

"Austin!" says Shane, emerging from the bar, but I'm gone.

CHAPTER 13

Is there sunshine on your side of the river /
'cause since you crossed there's been nothing here but rain /
let the waters rise, let them sweep away the memories /
wash clean the ledgers of all we lost and we gained

"You're late," says my replacement tutor.

"Sorry," I say.

My replacement tutor shrugs. "She said you would be," he says.

"Josephine?"

"Yes."

My replacement tutor is sitting in the spot where Josephine was when I first met her. He's a skinnyish, solemn-faced kid who looks to be about thirteen years old.

"I'm only about five minutes late."

He cocks his head slightly.

"She said I'd say that, too," I venture.

He doesn't respond, but I gather that I'd guessed correctly.

"Right," I say. "I'm Austin."

"I know. I'm Isaac. Isaac Kaplan."

"Yeah," I say. "I got the email." Is he thirteen? Younger?

"I'm in college-level calc," he says, either because he just read my mind or because I'm still hesitating in the doorway.

"That's impressive," I say. "How old are you?"

"Fifteen. Well, I will be soon."

"Okay."

"It's math, not arm wrestling," he says.

"You could probably beat me there, too," I say, and toss my bag on the table and take a seat.

* * *

It's been two days since the show. I haven't heard from Shane since then, and I haven't tried to reach him.

I don't know why I reacted like that in the bar. I just did. Everything had been so good, so perfect, and then it all broke and I hated Shane and felt like I was never going to stop hating him or being sad. It was worse because I was supposed to be happy—I had performed on stage, with my father, and everyone saw, and Josephine was there and she saw me and told me I was good, and all I was feeling was anger and darkness.

When I left the bar I was shaking so hard it was difficult to pilot my bike, the tears not helping much either.

I tossed and turned in my bed until five in the morning, feeling like the world had started and ended over the past twenty-four hours. Then I had a sweaty, fitful sleep, dreams of Shane and Josephine, a series of incoherent scenes and images with an unsettling musical score lurking underneath.

When the alarm woke me up, I was greeted by a thudding headache and exhaustion and my mom hectoring me, *Where were you, where were you,* all while I tried to eat breakfast and make a sandwich and get out the door.

I checked my email before I left and felt a burst of excitement and got angry at myself for feeling it: There was a new message from Josephine. Then I realized it was simply a forwarded message from Isaac Kaplan, who was agreeing to tutor me in her place. No extra message from her, nothing about seeing me perform, nothing.

We're not actually friends.

I wrote back a longish email, deleted it, wrote a medium one, deleted it, wrote *thx,* then deleted that, too. Then I went to work, parking my motorcycle in a hidden spot so that Todd and Brad couldn't once again use it as the canvas for one of their dog-poop-based art projects. Instead Todd used me as the canvas. "Hey, Methune!" I heard him shout, and when I was dumb enough to turn around I got my reward— *SPLAT*—a hefty, pungent lump of art material square in the solar plexus.

"Bull's-eye!" said Todd, high-fiving and celebrating with Brad. He was right, because I had chosen that day to commit the minor infraction of foregoing my Rick's Lawn Care Service polo in favor of a faded The Who T-shirt. The one with the logo that looks like a target. A target that now had a big glob of dog poop smack dab in the center. It was one of my favorite shirts, but it stunk so bad that I just stripped it off and left it in some bushes and finished the day topless and sunburned.

When I got home, there was a note from my mom: she and Rick were at a movie, pizza in fridge. *We need to talk.*

Which, no thanks. I made sure to be in bed and asleep before they got home, or at least in bed with the lights off while I hid under the covers and thumb-barfed bad lyrics into my phone.

I called and texted Devon a few times. He finally texted me back: *Can you f*** off for like a month?* Except he didn't use asterisks.

* * *

Now I'm sitting with Isaac Kaplan. I'll admit that I'd been sort of hoping Josephine would be waiting for me in the classroom this morning, despite everything. I have to give Isaac credit, though—he seems to know his stuff, and although it's early on I've yet to catch a single eye roll from him as I fumble around.

I take a breather from the quadratic equation that's taunting me from the page.

"Did Josephine say anything else about me?" I ask.

"She said you'd try to distract me from the lesson," says Isaac.

"Right." I try without success to refocus on the problem. "Nothing else?"

"Um . . ."

"Nothing about the concert?"

"She didn't mention it, no."

"Okay, right."

I pick up my pencil again and tap it against the paper. "Nothing?"

"No. Sorry."

"Right. Okay."

I go back to the problem, scribbling away, then pause again.

"We didn't really talk that much," he says, before I can start.

"Right."

Scribble scribble scribble. A good thirty seconds go by while I advance the field of mathematics.

"Would you say that she knows herself?"

"Knows herself?"

"I mean, when you think of her, do you think, oh, she's just some girl, or do you think, oh, there's someone who's complicated and knows herself and is comfortable with who . . ."

He blinks at me.

"Never mind."

"Okay." He looks meaningfully at the unfinished equation in front of me. I go at it again, or try.

"She didn't say *anything* about me singing?"

"No. You skipped a step," he says, indicating my mistake.

"Right. Okay."

Tap tap tap with the pencil on the page.

"I think she hates me," I say. "Do you think she hates me? She acts like she hates me. I think she hates me."

"I think," he says, "that I can teach this stuff pretty well but that I can't make you care."

"Jesus. How old are you again?"

We work the rest of the time in near silence. By the end

of the session I think I've actually started to learn something. Then, after we've packed up and Isaac is about to leave the room, he pauses in the doorway and drops this: "She's definitely not just some girl. And, you know, people have all sorts of reasons for the way they act."

Then Morpheus Kaplan gives me a little salute and goes off to be Delphic elsewhere.

* * *

I ponder that cryptic gem as I ride my motorcycle to the day's lawn-mowing venue, and I ponder it while I'm cutting grass, and I'm still pondering it when Todd casually pushes me off a hillock into a waist-deep decorative pond. *Huh,* I ponder as I flounder to the surface and get my feet under me and then sink gently up to my ankles into the soft muck, I wonder what sorts of reasons Todd has for acting the way he does.

Then at the end of the day I find out.

* * *

I find out because I forgot my Minnesota Twins ball cap on a rock by the pond. I left it there to dry after I splorched out of the water. I didn't mind the rest of my clothes being wet—it was a hot day and it actually felt pretty good. Or so I kept telling myself, while also cycling through several different fantasies about how I was going to extract my revenge against Todd Malloy. Leading contender: I'm giving a show in front of 10,000 people, and for some reason Todd is there in the front row—something to do with him winning a surprise concert from a radio station or whatever—and I see him and I stop the concert (which he's actually enjoying despite himself) and tell everyone, "See this guy? He is an awful person.

SHAME HIM." And they do, all 10,000 of them, jeering at him, and HOW DO YOU FEEL NOW, TODD MALLOY?!

I finished the day, my shoes still squelchy, and loaded my mower on the trailer, gave Kent his high-five ("Right on, bro!"), and realized that my cap was still on a rock about thirty miles from where I was. So I walked back across the lawn, dodging the swarms of early-evening gnats that hovered in pulsating clumps at head height, and retrieved my cap.

I took my time walking back toward the office building, a ten-story reflective glass cube surrounded by lawns and woods and mucky decorative ponds. The employees had apparently left for the day, the front parking lot entirely empty. Kent was gone. Todd and Brad appeared to be as well.

When I got closer, I started hearing voices. One voice, really—a man's voice, angry, shouting. It was hard to tell where the ruckus was coming from, but it seemed to be from somewhere behind the building. Why was a grown man standing somewhere behind this deserted office building on a Thursday evening, shouting?

Ten seconds ago, I got to the corner of the building and peeked around it. There was a rear parking lot, just three or four cars parked here and there out toward the perimeter.

There was another car, a dark-blue SUV, more or less in the center of the lot, parked at an angle so that it partially covered about four parking spaces. The driver-side door of the SUV was open, the engine running.

In front of the car was Todd Malloy. In front of Todd Malloy was a man who looked like a larger and even meaner version of Todd Malloy, a man who had to be Todd's father. And now everything makes sense.

It's his yelling I heard and am hearing right now. He's crowding Todd like a drill sergeant, face an inch from Todd's, screaming at him, alpha-dogging him, just like I've seen Todd do to other kids. Todd's doing the thing where you turn your head left and right and backpedal, trying to get away from his father without looking like he's running away, and his father is unloading on him, screaming abuse, and it's stomach-churning terrifying.

"YOU'RE GONNA BE A SMART-ASS TO *ME?* HUH??!!"

It's all stuff like that. I'm frozen in place. I shouldn't be watching this, but I can't stop. I hate Todd Malloy, hate him, but I'm getting nothing out of this, only a sense of fear and nausea. Todd is helpless, a little boy, completely drained of all his power, and I feel sorry for him, ashamed to see him brought this low.

Then it happens. His father is bellowing at him, forcing him backwards, and Todd brings up his hands defensively and sort of places them on his father's chest—not pushing, too scared to put any energy in the gesture—and his father bats his arms away violently, the noise a loud clap. This sparks a reaction in Todd, a burst of anger and aggression that blooms onto his face, his posture changing, fists clenching, and there's a primal moment where his father recognizes the challenge and *WHAM* he punches Todd straight on in the face.

Holy crap.

Todd's knees buckle and he staggers backwards, hands coming up to his face, and already there is blood pouring down his chin as he catches a heel on the asphalt and goes down hard on his ass. I'm jelly legged too, my chest heaving, heart thump

thump thumping, and I flinch as Todd's dad slams the door of the SUV shut and screeches away.

Todd is still sitting in the middle of the lot, holding his nose and sobbing. He tries to get up, but he's too wobbly, and he sits down, then tries it again, and again. When he tries it a fourth time, getting into a sort of a football-lineman position before tumbling forward onto his face, I start walking over to him, not even sure why.

He's still trying to get to his feet when I reach him.

"Stay down," I say. "Don't try to get up."

Like I know what I'm talking about. I've never had to deal with someone who maybe just got a concussion from his massive dad. Now Todd is in a sitting position, knees up, one hand over his nose. His eyes are glassy, and I'm not sure he's totally aware that I'm next to him. I stand there for what seems like five minutes, unsure of what to do—Put a hand on his shoulder? Call 911? Police? Fire? Ambulance? The principal?—and Todd stares straight ahead, holding his nose. Then, still not looking at me, he raises a bloody hand up toward me and slurs, "Help me up."

He nearly pulls me to the ground as he labors to get to his feet, grabbing my wrist with his free hand, me leaning away and taking two staggering steps back to counterbalance his weight. When he's finally up, I have to keep him from pitching forward, then steady him once, then again, until he waves me off with a limp hand and stands there, breathing in and out five or six times like he has to remind himself to do it. He wipes at his nose and looks at the blood. Only then does he look up at me, and the heavy locked gate to Todd Malloy is open for just a moment, a moment where we sort of acknowledge each other, where his eyes say, S*o now you know.* Then he drops his gaze and turns away.

"I gotta get home," he says. He takes a few uncertain steps in a random direction, then stops and looks around like a person trying to get his bearings in the middle of a forest.

"Maybe you should go to a doctor or something," I say.

He shakes his head.

"I just gotta get home."

"Won't your dad be there?"

"No, he won't come back for a few days now. That's what he does." He wipes again at the blood. "I just gotta go home."

He's still standing there.

"Uh . . ." I begin, not believing I'm about to say it. "Do you need a ride?"

* * *

Which is how I end up with Todd Malloy sitting on the back of my motorcycle as I drive him home. He's hugging me around the waist, either too stunned to be aware of just how weird this whole thing is, or aware enough of how stunned he is to know that he'd better hold on or he's going to be tumbling along the concrete at thirty miles per hour.

He lives in a generic house in west Edina that's only a few blocks from Josephine's. When we pull up to the curb, he has a bit of trouble getting off the seat, then just starts walking across the lawn toward his front door without a word. After a few steps, he stops, though, and turns around. We regard each other for a moment. The customary fierceness is seeping back into his gaze, like he's remembering who he is. I can see it coming: *You better not tell anyone,* he's going to say.

Instead, his voice quiet, he says, "Thanks."

Then he turns to go inside.

CHAPTER 14

I'm gonna call you up /
I'm gonna call you up so we can talk /
but first I have to finish this letter to you /
and before that there're fifty things / I have to do

"So glad you could join us," says Rick with a big smile.

Thank you! my mom is mouthing next to him. *Say thank you!*

"Thank you," I mutter.

She's now mouthing something else and I'm squinting at her, unable to figure out what she wants me to say.

For. Inviting. Me, she repeats, accompanied by a big round eye glare.

"Thank you for inviting me."

If Rick notices the whole exchange, he pretends not to.

"Of course," he says. "Always a pleasure to have you around."

Oh, shut up and eat your egg-white omelet, Rick.

Sunday brunch with Mom and Rick. *Yayyy.*

We're downtown, some place in a converted warehouse with high wood-beamed ceilings and really expensive gluten-free muesli on the menu. I rode my bike here, mumbling some excuse about having to meet Devon later on, but the real reason is that I couldn't stand to be in the car with them.

On Friday, Todd didn't greet me or even look at me when I arrived in the lot of the office park du jour. He had a purple bruise on his left cheek that sort of blended into a shiner. No eye contact when we had our morning meeting and did our "Go team!"

Afterward, Kent monitored us as we pulled the mowers off the trailer and arranged them to be fueled. Then he got a call on his cell and wandered off a ways to chat. I was working alongside Todd and Brad, but still Todd didn't acknowledge my presence or say a word to me. Like nothing had happened the previous day.

Brad acknowledged me, though. "What's up, faggot?" he said, which is about as good as it gets for a morning salutation from him. While we were standing near each other, putting gas in the mowers and weed whips, Brad kept going, telling me to hurry up, give him the stupid gas can already, lobbing lazy insults at me. Todd was silent.

"Dude, gimme the friggin' gas or I'm gonna smack you," said Brad.

Todd, adding oil to one of the walk-behinds, didn't look up as he said, "Shut up."

Brad stared at him.

"What?"

"I said, shut up," said Todd.

"Why?" said Brad.

Now Todd raised his gaze. "Because I friggin' said so."

Brad looked at him, surprised.

Todd straightened up, glared back. "You got a problem with that?" he said.

Brad blinked at him. "Naw, man. It's cool."

"Okay, then," Todd said, and yanked on the cord, firing up the engine, and rolled off. And that was it. Neither he nor Brad have said a single word to me since.

* * *

" . . . *Mrgle flrgle frmph* pretty great, right?"

Crap. Rick has been talking to me. They're both looking at me expectantly.

"Yeah . . . great," I hazard.

Rick laughs. My mom smiles. I cautiously smile.

"You're funny," says Rick, and I gather I just said something brilliantly ironic. " '*Great,*' " Rick repeats, imitating my delivery. He glances sideways at my mom. She smiles at him. He smiles back. He looks at me. "You know," he says, obviously about to introduce a new topic, just as I say, "Excuse me for a second."

More glances exchanged. "Of course," Rick says.

"Where you going?" says my mom, suspicious.

"Just the bathroom," I say, and slide out of the booth.

When I come out of the bathroom I stand there for a minute, looking across the room at my mom and Rick. He's got his arm around her shoulders, his hand massaging her, and I feel the same revulsion as when he touches me. She leans closer. They kiss. I taste semi-digested French toast and bile in the back of my throat.

You think I don't know what they've been working up to saying? You think I don't know they want to get married? I know. I'm not dumb. Okay, yes, at least about that.

Personally, I don't get what they see in each other: he's the World's Least Interesting Man and she's Kooky McKooksville. But that's exactly it, says Devon — it's like one of those movies: nerdy boring uptight guy meets free-spirited lady and whodathunkit they balance each other out and love and happiness and roll credits. And I will admit that my mom has been a lot more stable since Rick has been on the scene, and whenever he's with her he always has an expression like he can't believe his luck. So, fine. Maybe they *should* get married. It doesn't bother me in the least. I'm going to be gone in a year anyway.

Oh, BS. Of course it bothers me. I wouldn't be standing here having to reswallow my breakfast if it didn't bother me.

There's a family at a table near me, two young kids with the same curly hair as their father. He's saying something now, entertaining them, and they're both laughing. He seems like a good dad.

Kids can have all sorts of dads. You can have a good dad like that, which I assume is healthy and beneficial. Or you can have a dad who's a plastic politician and uses you as a Barbie doll in his CampaignLand™ playset, which probably isn't so healthy and beneficial. Of course, it's probably healthier and beneficial-ier than having a dad who regularly pounds the crap out of you, like he's beating you on an anvil to gradually deform you into a miniature version of his twisted self.

Compared with either of those choices, having a dad who skips out and isn't a dad at all might not be so bad.

My mom has a piece of fruit skewered on her fork, and she's teasing Rick with it, pretending to feed it to him and then moving it just out of reach when he tries to eat it. They're both giggling. In a moment I'll rejoin them and they'll say, *Austin, we have some exciting news for you.* Urrrrrrp.

The restroom is near the entrance, and through the glass I can see happy people on the sidewalk, enjoying the morning sunshine. I push through the door and step outside.

I recognize the neighborhood now. I check a map on my phone, and there it is, the recording studio, just a few blocks away from where I'm standing.

It's Sunday morning. He won't be there. And even if he is, I don't want to see him. Is what I'm thinking as I start down the sidewalk, away from the restaurant, away from my mom and Rick, toward the recording studio.

* * *

Rocker Dude is sitting at the incongruous reception desk, reading the same issue of *Guitar Player*.

"Shane here?"

The bored glance, the gesture with his head to go on in. *Rock on, dude.*

I get to the door at the end of the hall. I knock a few times but no one answers, so I turn the knob, open the door, and peek in. There's an anteroom, and then another door with a circular window like a porthole in it. I peer through the window and see a dimly lit audio-monitoring room, the mixing board glowing like a massive control panel in a spaceship. The board faces a big window into what I assume is the recording studio.

It takes a second for my eyes to adjust enough to see that there are two people in the control room—Ed the engineer and Shane, both listening to something on headphones. Ed is nodding his head. Shane is shaking his.

As I watch he takes his headphones off and tosses them aside, then slumps way back in his chair until he's practically facing the ceiling, rubbing his eyes.

I open the door and step inside the room. Ed looks at me, surprised.

"Hey," he says. "What's up?"

"Who is that?" says Shane. His eyes are still closed.

"It's me," I say.

He opens his eyes and tilts his chin down to look at me, then straightens up in his chair.

He doesn't say anything for a bit. Then he says, "You want to go fishing?"

"Fishing?" I say.

"Yeah, fishing. Isn't that what fathers and sons do?"

"Shane," says Ed, "we have a lot of work to do here, and you're about *this* close to Barry losing his patience and pulling the plug on you."

Shane looks at me.

"What do you say?"

What do I say? I say, "Sure."

* * *

So my dad and I go fishing.

First, though, we descend upon a Target and power-shop for fishing gear: rods, reels, a massive tackle box, a random assortment of grotesque lures to fill it, every "Do we need this?" from me met with a firm "Abso*lutely*."

"Hats," says Shane, so we try on all sorts, me settling on a straw cowboy hat, Shane getting one of those bucket things, and then we both get huge wraparound sunglasses.

Before we left the recording studio, I texted my mom: *Hey, sorry ran into a friend will meet you at home*
She texted back, *What? You are such an asshole.*
Then, *I am so angry at you.*
Rick is very disappointed.
You owe me a big explanation.
And so on, until I turned off the indicator so that it doesn't buzz each time a new threat arrives.

I ride in the giant red shopping cart. Shane pushes me at a near sprint. He hops on the back. We nearly plow into a very ample lady. Unhappy store manager in red Target vest voices polite disapproval. Sincere apologies are offered, somewhat undercut by stifled giggles. Items are paid for, Shane shoplifts a candy bar, we make our escape.

A drink run. A six-pack of soda, two six-packs of beer that we place on ice in the cooler—another Target purchase, very reasonable price.

"Um, where are we going?"

"Well, where would you normally go if you were playing hooky?"

"I guess I'd go to the place we call Whitmore's."

"Can you fish there?"

"Yeah, sure, I guess."

"Okay, let's go to Whitmore's."

As we drive we talk about music. We talk about guitars. We talk about artists we respect and shows we've seen and who we wished we'd seen. We don't talk about the other night or about anything that might point us in a direction leading to tears or anger or not talking.

We park the truck near the path and lug the rods and tackle box and cooler and Shane's acoustic guitar through the woods. When we get to the spot, Shane looks around and says, "Well, we got us a river and we got us some train tracks, and if that ain't the stuff of music, I don't know what is."

So now we're settled against a thick tree upstream from the railroad trestle, a hundred and fifty dollars' worth of fishing gear mostly forgotten in the long grass by our feet. Instead we talk a little and drink beer ("You can have *one*," said Shane, I think because he was trying to seem responsible, but pretty soon I noticed that he wasn't keeping track). Mostly what we do is take turns playing Shane's guitar and sing songs together.

For hours.

Do you know that Carter family song, "Long Journey Home"?

I'll teach you.

Do you know "Wild Horses" by the Stones?

Of course.

"Wish the Worst" by the Old 97's?

How's that go?

That's really good, says Shane, or Let me show you how to do that better, or Here's something you might want to work on . . .

Like, you know, a dad would do.

Hours drifting by, Shane and me, the creek swirling and changing color as the sun sinks lower, trains passing, clouds forming and dissipating.

We talk about rivers and trains in music, all the references, the delta blues. We sing "Take Me to the River," "Watching the River Flow," Joni Mitchell's "River." We talk about Jeff Buckley wandering into the Wolf River in Memphis, Tennessee, and drowning, and Shane sings me a beautiful song about that by another Amy, Amy Correia, a song called "Blind River Boy."

That's beautiful, I say, and he says, *Yeah . . .* Off somewhere, thinking about something. "I knew him, you know," he says.

"Yeah?"

"Yeah. When he was down in Memphis. I was a lot younger, just getting started." He thinks some more. "You know, you do this stuff, Austin, you create something, I think you have to be on good terms with the devil. But don't ever think you can be friends with him."

We're in a sunlit patch, warm, but I shiver.

Then he says, "Dat's some deep stuff, right?" and throws back his head and laughs, dispelling the shadows, and launches into "Friend of the Devil," and we have more sing-along time.

Being there with him, singing and talking and just sitting in silence watching the dancing eddies of the creek, I feel a sort of contented happiness that I've never felt before. And also a sort of terror. Like someone has said to me, *There's this thing called oxygen. You breathe it and it keeps you alive.* Now I'm having oxygen for the first time and it's so basic and so good, but now I also realize how much I've always needed it, and how I will go on needing it, and I don't want it to go away.

When it gets late in the afternoon, the sun down behind the trees, Shane says, "Let's get some food. But before we go, I want to hear something by Austin Methune."

"What?"

"Sing me something of yours."

"No, I can't. I don't have anything."

"Nothing?"

"I just have pieces of things."

"So play me a piece of something."

"I can't."

"Austin," he says, "here's the great part. It can stink—I mean absolutely *stink*—and it's okay, because it's just me."

I think about that. He smiles at me and passes the guitar over.

So I start strumming, then quietly sing something that came into my head last night during my under-the-covers songwriting session. "Oh, Josephine, Josephine / hear my plea / Someone has got to love me / and it can't be me. / I'm a liar and a deceiver / I can't stand me neither / But if you leave / well that's the end of me"

Then I stop.

"That's it?" he says.

"That's all I have. That's about as far as I usually get."

He's smiling, nodding.

"What?"

"Josephine—she's the girl from the other night," he says. Again, not so much a question as a statement.

"Yes."

He nods again.

"It's not about her," I say. "Or me."

"No, right."

"I'm just using her name for the song."

"Sure. It's a good name."

I wait.

"So . . . what do you think?" I say.

"I think you've got something really special there. Something really promising. Keep working on it."

"The song?"

"The song. And the girl. C'mon, let's go get some food."

* * *

We drive to Uptown, me a bit buzzed, Shane not showing any obvious effects from the numerous beers he downed. Which, yeah, I've been the unwilling witness to a fair bit of parental drinking in my time, and maybe there's a tiny red flag being waved somewhere in my mind. But this is different, because it's Shane.

We eat at some hipster place that's half restaurant and half bowling alley. I take a break to use the bathroom and check the by-now-impressive number of affectionate, supportive texts from my mom, the last of which suggests that I had better goddamn well be dead, because that's pretty much the only excuse for not responding that will cut it at this point. So I text her back and tell her, Yes, I'm dead, I'm texting you from beyond the grave and I bet you feel pretty awful right now, and my ghost is having dinner at Devon's and will be back later on and I still love you even though you hate me, your poor dead son.

When I get back to the table, Shane is fiddling with the check, pen hovering.

"The other night," I say, "that was the first time I've ever been able to get onstage and perform."

He lowers the pen. "What? You're kidding."

I tell him about my whole problem with audiences.

"I don't know why," I say.

"I do," he says, and starts scribbling on the check.

"So?"

"Because," he says, distracted as he adds numbers, "you think it's the only thing in this life you love to do, the only thing you *can* do, but you're afraid to find out that you really *can't*. Because if you can't, what have you got left?"

He signs his name with a flourish, then looks up at me, offers me the pen. "Here, you should be writing all my wisdom down. This stuff is priceless."

* * *

On the way to the car he says, "Speaking of performing, Amy's leaving tomorrow for a bit to do some shows in Chicago. We're having some folks over tonight, and she's going to sing some stuff, I'll sing, other folks will sing, we'll all sing together. It'll be a regular good ol' time hootenanny. You want to come?"

"Sure."

"You can bring someone, you want."

So I call Alison.

"Austin!"

"Hey there. Listen, there's this party thing tonight . . ."

We make a plan that we will swing by and pick her up at eight p.m.

"Here," I say to Shane when we reach her house, and Shane pulls over and stops.

Then I sit there in the passenger seat without moving.

"What?" he says after about thirty seconds.

"Actually, can we stop somewhere else instead?"

"Sure. What's up?"

"I just realized who I *really* want to invite."

CHAPTER 15

I thought that you were someone else /
I thought that I was too / but maybe if you were with me /
we'd both be someone new

"Hi. Jacqueline, right?"

"Uh . . . yeah?"

"So good to see you again!" I say.

"Uh–huh."

"Austin."

"Uh–huh."

She's standing in the doorway, looking at me with the same amused contempt as before. I smile warmly back at her. She has makeup on and she's fiddling with her hair, doing those occult things girls do. A date tonight, I imagine.

"Might I add that you look particularly ravishing this evening?" I say.

"What do you want?"

"Is your sister available?"

She snorts. "Hold on." She leaves.

Fidget. Pace. Turn a full circle. Phone buzzes. Another frowny-face emoji from Alison, who has sent me, like, five of them after I texted her and said I had to cancel because of a Mom thing.

"Hey."

I jump, quickly putting the phone away. It's Josephine, standing in the doorway, her expression cautious, confused.

"Hi! How are you? Are you okay?" I say.

"Yyyes . . . ?"

"Great. Great."

"Is there—"

"Do you want to go see some music?"

"What?"

"Music. Music. Want to come?"

"Now?"

"Yes. I mean, it's more like a party, but people are going to sing and all. Me and Shane are going. Shane and I." I gesture to the Range Rover waiting at the curb behind me.

"Oh. Thanks. I don't think so. Thanks. No."

"You sure?"

"Yeah, thanks. It's sort of late."

"Back by midnight. Maybe one."

"Thanks, no."

"Is there some rule? Against fraternizing with your former tutees?"

"No, I just can't. Curfew. I'd get in trouble. I'm already kind of in trouble from the other night."

"Right."

Shane taps the horn.

"Okay," I say. "You sure?"

"Yeah, thanks."

"Okay." My gaze flicks past her. Her sister is standing at the far end of the hall that leads to the door, arms crossed, watching us, not even trying to hide it. Smirking.

Josephine turns to see what I'm looking at, then turns back to me.

Our eyes meet.

"Let me get my phone," she says.

*　*　*

This is a disaster.

We're in Shane's car, me in back, Josephine in the front seat, and we're all nearly dead, suffocated by the toxic awkwardness that has displaced all the oxygen in the vehicle.

Things began going downhill the instant we started walking down the path from her house. Josephine took three steps and got a text and immediately started texting furiously back. I was trying to figure out if I was supposed to be walking next to her or not and ended up sort of splitting the difference, walking just ahead of her, twisting once to say, "Should be a fun party."

She didn't say anything, just glanced up from her phone to give a brief, grimacey smile, and right then it was plain: all she had wanted to do was stick it to her family, prove to them and herself that she was independent. Not actually *be* independent. But she was trapped with her choice now, heading off to some weird party with me, and like we'd both said, we're not actually friends. *It's okay, you beat them, you can go back to them now,* I was thinking of telling her, but by then we had reached

Shane's car and he was opening the passenger door for her, expansive and welcoming.

"Hi there. I'm Shane," he said, hand extended.

"Hi," she said, polite, but nervous and watchful. When she climbed in, Shane glanced at me questioningly and I gave a little shrug. Shane put the car in gear and did his best to engage her: You like the show? You see a lot of music? You in school with Austin? Josephine answered in nervous monosyllables and then fell silent, still fielding texts on her phone.

Shane glanced at me in the mirror. Again I shrugged.

Now I'm rifling through every drawer in my brain, trashing the place, hoping to find something to say. Shane drums on the steering wheel. I jiggle my foot. I'm watching the anxiety reflected in Josephine's left hand, which is resting on her left thigh but is squeezed into a slowly churning fist, clenching and unclenching like she's kneading a small ball.

"Mind if I . . . ?" says Shane, indicating the radio.

"No, please, great, sure, great," Josephine and I rush to say, and Shane switches on the radio, a merciful bolt gun to the temple of this wretched moment, putting it out of its misery.

Amy welcomes us at the door of the house, a two-story near Uptown, and she hugs Shane, hugs me, ignores Josephine's proffered hand to pull her in for a squeeze too. "You're friends with them, you get one of these!"

"Why don't you give them a tour of the house?" suggests Shane. He seems somehow amused, enjoying the awkwardness.

"Sure," says Amy.

"Here, first you have to touch the horseshoe," she says without any explanation, indicating a beat-up horseshoe nailed to the front door, so we touch the horseshoe before stepping inside.

Then she shows us the upstairs, the downstairs, keeping a cheerful patter running the whole time, and takes us out back to the unused granny apartment over the detached garage, leading us up the ladder-like stairs to the mini-home with its tiny fridge and one-burner stove and Isn't it adorable? she says, and we agree, and frankly I'm grateful to her for giving us an excuse not to talk.

When we come back into the house it seems that everyone is arriving all at once, Shane giving embraces, backslapping, laughing, that same intoxicating aura that he had in the bar, the all-is-splendid-with-life-and-the-universe glow. People touch the horseshoe as they step in, one guy with neck tats saying, "Aw, you brought it!"

"Always," says Shane.

I recognize many of them from the show, some of them recognizing me back, saying, Hey, great job the other night. I even see the bassist from the first time I went to Shane's studio, Rob, the one who had stormed out, and he gets the same treatment from Shane, like the screaming argument never happened.

"Isn't that . . . ?" I say to Amy.

"Yeah," she says. "Everyone loves Shane. Just not in the studio."

Shane makes sure to introduce us around: Alex, this is my son, Austin, and his friend Josephine; Becky, this is my son. . . . I don't think I've said three words to Josephine since we got in the truck, and I feel like I can see us from above having parallel party experiences, attending the same event but not *with* each other.

"Okay, everyone, we should head out back," announces Shane, so we all head through the kitchen to the backyard. Josephine is texting as she follows the herd. Shane puts his arm around me.

"Doing okay?"

"Yeah, yeah, all good."

There are Christmas-style lights draped along the wooden fence and in the overhanging branches of the trees, stars visible beyond. People crowd onto three old picnic benches and an assortment of lawn furniture and indoor chairs that had long ago become outdoor chairs, everything arranged in a rough semicircle, Amy tuning up her guitar in the middle of it.

There is an old sofa out there too, and Shane says, "Why don't you guys sit?"

"No, you sit," says Josephine, and then we do the whole back-and-forth negotiation, going through every possible permutation of who sits and who stands, and finally Shane practically shoves me and Josephine into the sofa's marshmallow embrace just as Amy is saying, "Hey, everyone!"

It's small—a love seat, really—and the instant our butts hit the cushions we both casually lean away in opposite directions like magnets repelling each other. But it's almost impossible to sit without some part of our bodies touching, the sagging U-shape of the frame and the soft cushions colluding to bring us toward the center and each other.

"Thanks for coming!" Amy says, and everyone cheers

and claps, and I swear the next is directed right at me and Josephine: "So glad you're here."

I'm so glad *one* of us is glad.

"I'm gonna get started in *juuust* a few seconds," Amy is saying, doing some last-minute tuning tweaks. Low murmurs of conversation from the others, the rhythmic pulse of crickets. I can feel the heat radiating from Josephine, feel it along my left flank and especially along my leg, our thighs half an inch apart. She shifts slightly and our hips bump and we both try to readjust without making it obvious that that's what we're doing. We've both got our outside arms draped over the armrests, squeezing ourselves to them like we're clinging to life rafts. This is not going to work. I could say I need to use the bathroom or that I'm going to get a drink. "I think I might—"

Then Amy starts to sing, and I forget all that.

Her voice . . . a voice that glows, a voice filled with heartache and longing and all the sad and happy things that life has to offer. Everyone goes hushed quiet, church quiet, no one wanting to move and mar the loveliness.

I feel transported. Enthralled. I'm embarrassed that Josephine is going to catch me all starry-eyed and weepy, and I feel a surge of resentment toward her for being here, even though her being there is my fault. I fight against and then give in to the urge to look at her, knowing my glance will be met by an arched brow and an eye roll.

But no. When I look at her, I get a jolt of recognition because I see she's captivated too. And I want to touch her on the shoulder and say, *I know you now, I know you. We understand each other.*

146

At that moment she must sense my gaze, because she glances at me and our eyes meet and we both quickly look away, like we've walked in on each other naked.

I don't know how many songs go by with us sitting like that, each fighting the sofa's gentle encouragement to lean against each other. When we applaud, our arms touch. We don't look at each other except a few times, and when we do we trade quick shy smiles and both look away.

Amy sings songs about falling in love and about falling out of love and about wishing someone loved you and wishing they didn't. She switches between a guitar and a mandolin and a baritone ukulele, which you would think would sound silly but in her hands sounds spare and solemn and powerful.

I'm aware that Josephine smells nice. I hope I don't smell bad. I try to surreptitiously smell my own breath, jutting my lower lip out to direct my exhalation toward my nostrils, but does that even work?

Amy says, "C'mon, Shane Tyler, come on up here and sing a song with me." Shane says, "Oh, I'm coming, Amy Adler," and rests a hand on my shoulder as he passes by, turning to wink at me and Josephine. Now I look at Josephine, and she smiles at me, still shy, but this time with something approaching delight.

They play one of Amy's songs together, and halfway through I realize that Josephine and I have both given up our battle with the sofa, that we're leaning against each other. When they finish the song, Amy says, "Can we sing one of yours now, Shane Tyler?"

"Well, certainly, Amy Adler," he says, "but can we bring a third up here?"

She laughs, like a shimmer of bells. "Why, sure. The more the merrier. Who you got?"

Everyone in the crowd is twisting again, looking around curiously. Josephine whispers, "He means you."

"Austin, you want to come join us for a song?"

I'm suddenly embarrassed, aware of everyone looking at me. I shake my head at him. *Please, let me be.*

"Go on!" says Josephine. "Go!" and she nudges me forward. I look at her, and she nods at me encouragingly—*go!*—so I get to my feet and make my way to the front.

"Austin Methune, everyone," says Shane. "You know 'Seeing by Starlight'?" he says.

"Sure, yeah."

"You could play it on the mandolin?"

I do some quick chord conversions in my mind.

"Sure."

The three of us crowd together, Amy in the middle, the two of them on guitar and me on mandolin. I sing the middle harmony on the song and add some mandolin fills that suggest themselves to me, no effort on my part. Josephine is watching me, her eyes shining wide and luminous, her lips parted, and I feel a tiny explosion inside and have to hide from that gaze.

We finish the song, everyone applauding, Amy hugging me, and when I go back to the sofa there's the shy smile again from Josephine, and I sheepishly return it before sitting.

"All right, who's next?" says Amy, and everyone here seems to be a musician, and so she sings with another person, and then that person with Shane, and Shane with someone else, everyone joining in on the sing-alongs or listening respectfully to the quiet, sad ones.

I'm once again aware how close Josephine and I are sitting, our sides touching, and it's okay, but then she adjusts her position and pulls away a bit, so I do the same so as not to give her the impression that I'm trying to touch her, and she maybe pulls away a bit more, and we get stuck in that loop of *What is the other person thinking/doing?* Or maybe *I'm* stuck. I don't know. I think this is how wars start.

Shane is leading us in "Let It Be" when I realize that Josephine is singing along. And has a nice voice. Not beautiful and polished like Amy's, but simple and on-key and pleasant. Unadorned, I think. Then she notices me looking at her and blushes and clamps her mouth shut.

"Come sing another with me," says Amy, so she and I sing Dylan's "You're Gonna Make Me Lonesome When You Go."

When we finish, I see something in Shane's expression, the same inner entertainment I saw earlier in the evening, and just as I'm thinking, *Wait, what is he up to?* he points to Josephine and says, "Your turn!"

Her eyes widen. "No no no no no," she says, waving her hands.

"Yes yes yes. I heard you singing."

"No no no, I don't know any songs."

"Everyone knows a song. Austin, I bet you can figure out at least one song for the two of you to sing."

"How about 'Time After Time,'" I suggest, and I know she knows it, because they sang it in choir.

"I'm too embarrassed."

"You have a beautiful voice," says Shane.

"I can't."

"You can!"

And so on back and forth, but it's *Shane,* see, irresistible and wholehearted and sincere, and the night is magic, it's magic, and it's inevitable that she'll say yes, and all the guests are saying, *C'mon, you can do it!* and Amy closes the deal by linking arms with Josephine and saying I'll sing with you too.

So it happens. Amy and Josephine and I sing "Time After Time," Shane on guitar, Josephine restrained and hesitant at first but gaining strength, and I'm aware of Amy smiling at me as she gradually eases back until by the second half of the song it's just Josephine and me singing. I can feel everyone focused on us, everyone listening. It feels like the whole universe is listening. We're singing, harmonizing, but Josephine won't even look at me, keeps her eyes downcast like the lyrics are on the ground before her. Then just when we get to the part about finding the other person if they're lost and catching them if they fall, she looks up and our eyes lock and it's searing and so intense that my voice falters for a moment and we both have to search for the words somewhere on the lawn.

When we finish, we end up back on the sofa and can hardly look at each other. A few more people sing songs, a big rousing finish with "All You Need Is Love." I can barely hear any of it. Everyone is standing and hugging and shaking hands, and I feel a light touch on my shoulder and it's Josephine, pulling her hand back hurriedly.

"I should go," she says.

"Right Yes. Of course. Uh, let me figure out what we should do," I stammer.

"Why don't you take the truck," says Shane. "Bring it back to me whenever."

Amy does a quick field-sobriety test, consisting of her grabbing both my ears and saying, "Breathe on me."

I breathe on her.

"Have you been drinking?"

"No! Not a drop!"

She lets go of one ear but starts twisting the other.

"Austin, I will beat your ass if you're lying to me."

"Not a drop! Ow! Let go!"

"Okay, then." She leans in close and whispers, "I like her a lot. Go."

On the ride to Josephine's it's a whole new variety of wordless awkward. Like by singing that song together we'd somehow gone way too far, experienced something far too intimate. More intimate somehow than, well, being *intimate*.

Two frozen centuries into the ride, she finally says, "So . . . tell me about Shane," and I'm grateful to have a way to fill up a few miles and minutes. I tell her everything that has happened since he first showed up on the doorstep, everything I know about him, about my mom lying to me all this time since I was a kid.

"Austin, that's incredible."

"Yeah. Of course, it's possible that he's not really my dad."

She's quiet.

"No," she says, "he's your dad."

More silence.

We get to her house and I park.

"Well . . ."

"Yeah, well . . ."

"That was really fun."

"Yeah."

"Thanks for inviting me."

"Yeah, sure, of course. Thanks for coming."

The radio is on, so at least the silence isn't silent.

"You want to hang out again sometime?" I say.

"Sure, yeah."

"What are you doing tomorrow?"

She laughs softly. "Can't tomorrow. Phone calls. Raising funds."

"Right."

Well.

Well.

It's time for her to go.

The song on the radio is ending.

She has to go.

She's not moving.

The song ends. The song "Heirloom" by Sufjan Stevens starts, and I'm about to say, *I never liked this song,* but suddenly it's the most beautiful thing ever, and it's like the song is showing me the way, the song is saying, *Now, the moment is now, don't wait,* and it's like Josephine and I both know and we turn to each other and we're kissing.

We're kissing and her lips are soft and my hands are on her face and I can feel her warm hands on me and I'm thunderstruck, I'm trembling, and we kiss more and kiss more, my eyes closed, the heat of her body, her breath, the smell of her hair, the feeling of floating in a sea of stars.

Then suddenly she stops. She stops and pulls back, a hand on my chest. She pulls back and pushes away and looks at me, then wait she's turning to open the car door and wait

152

she's climbing out and closing the door and wait she's walking up the path toward her house—"Wait," I say—and her walk goes faster and turns into a run and then she's at the front door—"Wait!"—and the door opens—"Josephine, wait!"—and she's inside and the door closes and she's gone.

CHAPTER 16

I believe in things I cannot see /
I believe in you and me / I believe /
I believe that we'll be together

"Where is he?!"

"Whuh?"

"WHERE IS HE?!"

Really bad way to wake up: My mother shaking me violently by the shoulders and screaming in my face.

"What? What's happening? What's going on?"

"Where. Is. He?"

The various components of my consciousness that go off and do their own thing when I'm asleep are still struggling to return to headquarters so that my brain can function.

"Mom, whuzzuh . . . What's going on? Where is who?"

"Don't give me that crap! Where is Shane!"

"Shane? He's not here! What are you talking about!"

"Why is his goddamn car here?!"

Oh, crap. The car. Right. I drove home from Josephine's, dazed, three-fourths baffled, one quarter love-dopey, and parked in front of the house, figuring I would wake up before dawn and drive it to math class and then to work before my mom was the wiser. Fail.

"I said, why is his goddamn car here?!"

Lesson number one: Don't plan tactics when you're baffled and/or love-dopey.

"What time is it?" I say, then look over at the alarm clock — "Oh, crap!" — and leap out of bed and rush out of the room and down the hall, my mom in hot pursuit.

"What the hell is going on here!"

"Mom, shut the door! I'm peeing!"

"Why is his car here?!"

"Mom, I *will* pee on you!"

Really shocking statement from my mom about what she, in turn, will do to me.

"Jesus, Mom!"

"I'm serious! Where is he?"

"He's not here! I just have his car!"

"Have you been hanging out with him? You *have* been hanging out with him! I'm going to—"

Truly harrowing, scrotum-puckering description of the traumatic punishment that awaits Shane.

"Mom!"

"What the hell happened yesterday! Where were you last night? What have you been doing!"

What was I doing last night? Did all that really happen? It can't have. It's impossible. It was a dream. I made it up.

"I'm talking to you!"

"Mom!"

It goes on like this for the next several minutes as I yank my clothes on—"Answer me!" "I'm trying to put my pants on!"—and head downstairs—"Where are you going!" "Breakfast!"—and pour myself some cereal and shovel it into my mouth while standing at the counter, my mom at my elbow, harrying me.

Mom (pulling cereal bowl away; milk and cornflakes slopping on the linoleum): "Look at me when I'm talking to you! How come you have his truck?!"

Me (pointing to mouth stuffed with cereal): "Mmmm! Rmmph mmph mmmm!"

Then I grab the box of cereal and scoot out the door—"I gotta get to class and then work! It's in the contract!"—and hop into the truck, my mom banging on the window.

"We are gonna talk, mister!"

"I love you!"

"You tell him he's dead!"

"I love you bye!"

SCRREEECH!

I Fast & Furious it backwards out of the driveway and accelerate away before my mom can leap on the hood, punch through the windshield, and pull my heart out of my rib cage.

* * *

Last night when I got home, I texted Josephine:

Is everything okay?

It was the only text I sent. I'd like to say it was self-control, but what really happened is that the music came flooding in and I fell asleep while I was waiting for a reply. Now I'm late

156

to math class, but the anxiety is growing so intense that I have to pull over to send another text:

All ok?

I wait on the side of the road, hoping she'll get back to me. Minutes pass. She doesn't. I swear and put the truck in gear.

Math class is special agony because I desperately want to check my phone, but there're only seven of us in the class, all known troublemakers, and Mr. Westphal's gaze never wavers.

Class ends. No communication. I arrive at the office park we're mowing today, everyone else already out there fighting the good fight against grass. No texts.

I pull a mower off Kent's trailer of fun and get to work.

My back-and-forth progress across the lawn is herky-jerky, my forward motion interrupted every thirty seconds when I check my phone. I know I shouldn't do it, but I can't resist: I start sending more texts:

Are you angry?

All okay?

Can we pls talk?

I see Kent in the distance, observing me, and so I start forcing myself to wait until the turnaround point at the end of each row to check for responses, but a good acre goes by with nothing, and then another acre, my misery growing with every swath of freshly mown turf.

What has happened is clear: Josephine, having realized she'd lost her goddamn mind, fell asleep last night midscream and woke up this morning to finish screaming, and now she can't shower enough to rid herself of the repulsive memory of my touch, completely Lady Macbething it, probably brushing her teeth with obsessive ferocity at this very moment as she tries to scrub away my kisses.

I replay over and over again the moment she pulled away from me, her expression worse with each iteration, a scene shot ten different ways: Confused. No. Scared. No. Angry. No. Furious. No. Barely contained nausea-inducing revulsion.

"She hates me!" I shout, a squirrel in a nearby tree watching in consternation. "Hates me!" I repeat to the squirrel. *Oh, dear,* thinks the squirrel, or whatever it is squirrels think, then evidently decides it would be wiser to put several more trees between him and the screaming human.

More mowing, the sun rising higher, the temperature and my despair climbing with it.

My phone buzzes. *YES!*

Yank it out, fumble and bobble it, nearly dropping it under the mower.

NO! IT'S JUST MY MOM!

i expect you here for dinner you have lots of explaining to do
mom ok ok it's all fine don't worry

I mow angry. I mow bereft. I mow with denial. I mow with four of the five stages of mourning, skipping the acceptance part. During the lunch break, I seat myself on a bench away from the others to eat my boloney sandwich, which tastes of a very complicated mix of emotions that add up to WHY GOD WHY DO YOU HATE ME WHY WON'T SHE CALL. I cling to my phone, stare at it, issuing high-level, threat-of-death orders to myself not to send another text, *no no no, do not, will not, won't, no way, I'd rather die than okjustthisone:*

Please respond.

Three minutes later, she does. And I wish she hadn't.

Austin—I'm sorry. The party was really fun, and thank you for inviting me, but I feel like I made a really bad mistake last night and need space. Sorry.

It's like a physical blow, a kick to the stomach. I'm sitting on the bench, gasping for breath, my hand shaking as I read and reread the text. Then I realize that Kent is standing in front of me, hands on hips, grinning his coach grin.

"What's wrong with you?" he asks. "You have girlfriend trouble or something?"

It's only about five minutes later, when I'm driving away too fast in Shane's truck, that I say, "I *quit.*"

* * *

Ed the engineer is coming down the hall from the audio-monitoring room as I approach.

"Hey, kid," he says.

"Hey. Where you going?"

"Out to smoke. And probably drink."

"Oh. Shane here?"

"Yep. That's why I want to go drink."

"What happened?"

"What happened? Nothing happened. That's the problem. You don't by some chance have a band with you, do you?"

"What?"

"Nothing. I'm gonna go smoke."

I enter the control room and let my eyes adjust to the dim light. "Shane?" I say. He's not there. I look through the window and don't see anyone in the actual recording area. I stand there for a minute, perplexed, wondering if he somehow managed to sneak out another way. I'm about to leave but then decide to check out the recording room.

It's a much larger space than I'd expected, maybe half the size of a football field, the exact dimensions hard to make out because of the subdued lighting and the black audio insulation that covers the walls and ceiling. It takes me a moment to realize that Shane is lying on his back in the middle of the floor, eyes closed.

"Shane?" I say.

He opens his eyes, turns his head to confirm it's me, returns his head to its previous position, and closes his eyes once more.

"Hey," he says. "You bring the truck back?"

"Yeah."

"Thanks."

"Sure."

"Fun party last night, right?"

"Yeah."

"Glad you could make it."

"Yeah, thanks for inviting me."

"Josephine have a good time?"

"Yes. Or no. I think. I'm not sure."

"Sounds complicated."

"A bit."

"That happens sometimes."

"Right."

I'm still leaning through the doorway, holding the heavy insulated door half open, wondering if I'm supposed to enter the room or excuse myself and leave.

"Uh . . . Shane?"

"Yeah."

"Everything okay?"

"Nope," he says. "I'm stuck."

"What? Did you fall? Are you hurt?"

"No. Not that kind of stuck. This is more of an existential stuck."

"Oh."

"Yeah. Stuck. It's over."

"What is?"

"Everything. This." He makes a squiggly finger gesture toward the ceiling.

"The record?"

"Yep. Done. Over. Remember how Ed said Barry was going to run out of patience? Barry ran out of patience. I don't blame him."

Now I step in, the door closing behind me with the sucking sound of an air lock sealing.

"He pulled the plug?!"

"Yep. The plug, she is pulled."

"That's it? How can he do that?"

"He's the person who inserted the plug in the first place, so he has full plug-pulling authority. It's his dime. And his plug."

"But . . ."

"That's Barry."

"What does that even mean?"

"It means Barry's the sort of guy who calls you up one day, probably sitting by his pool in Beverly Hills, and says, 'Hey, get in the studio.' He's also the sort of guy who calls you up, you know, still sitting by the pool, and says, 'Send me something good tonight by eight p.m., or get out of the studio.' Which he did."

"So send him something!"

"That's the point. There is no *something* to send him. I have nothing."

"But—"

"The other night when I performed—how many of those songs did you know?

"All of them."

"Right. Every single one. What does that tell you?"

"But you've been in here—"

"For three weeks. And I have nothing. I didn't have anything going in, and nothing's happened since I got here."

"Nothing? All these weeks?"

"Well, lots of arguments and me being an ass. Lots of that."

"But—"

"Did you not hear me about the stuck thing? I have a bunch of partial songs, all of which, even in their partial form, are crappy to begin with."

"Half songs," I mutter, not even intending to say it out loud.

"You say 'half songs'? Yeah, that's what I have. Half songs. I have maybe one song that's any good."

"So give him that!"

"You have a band hiding behind you?"

"Can't you just record something solo?"

"He wants a song, Austin," he says, finally looking at me again. "Not a sketch of a demo of a demo."

"Well, what do you need?"

162

"I need a *band*. A drummer, a bass player, rhythm guitar, blah blah blah."

"But you know so many musicians!"

"Yerp. And they know *me*. That's the problem. Frankly, even *I* don't want to work with me anymore."

"You could use —"

"Do *not* say a drum machine. I will *not* use a drum machine. I need a real drummer. And everything else. In, like, an hour or so."

"I can do that."

"Great. I'll be here. A drummer, guitarist . . ."

"How about a girl to sing harmony?"

"Sure, why not. A horn section. Strings. Bring it all."

"I'm serious."

"Fantastic."

"I'm *serious!* Stay here! I'll be back in an hour. Two, tops!"

As the door is closing I hear him say, "Austin, wait," but I'm already on my way.

CHAPTER 17

Put it back on my back / I will carry it, I'll carry it /
I'll carry it for you / I will carry you too

I drive across the office parking lot all the way to where it meets the lawn. Kent's truck and trailer are nearby, but I can't see anyone. Then, at the far edge of the field, which looks to be ten miles away, I see a tiny figure pushing a lawn mower. I take another look around to make sure Kent isn't in evidence, then put the Rover in gear and ease it over the curb and onto the grass.

I drive across the lawn, sticking to the edge, careful not to gun the engine and tear up the turf. The tiny figure is getting less tiny, growing in size until I'm fairly certain it's Todd pushing the mower, then a hundred percent sure. I increase my speed to medium.

I drive along next to him for a good five seconds before he realizes I'm there and does a double take, coming to a halt. I stop even with him. He stares at me, then twists to see the path I took to reach him, checking to see how much damage I've done, before taking off his headset.

"What the hell?" he says, over the competing sounds of the Rover and lawn mower engines. "You're screwing up the lawn! I'm almost done!"

"You want to finish it?" I say.

"What the hell are you talking about?"

"What I mean is, I think I've got something a lot more fun to do."

* * *

We keep the windows rolled down as we drive, because Todd smells like someone who has spent the better part of the day mowing a giant lawn.

Out there in the verdant fields, I had to repeat to him three times what I was asking, until finally I leaned my upper body out the window of the Rover and reached down to shut off the mower engine. Then I said, "I'm saying, I want you to come right now to a real recording studio to play drums on a real song with a real-live straight-up famous person."

When he just stared up at me, still confused, I said, "Listen. The way I see it? You owe me four thousand bucks for that mandolin. You come now and play drums for this recording session, and we're even."

"You want me to play drums in an actual recording studio."

"Yes."

"Right now."

"Right now."

We left the mower where it was in the middle of the field. He didn't ask a single question more at that point, just circled around in front of the Rover, climbed in the passenger side, and said, "Let's go."

We've barely talked at all. Once when we get to a light, he says, "Do they have a kit there? My dad got pissed off and sold mine, like, two years ago."

"They have a kit. You think you can still play?"

"Hell, yes," he says. "I think."

Other than that, it's quiet until I pull into the parking lot at our next destination.

"What this?" says Todd. "This the studio?"

"No," I say. "I'll be right back."

It's a midlevel strip mall, angled parking out front. Between one of those frozen-yogurt places and a bakery is a storefront with a sign on the awning: LINDAHL CAMPAIGN HEADQUARTERS. There's a similar rubdown transfer on the big tinted picture window. I lean my forehead against the window, cupping my hands around my face so I can see inside. If this was once a store, there's no evidence of it—it's just a big square room. There are campaign posters and maps on the walls. There are two long folding tables set up, the kind they use for buffets at weddings, and about two dozen people sitting at the tables talking into headset phones and typing notes on laptops. They're mostly middle-aged suburban women, and one guy who looks like he's in his twenties. I don't see the candidate.

And there.

Josephine.

A few of the women look up at me curiously when I walk in. I feel like some of Todd's lawn-care smell has clung to me. The one guy is finishing his call, half standing as he does so.

"Can I . . . ?" he says.

"I'm just . . ." I say, hoping that suffices, and point to Josephine, who's talking on the phone and hasn't noticed me yet. I can hear her voice among the others in the room, reading from her script: " . . . values your continuing support and is hoping he can count on you to help him reach his fundraising goals."

I shuffle sideways and kind of lean over a bit until I'm in her line of sight, raising a hand, and her eyes widen in surprise.

"There are several, uh, several levels . . ." she's saying, stumbling over her sales pitch, then diverts her gaze from me back to the written script on her laptop and gets herself back on track: "Several levels of support that you could select."

I stand there, shifting from foot to foot, hands in pockets, trying to ignore the other women. Josephine is listening to the person on the phone now and *uh-huh*-ing and *mm-hmm*-ing, and gives me a fierce *WTF are you doing here?* look.

I have to talk to you! I mouth, and she mouths, *What?* Then as I'm remouthing what I'd previously mouthed she holds up a hand to stop me and says, "Well, the candidate's view is that raising taxes on job creators is counterproductive. Mm-hmm. Right."

She continues with the *mm-hmm*s and *right*s as she pushes her chair back and stands up and crosses to me, her gaze half focused because she's still listening to the person on the phone. I back up as she approaches, to create some distance between us and the rest of the people, until we're at the front corner of the room, the window behind me. When she gets close, she presses the mute button on the side of the headset and says, "What are you doing here?!"

"I need your help," I say, but she's talking over me, saying, "I'm sorry, I was talking to someone else. No, I'm still listening. Yes." She gives me another interrogatory glare.

"I need your help," I repeat. "Right now."

"Yes, he believes deeply in the sanctity of human life," she says, then goes to hit the mute button again and instead covers up the little microphone with her hand and whispers, "What are you talking about? I'm working!"

"This is more important!"

"Yes, from conception," says Josephine in her friendly, reassuring voice, then shifts to whisper again: "Would you get out of here?"

"I need you to come sing—"

"Gay marriage? Uh, he's morally opposed to gay marriage but respects the law of the land."

"—with Shane in the studio."

"Sing?"

"In the studio! With Shane!"

"Is everything all right over there, Josey?" says the Guy.

"It's fine, Dan," says Josephine. "Sorry, sir. Yes, I'm listening. Right, he's morally opposed to it, but—uh-huh. Yes."

"Listen to me," I say to Josephine, and speak fast to get it all in while she's not talking into the headset. "I'm sorry if I did something wrong last night. You don't have to like me. We don't ever have to speak again after today, if that's what you want. You don't even have to talk to me today. But this is—"

"Yes, sir, that's correct. Right."

"This is an *emergency*. It's for a recording. I need you. Shane needs you."

"Is this a joke?"

"No!"

"You want me to sing. In a—"

"A recording studio. Yes. You. Sing."

"He knows a million people, people who do that for a living!"

"There's no one available!"

"I can't go now! What? No, as I said, on a personal level he is morally opp— Okay, sir, I don't think that language is very appropriate."

She listens for a moment. I open my mouth. She holds up an index finger, turns her head a few degrees away from me.

"I *appreciate* your feelings, sir, but I don't think that language is *appropriate*."

Her voice is rising, sharpening. More heads are turning this way. Dan is sitting sideways in his chair, chewing a fingernail, watching us.

"Josey," he says. Josephine, brow furrowed as she listens to the headset, ignores him.

"Josephine, please," I say. "If you—" Now she replaces her index finger with her whole palm, still focused on whatever she's hearing.

"Well, on a personal level, I find what you're saying offensive," she says.

"Josey," repeats Dan. Now *he* gets the palm treatment, a straight-arm like she's warding off an approaching tackle.

"Yes, that particular word is offensive," she says. It seems like all the other people in the room have given up on their conversations and focused on Josephine's.

"Okay, sir? Sir?" she's saying, trying to cut the other

person off. "Sir?" she says. "Yes, I understand you have a son. I heard you. Okay, that's— Sir, please. What?! Okay, you know what? I HOPE YOUR SON MARRIES A BLACK MAN AND THEY ADOPT FIVE BIRACIAL BABIES."

"Josey!" says Dan, horrified.

"It's *JOSEPHINE!*" she bellows, then tears off her headset and hurls it across the room to rebound off the wall. Everyone is silent, gaping at her. Including me.

"So?" she says to me. "Let's *go* already!"

I have to hurry to keep up with her, Josephine out the door before I'm even halfway across the room. As I pass Dan I lean over slightly and murmur, "She *really* prefers Josephine."

* * *

When we reach the truck, Josephine sees Todd in the front seat and stops dead, then looks at me.

"Yeah," says Todd. "This is pretty weird for me, too."

* * *

Here's what's killing me not to say while I'm driving: *WTF happened last night?!* But of course Todd is sitting here and I can't say anything, so all I do is give them both the barest minimum of a rundown: Shane needs—

"Shane's the famous guy?"

"Yes, Shane's the famous guy."

Shane needs help recording one song, just one song, and he's got to send it off to the big producer in LA tonight, because, you gotta understand, that's just how this stuff works (like I have even the slightest clue what I'm talking about, and it sounds a hundred percent ridiculous, but I present it with so much confidence and authority that even *I* sort of believe me).

It's hard to come up with a worse formula for casual

chitchat than Josephine + Todd + me, so besides my brief primer on what our mission is, any talking that occurs in the vehicle remains inside our respective skulls.

We park. A short walk, me moving fast and keeping ahead of them so I don't have to talk.

When we get to the studio, we file right past Rocker Dude, who's playing some sort of computer game and doesn't spare us a single one of his five brain cells' worth of attention. I have a brief fantasy of renting several llamas and parading them by, just to see if he'd notice.

Ed is slouched in his chair in the control room, texting. He looks up when we come in. The recording studio appears to be empty.

"He leave?" I ask.

"He's still in there," says Ed. "Sort of."

Todd is taking in all the glowing buttons and slider controls and monitors.

"Whoa," he says.

"I told you," I say. "It's real."

Ed is still in his slouching position, his eyes going back and forth between Josephine and Todd.

"Uh . . . hi?" he says.

"You know Josephine, right?" I say. "From the other night. The party."

"Hi," says Josephine, giving a little wave.

"Right. Hi."

"And this is Todd."

"Oookaaay," says Ed. He still hasn't moved. "So . . . ?"

"They're with the band. C'mon," I say to Josephine and Todd, moving them toward the recording-room entrance, catching in my peripheral vision Ed reaching a hand up to massage the bridge of his nose.

"What is this? No one's in here," says Todd when we enter, squinting to peer into the dimly lit space. Then we hear it: a distinct snort, coming from the far end of the room. There's a pause, somewhat unsettling in its length, and then another snort followed by more regularly paced wood sawing.

"I think there's someone sticking out of the drum set," says Josephine.

There is. Shane is sticking out of the drum set. He's lying on the floor, his head inside the bass drum, resting on the pillow that's inside there to dampen the sound. The snores we hear are his.

We walk across the room and form a triangle, peering down at him.

"That's the famous guy, huh?" says Todd.

I ignore him. "Shane," I say. "Shane." He keeps snoring.

Before I can move closer to him, Todd does, squatting down a bit to take a better look.

"He okay?" says Josephine.

"Famous guy looks drunk," says Todd.

"He's just asleep," I say, even though I know Todd's right.

"Smells drunk too."

"He's been working really hard."

Todd looks at me. "Uh-huh. This is what you got me fired for?"

"Shane," I say again. "Shane!"

"Maybe we should go," says Josephine. "I mean, look at him."

I do. It's not pretty. His mouth is open, his T-shirt riding up enough to reveal a few inches of thirty-seven-year-old belly. I'm burning with shame and embarrassment, both for him and for me.

I note that there's a large and disordered pile of papers nearby, many of them crumpled up into balls. It's the sort of mess I'm very familiar with, the aftermath of an *aw, screw it* moment. Or many, many such moments.

Todd, meanwhile, has circled around to the back of the set. He steps lightly on the bass pedal. Muted thud.

"Mmmrr," says Shane.

Todd takes a seat on the drum throne, picking up the drumsticks from atop the snare, and stomps on the pedal again, louder. *Thud.*

"Gwuuuh," says Shane.

BIDDA-BIDDA BADDA-BADDA BUDDA-BUDDA *PISHHHHH!*

"GAAAAH!" says Shane, sitting up abruptly and hitting his head on the inner surface of the top of the drum. "OW!"

Obscenities issue forth from the finely crafted wooden frame of a Gretsch bass drum.

"I think he's awake," says Todd.

Shane groans. Then we wait as he laboriously extricates himself, grunting, swearing a few more times, finally rolling to his side and propping himself up on an elbow. He rubs his face, blinks at me.

"What is going on?" he says.

"I got us a drummer."

Shane manages to sit up. He looks at Todd. Todd looks back at him.

"Him?" says Shane.

"Dude," says Todd, "you're lying on the floor, messed up, and you're disappointed in *me?*"

Shane looks at Todd again, then back at me. "Well," he says, "he certainly *acts* like a drummer."

Then he struggles to his feet, a multistage undertaking with pauses for short breaks: first while he's on his hands and knees, then sitting back on his heels, then up on one knee, then finally straightening. I avoid looking at Todd or Josephine during the process.

It's only when he's on his feet and has finished rubbing his face with both hands that he notices Josephine.

"Oh, jeez," he says, embarrassed. "Hey. Hi."

"Hi," she says.

"You remember Josephine, right?"

"Of course. Hey."

"Are you okay?" she asks.

"What? Yeah, of course. Great to . . . see you. Jeez." He awkwardly brushes off the front of his shirt and his jeans. He darts a look at me, part rebuke, part question.

"You said you needed a girl, too."

"Did I?"

"Yes. For harmony. I got a drummer and a singer, and figured I could play bass and sing, too. So we can do the song."

He looks at the three of us in turn, like it has taken this long for the needle on the sobriety meter to reach the point where he actually comprehends what I'm suggesting.

"Oh," he says. "Austin, I didn't think you'd actually . . ."

"Well, I did."

More face rubbing. "Austin," he says, "I appreciate all this, but . . ."

"What?" I say. He looks at Todd and Josephine, then motions for me to join him as he takes several steps away from them. I do. He crouches over a bit, hands on his thighs, like a football huddle. I follow suit. He smells like whiskey.

"Austin, what are you doing."

"I'm trying to help you."

"Help me."

"Yes."

"How are you helping me."

"With them! A band!"

He makes a sour, pained sound that almost passes for a chuckle.

"Austin, this is not some kind of old movie musical," he says. "'Hey, kids, my dad's got a studio, let's make a band and put on a show.'"

"You said you needed a girl, a drummer, and a bass player. You have a girl, a drummer, and a bass player."

"Kid," he says, "c'mon . . ."

"You know Josephine can sing. And you know I can too."

"Of course. That's not what I'm saying."

"We could at least *try*," I say.

"I'm not in any shape to try. I don't *want* to try."

"Shane . . ."

"Sorry, kid. It's over." He straightens up and turns to Todd and Josephine. "Sorry, guys—thanks for coming, but I just don't have it right now."

With that he turns to go, and we watch him trudge slowly toward the sound-insulated door on the other side of the studio. None of us says anything. Then,

"Hey!" says Todd. "Hey!"

Shane pauses, turns around to face us again.

"That's it?" says Todd. "You're just leaving?"

Shane sighs. "Listen," he says, "I appreciate that y'all came out. Josephine, you've got a lovely voice, you really do. And Austin . . . But I've got about two hours to get this thing done, and what I need right now are experienced professionals."

He starts to turn again.

"Yeah?" says Todd. "Well, guess what. What you have is *us*. And maybe you don't know me," says Todd, "but I don't know *you*, either, and I friggin' quit a job to come here today. So the least you could do is man up and put your skates on!"

Shane doesn't say anything for a moment. Then, "Put my skates on?"

"Hockey player," I say.

"What I'm saying is, stop acting like a pussy and let's do this thing!" Todd clarifies.

"Yeah, I got that," says Shane. "Man. You really are a drummer, aren't you."

"Yeah. A good one."

A pause.

"Shane," I say, "let's just *try*."

One more big sigh. One more face rub.

"I can't believe I'm doing this," says Shane. Then he walks back toward the drums, crouches by the pile of paper, and sorts impatiently through it, muttering to himself as he picks up, examines, and discards one sheet after the other. Finally he seems to find what he was looking for and straightens up again.

"Here," he says, slap-pressing two wrinkled sheets onto

my chest as he walks past. "You'll have to share it. Give me a few minutes." He exits.

I look at the sheets. There are lyrics and chord changes and handwritten musical notation scratched on them, without much to indicate which are the verses and chorus.

"How do you know this guy?" says Todd.

"He doesn't know?" Josephine says.

"No. He's . . . my dad," I say.

"Huh," says Todd. He leans over and picks up a half-empty fifth of bourbon that was sitting next to the kick drum. He opens it and gives it a sniff.

"Your dad's a drunk," he says.

"He's *not* a drunk."

"Look, it's fine," he says. "So is mine."

He holds up the bottle in a toast, takes a shot, then shoves the cork back in and tosses the bottle to Josephine. Then he picks up the sticks and absolutely assaults the drums, an ear-crushing blitz of aggression and anger that has Josephine and me clutching our skulls.

"Man," says Todd, sweating and panting after about three solid minutes and 120,000 beats. "That feels *great*."

Winfield Public Library

CHAPTER 18

Love you like my dreams / love you like a ghost story /
love you like the cards looking forward through history

"No. No. No, no, no!"

It's been twenty minutes since we started trying to record, and I now understand why no one will work with Shane.

After he left the studio, it took him nearly half an hour to return. Todd spent the time beating out different rhythms, adjusting the drums and cymbals, playing some more, doing more tweaking. Josephine and I stood by a music stand, and I played the chords on the guitar while she sight-read the notes, and we went through the song a few times, experimenting with different harmonies and trying to decipher Shane's hieroglyphics. All the while pretending that this wasn't all completely bizarre, and that last night didn't happen.

Ed came in and started placing and adjusting the microphones, one for me, one for Shane, and one for Josephine, spacing them far enough apart so that they'd only pick up audio from the person they were in front of. He had the deliberately blank expression of a man trying not to reveal the disapproval he's feeling, but also wanting to signal that, no, he doesn't approve.

"How's that?" he said as he adjusted the height for Josephine.

"Um . . ." said Josephine uncertainly.

"Never mind," said Ed. "It's good."

Then Shane came in and said, "No. We're doing this old school—one mic, one take. Get the EQM double-wide sixty-five thousand," or something like that, and Ed did his Ed sigh and disappeared and reappeared with another type of microphone, swapping it out for the one in the center.

Shane said to Todd, "Can you play a train shuffle?"

"Yeah, sure."

Shucka SHUCKa shucka SHUCKa . . .

Shane held up a hand to stop him. "Can you play a *good* train shuffle?"

And so it went.

*　*　*

We stop, we start, we do take after take, each time Shane finding something that isn't quite working—let's change this harmony, don't come in there, augh, this wording is wrong, let's do it again. It's challenging to fit us all around the mic, me inexpertly plucking at the electric bass, Josephine leaning in for the harmonies, Shane with his guitar and his petulance. I don't look at Todd, but I can feel his frustration growing behind me. Josephine doesn't meet my eyes, but her expression has evolved from confused to concerned to cross.

Finally, inevitably, Shane simply stops singing. He stops in the middle of one of the takes, stops singing and stands there. Not angry this time. Just staring off passively like he's observing clouds forming over distant hills. The rest of us keep on for a few more measures before coming to a disorderly, ragged halt.

Shane is still contemplating the distant weather system.

"Shane?" I say. "Shane."

"It's the song," he says. "The song is no good. *None* of them are any good. I haven't written a single worthwhile song since 'Good Fun.'"

He takes a deep breath, then sighs it out: *haahhhhhh*.

Only then does he shift his attention to us, turning and stepping back so that he can address us all. The old Shane, generous with his warmth, eyes crinkling in the corners. Happy now, relieved, because he has given up once and for all.

"I'm sorry, everyone. You're all doing great. It's my fault, not yours. Thank you all for your time."

"You're giving up?" says Todd.

"Yep. Taking off my skates. C'mon, why y'all looking so glum?"

"We still have some time left," I say.

"It ain't time that's the problem," says Shane. "I've been stuck for ten years—it's not something that I'm going to fix in the next hour."

"We wrapped, Shane?"

Ed's voice, coming over the studio address system.

We all look at Shane.

"Shane, are we wrapped?"

Shane looks at us.

"Shane?" says Ed.

Now Shane looks at me. Then at Josephine. Then back to me. Then a few more repeats: me, Josephine, me, Josephine. Uh-oh.

"No," says Shane. "No, we're *not* wrapped."

The reflections and glare make it hard to see through the double-thick glass, but I think I can discern Ed clapping a hand over his eyes.

"What we're gonna do—" says Shane, and I'm already saying "Shane, no . . ."

"—is sing one of *Austin's* songs."

"No way. There are no Austin songs."

"You got that song we were singing together yesterday by the river. We're gonna take that half song and make it a whole song."

"Shane, don't sing that one. Not now."

Shane gives a sly sidelong glance at Josephine, and as I feel the panic rise he starts singing, *"Oh,* Rosalie, Rosalie, *hear my plea / someone has got to love me and it can't be me . . ."*

Winking at me on the "Rosalie."

He keeps going, strumming the chords skeletally, twisting to give a nod to Todd, who starts a tentative rhythm that quickly gets stronger.

"Shane, come on," I say, but he keeps going, adding verses: "She calls me on the phone to say / she won't call me no more / She tells me to come over / just so she can slam the door . . ."

He comes around again to the chorus, looking at Josephine with raised eyebrows, singing the words to her with the exaggerated emphasis you use when you're teaching someone, and Josephine is starting to smile, then leans in to the microphone to add her voice, Shane signaling to keep the chorus going so he can add a harmony (me saying, "Shane, I don't think . . ."), and he responds by giving me a soft kick in the ass and I start singing too.

We get to the part where the bridge should be, except there's nothing but river between the first part of the song and the second, and Shane twirls his finger to encourage Todd to keep going and shifts back and forth on his feet, eyes rolled skyward, muttering to himself, running experimentally through different series of chords, then hits one and sings: "I'm tired of all my old mistakes / we can do it wrong but let's make it new . . ."

And he trails off, muttering again and thinking, and I surprise myself by singing, "It would be good for me / if you were good to me / I think I might be good for you too . . ."

And Shane laughs out loud and we all sing, *"Rosalie, Rosalie, hear my plea . . ."*

We have a song in about twenty-five minutes, Shane putting out some lyrics, me responding, Shane scribbling them down as we go, and before we can catch our breath or stop to think he says, "Y'all got it? Got it? Yes? All right, let's go. One take. Let's do it."

So we do it. We stand around that microphone and Todd plays and I play and we all sing and Shane has the happy look he had last night at the party, and so does Josephine, despite herself, and I know I do too, just having fun singing a song together, sloppy and unpolished but true, all our problems and arguments and anger put away for three minutes and ten seconds, and when we finish we don't all collapse into laughter like it's a movie musical, but we do take a moment to grin stupidly at each other—well, not Todd, he just sits there blank faced—until Ed's voice comes over the speaker again: "Okay, clear. Can I go home now?"

* * *

Shane needs to stay to do some mixing on the song. Todd and Josephine need to go home. I need to figure out how to get them home, get myself home, get my bike home, and (I hope) arrange it so that Josephine rides with me as part of the deal. I mention this in a low voice to Shane and he gets it immediately, and when Josephine steps away to use the bathroom he hands Todd $100 in twenties and says, "Good job today. You can take a cab home, right?"

Todd blinks at the money, then shrugs.

"Sure."

I walk with him down the hallway toward the exit. You'd think we'd have bonded and we'd be chatting in an animated fashion, saying, *What an unusual experience we underwent today, new friend!* But no. Todd is hermetically sealed. At the door he gives me a nod without really looking at me, muttering an impersonal *thanks* as he exits, the sort of thing you say to the driver as you're getting off the bus. Then he pauses.

"You ever want me to play again, lemme know."

When I get back to the control room, Shane and Josephine are listening to a playback of the song, Josephine looking stricken. When it ends, she says, "I ruined your song."

"Nope," says Shane, "you made it work. And it's not my song, it's Austin's." Then he stands up and gives her a hug, gives me a hug, and says, "Thank you both." He puts the big headphones back on. "Go. We'll catch up later."

Walking down the hall again, this time with Josephine.

"Where's Todd?"

"Took a cab home. Which you can totally do. Or I could give you a ride on my bike?"

A few too many more steps as she considers it.

"Yeah, okay," she says.

* * *

Her hands are warm on my sides. She's got them in the I'm-not-sure-where-to-put-them position, tentatively placed on my ribs, her fingers gripping reflexively each time we go over a bump. Which tickles like hell, but I'm not about to say anything.

I go down Hennipen Avenue to the route that curves us around Lake of the Isles, huge lawns sloping up to giant old mansions to our right, the lake to our left. It's hard to have any sort of conversation when you're on a motorcycle, so we don't. Nor was she especially responsive to my attempts when we were walking to where my bike was parked near the restaurant:

"Thanks for coming today."

"Sure."

"Pretty fun, right?"

"Yes."

"You know, you have a really nice voice."

"Thanks."

"Oh my God would you please please please tell me what is going on because last night we were kissing in a sea of stars and today you hate me again but you still came with me to the studio and it's all insanely weird and driving me friggin' crazy."

(Thought, not said.)

So now we're riding, and I'm going to drop her off and she'll go in her house and we'll be exactly where we were when I received her *Let's not even be friends* text. Then, just as we're coming into a wooded area she says, "Stop."

"What?"

"Stop. Pull over."

I do. She gets off the bike without explanation and crosses the road toward the lake, taking off her helmet, walks across the grass and foot and bike paths until she's standing by the fringe of reeds at the edge of the lake, looking out at the water.

"You okay?" I call out, but she doesn't answer. A car beeps behind me, Minnesota polite. I give the driver an apologetic wave and steer the bike to and then over the opposite curb, parking it on the grass. It's dusk. There're a few joggers and strollers and bikers out. A middle-aged woman with silver hair notes the bike and gives me the side-eye but doesn't say anything. Minnesota disapproval.

"You okay?" I say again when I get close. She doesn't answer. Instead she spins around and says, *"Why?"*

"What why? Why what?"

"Why did you kiss me last night?!"

"I'm *sorry*. I told you I'm sorry! I'm sorry if I insulted you!"

"I'm such a fool!" she says. I have a flashback to her saying that as she stormed out the first day we met. "It's all just a game to you! You just collect people!"

"I don't know what you're saying! I don't understand!"

"I'm just another stupid girl to you," she says, "Another girl on . . ."

"On what?"

"Your frigging playlist!"

185

Oh, Devon, you stupid, loudmouth idiot . . .

"'Playlist'? What are you *talking* about?"

"You *know* what I'm talking about! *Everyone* knows about your playlist!"

"It's not . . . I don't . . . it's not even my idea!"

Taking a shovel to an already deep hole.

"Oh, so you *do* know what I'm talking about! It's real!"

"No, it's *not*. Or *yes,* fine, but *no*—it's not my idea! I never called it that!"

"Oh, really? What do you call it, then?"

"Call what?"

"Your cute little list of all the girls you've had sex with!"

"I've never had sex with anyone!"

It jumps out of me way too loud, way too emphatic. Timed just as some college-age guy jogs into earshot, his smirk pretty clear evidence that he heard me.

He's at least fifty yards away, receding in the distance, before Josephine can muster, "What?"

"Nothing!"

"You've never . . . ?"

"No! Yes! No! Whatever! Leave it!"

"You're a *virgin?*"

"Would you please?"

"But—"

"I've done lots of other stuff, okay? I just haven't— You know, this is embarrassing for me, and I don't want to be standing here talking about—"

"Why?"

"Why don't I want to talk about it? Because I—"

"Why are you still a virgin?"

"Is that bad?"

"No! But why?"

"I'm still a virgin because my mom had me when she was eighteen, and look how great *I* turned out."

"Oh."

"And . . . because it's special. Okay? I want it to be special, and with someone special. Is that all right with you? Now can we go? Please? Or do you just want to yell at me some more for kissing you, which I thought *you* wanted to do too, or yell at me because Devon made up the whole playlist thing, or make fun of me because I haven't done it yet, which, yeah, I'd prefer you keep to yourself, if you can manage that. Oh, what now? Why are you shaking your head?"

"Who *are* you?"

"Augh! I don't know what you're talking about, Josephine!"

"Who *are* you, Austin?"

"What do you mean?!"

"Who are you? Are you the guy who has a joke for everything, and a playlist, and it's all charm and laughs and your motorcycle and BS, or are you that other person?"

"What other person?!"

"The person who . . . The person I see when you're singing."

That stops me.

"I don't know, Josephine. Maybe I'm all of that." I scrub at my face with both hands like I'm trying to wash this all away.

"Let's just go. And we can forget today and forget last night and forget everything that happened since I met you. I projected all this nonsense on you, thought you were something. Why did I kiss you? I kissed you because I *hate* you. I kissed you because I think you're stupid and boring and ugly.

"I kissed you," I say, "because I can't stop thinking about you, and having dreams about you and pretend conversations with you, and wishing I was with you, because you're twice as beautiful as your awful sister and you don't even know it, and because you're smart and funny and you're like the songs I hear in my head, like every song I've ever tried to write. And *you* feel like a fool? *I'm* the fool. I'm the idiot, for liking you, and for thinking you might somehow like me back, and—What, what are you—"

—is as far as I get, because we're kissing again.

CHAPTER 19

I've painted all around the lines / in every shade of blue /
I'm asking you / don't fake with me / I'm true

"In New York," Josephine says, "we will have a cat."

"I hate cats."

"In New York we will have five cats."

"C'mon."

"In New York we will have no cats."

"A dog."

"We will have a very small dog that behaves like a cat."

I am naked next to Josephine Lindahl. She is naked too.

We are lying pressed against each other under the stars, the swim platform gently rocking with the motion of the lake.

"Okay. And we should probably get married, right?"

She says, "Absolutely."

"Good. Because I'm in love with you, and that's, you know, that's it. There's no other way. So I think we have to."

"Yes."

"Okay, good. That's settled."

After we did our kissing on the shores of Lake of the Isles, she said, "I don't want to go home yet."

So we came to do more kissing in the hidden cove on Cedar Lake. The place where it all started, the place from which I set off in a canoe to sing songs to the cheerleaders and got clubbed over the head for my efforts. Maybe the best thing that ever happened to me. Because if it hadn't, Josephine and I wouldn't be here right now.

We lay there and kissed and talked and kissed and talked, desperate to do both, in a breathless rush to reveal ourselves to each other, to tell all the stories and secrets we'd been saving up our whole lives to share with the right person.

There was this time when . . . Did you know that I . . . I've never told anyone this, but . . .

Able to tell each other exactly what we had been thinking since we met.

I said to her, I fell in love with you when I walked into that room.

And she said, I fell in love with you when I saw you singing, because I could see the real you.

And then a little later she said, "Actually, can I tell you something? It wasn't an accident that I was your tutor."

"What?"

"I fell in love with you when you were onstage. But I've had a crush on you since tenth grade."

"What? Why? How would you even know me?"

"Because I saw you in the hall. Todd Malloy was pushing Ed Risse, the kid with cerebral palsy. And you stopped him. You got in a fight with him."

There *was* a girl watching! THE girl! It *WORKED!*

"That wasn't a fight. That was Todd Malloy punching me in the face."

"It was very noble," she said.

"No one has ever called me noble."

"No one has ever called me beautiful."

I said, you were so mean to me when we first met.

"You showed up late, and I felt like such an idiot, this big plan where I'd be your tutor, and then . . ." She shook her head. "Haven't you ever wanted to hurt someone first?"

"After the party, when we were kissing . . ."

"It was the same thing. I felt dumb. I kept fighting it, promising myself I wouldn't be the dumb girl who falls for the bad guy with the motorcycle and the guitar."

"You're not. You're the *smart* girl who fell for him."

She propped herself up on her elbow. "My little cousin, she's four. I was teasing her, telling her animals can talk or something. And you know what she said? She said, 'Don't fake with me—I'm true.'"

"That's cute."

She looked at me. The moon was bright enough to light up the lake, light up the swim platform, which was about thirty yards offshore.

"What?" I said finally.

"Don't fake with me, either, okay? Because I'm true."

"I'll never fake with you, Josephine. Never. I'm true too."

Then we did more kissing.

And also mosquito slapping, because it's Minnesota. After more kissing and talking and mosquito slapping, Josephine sat up and gestured to the swim platform.

"I want to swim out there," she said.

"What, now?"

"Yes."

"I'm a terrible swimmer."

She stood up, said, "I'll save you. I won't let you drown. Close your eyes."

I could hear her zipper, the rustle of clothing. "No peeking," she said. *Splash splash splash* as she waded into the lake, then a bigger splash as she dove, then surfaced.

"Now you," she called. She was a few yards from the beach, just her head above water.

"Okay, but you turn around."

"Okay." I stripped down with my back to her, putting my clothes next to hers on the beach. When I turned around, she was looking right at me, smiling.

"Hey!" I said.

She laughed and said, "C'mon!" and started swimming out, and I ran in with a whoop and dove and dog-paddled after her. She was waiting for me when I reached the platform, and kissed me, our hands brushing each other's bodies.

"Man," I say. "When you make up your mind, you make up your mind."

She laughed and said, "C'mon" again and hoisted herself up out of the water.

"You coming up?" she said.

"I'm embarrassed."

"I already saw you naked."

"I'm sort of naked plus."

"Oh."

"I'm shy."

"I want to see you. Naked plus."

So I climbed up too—gingerly so as not to snag anything important—and she said, "Naked plus."

"Yeah." Then I said, "Hey," because her hand was somewhere.

"Is that all right?"

"Yes."

My voice was raspy.

"Can I touch you?" I said.

"Please."

It wasn't the most comfortable of surfaces for what happened over the next while, but that was okay. Since you're concerned, yes, I maintained my precious virginity. Afterward we both dove into the lake again, and then we climbed back on the platform and we're here now, under the dome of stars, holding each other gently for warmth. We talk and it's perfect, we're silent and it's perfect, we're together and it's perfect.

I murmur, "Why me?"

She says, "Because I know who you are now."

"Because you saw me perform?"

"That's part of it."

We speak slowly, quietly, long pauses between sentences.

"But not just because you're good at it," she says. "Because of the person I see."

"And who is that?"

"When you sing, you're so open. You look . . . like a child. Or like a person talking to God."

I absorb that.

"But it's just a show. It's just me performing."

"No. That's when you're performing the least."

* * *

When I drive her home, she steps off the bike and comes around and just stands there and we look at each other forever, smiling. She kisses me again, then turns and weaves a curving path to her front door with her arms out like wings.

* * *

I do the same when I get home: park my bike in the garage, glide to the back door, glide through the kitchen, glide up the stairs, fingertips brushing the walls, glide to my darkened room, shut the door and lean against it and . . .

AHHH!!! SCREAM WHEN THE LIGHT SUDDENLY GOES ON!!!

"Buddy," says my mom, "you are in some deep trouble."

CHAPTER 20

When the smoke is clear / then I won't be here /
but go on keep the ashes / and you can have the tears

"Mom! What the hell are you doing!!"

"What the hell am *I* doing? You've got some nerve asking me that!"

She's sitting at my desk in her nightgown, having switched on the desk lamp when I came in, like a frigging spy movie, and I come pretty close to having the kind of pants-filling accident that I haven't had for thirteen years.

"You and me have a lot to talk about," she says.

"I don't have anything to say."

"That's fine—I plan on doing most of the talking anyway."

"Mom, can we just do this tomorrow?"

"Nope. Sit your ass down on the bed, because we're going to talk about it right now PUT YOUR GODDAMN PHONE AWAY."

I shove my phone back into my pocket, dying to check the text I just got.

"Mom, I want to go to sleep."

"Me too, but instead I had to wait up for you to come waltzing in here."

"Mom, get out of my room."

"Do not talk to me in that tone of voice, Austin Methune! Do *not* take your phone out again!"

"Mom, *please* get out of my room."

"Sit down and shut up!"

"Fine, I'm going to sleep downstairs!"

"NO YOU ARE NOT!"

"YES I AM!"

I grab the pillow off my bed. My mom springs to her feet and snatches it from me and body slams it on the floor in front of me, which is not so effective because it's a pillow, but still pretty dramatic, and I immediately kick it at her, which is just stupid, and she bats it away, and it nearly knocks over the lamp, the illumination in the room lurching crazily as the lamp totters, and then we really start shout-arguing, full-on top-of-our-lungs going at it.

I don't know what's coming out of my mouth, but it all *COMES OUT LIKE THIS* and my mom screams her part *LIKE THIS,* asking me who do I think I am, and what the hell am I doing hanging out with Shane who is a *NO-GOOD PIECE OF CRAP* and she's the one who raised me and *BELIEVE ME IT WASN'T EASY,* and I say *WELL AT LEAST HE UNDERSTANDS ME,* and she starts laughing derisively and saying, *OH HO HO HO, REALLY,* and then Rick makes his entrance, squinting at the light, making patting gestures with his hands to try and cool things down—"Guys, c'mon, it's one in the morning"—and I shout, "It's none of your damn business!"

"It *is* his damn business, because he is a member of this household!" yells my mom.

"No he is not!"

"Yes he damn well is! Rick is moving in—*has* moved in—and we're getting married and you'd better start getting used to the idea!"

I'm gaping. Rick says, "Hon, this really isn't the time to . . ."

"It *is* the time, and Austin here does not get to set the terms!"

"What do you mean he's moving in! He's not moving in!"

I don't know why I'm saying this. It's not like I'm actually surprised.

"Uh, yeah, actually, he is, he *has* moved in, and if you had decided to be here at all over the past week, we could have had an actual discussion about it!"

"Oh," I say. "This is crap. I'm out. I'm going to Devon's!"

"Austin. Austin!"

Screaming at me, *"AUSTIN, AUSTIN,"* as I grab a handful of clothes and stuff them into a bag and storm out of the room and down the stairs, picking up speed, my mom yelling, "I'm putting you in that goddamn military academy!! Austin!!" but I'm already kicking my way out the back door, speed marching to my motorcycle, and buzzing along the driveway and into the empty night streets before she can make it outside.

Two blocks later, I remember the string of texts I was getting, and I pull over and check them.

OMG my parents were waiting up they're so pissed
I'm grounded like I'm a kid
This is absurd
I call her and she answers immediately.
"Austin, I'm so screwed."
"Me too. I just left. I'm not staying at home tonight."
"Where are you staying?"
I tell her.
Silence.
"You still there?" I say.
"Come and get me," she says.

CHAPTER 21

I'll lift you up high so that you can see /
till the lifting's all that's left of me

The chirping of my cell phone wakes me up, and I accidentally knock the phone off the night table, sending it thud-thumping onto the uncarpeted floor when I paw at it to silence it. Next to me, Josephine stirs, changing position. The phone, undaunted, continues to chirp.

"Who is it?" Josephine says sleepily, half into the pillow.

She's here. She's next to me. It wasn't/isn't a dream.

"Who is it?" she says again.

Not my mom, I think. Each time I've stomped out of the house and stayed at Devon's—three occasions now?—she's given me the silent treatment. No call, not even contacting Devon's mom to make sure I'm alive until at least two days have passed.

"What time is it?" Josephine slurs now.

I lean over the edge of the futon bed and grab the phone, squinting at it. 7:48 a.m. And it's not my mom calling.

"Hey," I say. "Hey, Shane."

"Hey! I wake you?"

Full of energy, keyed up.

"No, all good."

"Good. Excellent. I wanted to get you before you went to work. Listen—I wanted to thank you for yesterday. I haven't had that much fun in the studio since—I mean, look, I know the first part was rocky—but the end? Creating that song together with y'all? Pure joy. Honestly. I'd forgotten that you can try to create something and that the process can be fun. Did you have fun?"

"What? Yeah, yeah, definitely."

"Excellent."

"Did Barry like it?" I ask.

"Barry? Yeah, Barry, it's all good with Barry."

"He liked the song?"

"Yeah! Where are you now? You heading in to work? You still home?"

"Uh . . . yeah. Still at . . . the house. At the house. Yes."

Which is not a lie. I am still at the house. Or *a* house. Shane's house. Or on the property thereof. The granny apartment over the garage, to be exact. If Shane opened his bedroom window, and I did the same, we could dispense with the phones altogether and have this conversation across the backyard, barely raising our voices.

"I've been stuck for so long, Austin, and there was something about yesterday, the freedom of it . . . I'd forgotten all about that. That's what it's supposed to feel like."

"I'm glad."

Josephine has rolled more onto her side, resting her head up on her hand to watch me. She's got an oversize T-shirt on, one of the items that she had stowed in a small backpack, along with a toiletry kit. She had the bag slung over her shoulder when I pulled up to her house last night, Josephine emerging unexpectedly from the shadows and marching across the front lawn to me. Organized and prepared even when fleeing into the night with an unsavory kid on a motorcycle. She walked up to me and grabbed me and kissed me on the lips.

Then she said, "You asked me if I'd ever cross against the light. This counts, wouldn't you say?"

"Yes, ma'am, I'd say it does." Then, "Wait. That's not why you're doing this, right?"

She kissed me again.

"You know it's not."

She clung tightly to me as we drove through the darkened streets, clung to me as we headed toward east Edina, the houses old and older, kissed my neck as we left Edina behind and sped toward and then around the lakes again to Uptown and Shane's house. I parked the bike a block from Shane's and we walked the rest of the way holding hands. We went down the back alley and I used the blade of the small knife on my key ring to lift the latch of the back gate and we were in the backyard. I found the key hidden under the mat outside the door of the granny apartment, and we eased the door shut behind us and ascended the stairs, Josephine giggling as I picked her up at the top and staggered across the threshold.

Then a sudden shyness, both of us. We had been lying

naked together on the swim platform an hour or so earlier, comfortable with each other, but we got quiet, the two of us alone there in that room with its miniature kitchenette and round table the size of a pizza tray and tiny bathroom. A play house for us to play house in.

"You want to shower first?" I said.

"I showered—you go," she said, and I breathed a sigh of relief, glad I didn't have to figure out yet if I was supposed to pee in front of her.

When we got into bed, we lay on our sides, facing each other, and she traced the contours of my face with her fingers, and we leaned close and we kissed, not the passion of before but tenderly, sleepy and slow, and I heard the music again, so present that I wondered if she could hear it. Our foreheads were touching, our hands resting on each other's cheeks, and I murmured, half asleep, "I don't know how this song ends."

"I guess we'll find out," she whispered. And while I was thinking about that, the music swirled gently about me, and I fell asleep.

* * *

"You know I have to move on soon," Shane is saying now.

"Yeah."

"So I had a thought. I was just wondering if, I don't know, you'd like to spend some time together before I do, maybe come into the studio and play around some more."

"Seriously?"

I sit up in the bed. Josephine responds by moving to a sitting position too, facing me, now propping herself up with her arm.

"Yes, seriously," says Shane. "I've got the studio until the end of the week. Might as well use it."

"What about the album? What's happening with that?"

"Yeah, don't worry about the album. I'll get back in a studio in a few months and finish it."

"Barry's okay with that?"

"Yeah, it's all good with Barry. Don't worry about Barry. What I want to do is use this time to have fun. To make stuff. No pressure, no demands, just make music. I haven't been able to do that for so long, and I don't want to lose the feeling while it's here. You down with that?"

"Yeah, of course, of course."

"You've got work, though, right?"

"Uh, no. No, I'm off this week. All week. I can do it." Looking at Josephine as I talk. She looks back, questioning.

"Great!" says Shane.

"Hey, can I bring Josephine?"

"I was gonna suggest that!" he says. "And you know what? Bring that other kid."

"Todd?"

"Yeah, Todd. He's an asshole, but he's a pretty good drummer."

"You just want to mess around with stuff?"

"Right. Also, if things go well, I had an idea."

* * *

When he finishes telling me about his idea, I hang up the phone, thoughtful. Josephine says, "What was that about?"

"Can I tell you in a minute? Because first I just want to look at you for a while."

"Okay."

And that's what we do: just lie there on our sides and look at each other, smiling, laughing sometimes, Josephine saying, "Okay, kissing break."

Around kissing break seven or eight, her phone rings. She looks at it, grimaces.

"I'd better do this." She takes a deep breath and sighs it out. "Hi, Mom."

I step into the bathroom, listening to her end of the conversation:

"Yes, Mom, I'm with a biker gang, and I'm smoking crack and having unprotected sex with all of them. They're Muslims. What? 'Running away'? Mom, this is not one of those TV movies you watch. I'm staying over at a friend's house. I promise, it's not going to affect my GPA. Okay, can I remind you of something? You let Jackie stay over at Kyle's house all the time. No, she was *not* much older, she was a *year* older than me, and let's be honest, she behaved like — actually, *still* behaves like she's *twelve.*"

I take the opportunity to message Todd.

Want to come to the studio to play more music today?

A minute passes, then, *K.* Just like that. Not that I was expecting an emoji or anything. So I text, *I'll pick you up at 10* and suggest a rendezvous point.

K.

Josephine's still on the phone when I come out of the bathroom and sit at the small table.

"Mom, here, let me help you with your parenting. This is one of those situations where you look the other direction and everything turns out okay. No, I *told* you, I'll be back tonight. What? No. No, I'm not going there today. That's correct. Let's say that I'm respectfully tendering my resignation to the Lindahl campaign so I can spend less time with my family. G'bye."

When she hangs up, we do more of the looking and smiling at each other, her sitting on the bed. Finally she says, "Is this crazy?"

"Yes."

"A really crazy song."

"The best song ever."

"The best. What did Shane say?"

"He wants us to come by the studio today."

She nods. "Okay."

I say, "Also, there's something else. He has an idea."

"What?"

"I'll let Shane tell you."

* * *

"Shane Tyler and . . . ?" I say.

"Shane Tyler and the Children's Crusade," says Shane. "Good name, right? One night, one show. This Friday."

"Us?" says Josephine.

"Yes, you. And you and you," says Shane, pointing in turn to Josephine, to me, to Todd. "And me," he adds. "I have a show anyways. I'll play my set, and y'all will join me on our songs."

We're eating at the bowling alley diner, tired and exultant after a day in the studio that went by like a half-remembered dream.

There are hazy clips in my mind, all starting with Shane saying, "Okay, gimme a line," and me singing one of the

205

fragments in my head, something that had come to me the night before while I was lying with Josephine. "Great!" Shane said, and scribbled it down, then did the thing where he looks up at the ceiling and sways back and forth, muttering. Then sang a line, wrote that down, and the day zoomed by, a journey full of obstacles large and small, each surmounted in turn, each demanding full focus and attention so there was no time for doubt or distraction. Shane being musical director: Josephine, you sing this, let's change key, Todd come in here, Austin, you take the high harmony . . .

Before I knew it, it was late afternoon and we had two songs—two full songs, with verses, chorus, bridge, all of it!—and we were emerging, blinking in the light, and Shane took us out to dinner and we sat and ate and talked and laughed and recounted the day. Except for Todd, who focused pretty much entirely on eating at the expense of talking/laughing/recounting. As we were finishing our food, Shane said, "So, I have a crazy idea for y'all," and told them what he had suggested to me on the phone this morning.

"What did we do today, two songs?" says Shane now. "With the song we did yesterday, that's three songs total. We've got three days left to prepare, and we could have, say, six songs to play together. So what do you say?"

Josephine looks at me, smiles.

"Yes," she says.

"Austin?"

"Yeah, of course, you know it."

We all turn to silent Todd, who is more present to the remains of his french fries than he is to us. It takes him a bit to realize that we're all waiting for his response. Which is: (shrug) "Sure, why not."

Hey, kids, my dad's got a studio, and we're makin' a band and puttin' on a show.

* * *

As the newly established Shane Tyler and the Children's Crusade finish their collective band meal and file out of the restaurant, the bandmates sharing exuberant handshakes and hand slaps and hugs (save the drummer, who partakes not), the young female vocalist leans close to the young male backup vocalist/instrumentalist and murmurs, "Are you going back home tonight?"

The young male vocalist ponders that ludicrous idea.

"No way."

"Okay," she says. "Then I'm not either."

CHAPTER 22

Spirits whisper this is everything and all /
there is no more / there is no end / amen amen amen

Think of the best part of the best song you know.

That part that makes the world disappear, the part that makes your heart ache as you listen to it over and over again and ache more when it ends.

This time is that music.

Three days of the world's least responsible summer camp: Studio. Writing music. Group dinner. Josephine and me together every minute of the day, then together each night in our secret hiding place, our private world.

Lying there in my arms, she whispers, "I want it to always be like this. I want this song to go on forever."

We buy eggs and bacon and cereal, and in the morning I make breakfast for us, a skill you learn early on when your mom tends to spend the first part of her days sleeping off the night before. We eat at the tiny table, talking and laughing, our chairs scooched side by side, and wait until the garage door opens beneath us and Shane drives off to the studio. Then the complicated choreography: Josephine takes the bus downtown, and I ride my bike back into the wilds of Edina to pick Todd up, then to the studio to make stuff with Shane.

Who is glowing, tireless, joyful, as merry as I have seen him. Our endlessly encouraging and positive ringleader. The other Shane, the angry, impatient one, the defeated one, it feels as if he never existed.

He never says anything directly to me about Josephine, but sometimes I catch him looking at us, that mysterious smile on his face. Amused and maybe proud and maybe something else, the closest that he gets now to melancholy, the way he looked during his show when he was peering skyward at those high notes that are gone forever. When he sees me observing him, his eyes crinkle more and his smile grows, and once he gives me a nod.

I want this song to go on forever.

And so do I.

And I know that it can't. Know in the back of my mind that gravity still exists. That it will eventually assert itself over whatever shoe or shoes are out there waiting to drop. The little red flag again. I look the other direction.

I still haven't spoken with my mom. But I started getting texts from a number I didn't recognize. I opened the first one and it said, *Hi, it's Rick.* That's as far as I got. I've ignored the rest.

The morning of the second day Josephine and I did a ninja visit to her house so she could grab more clothes. That night she had a phone conversation with her family, a sharp argument with her mother:

"Oh, you're going to call the police? How's that going to look in the paper? Mom—would you—Mom, listen to me—fine. Put him on. Put Dad on."

Pause.

"Hi, Dad."

She listened.

"Dad—hold on. Dad. Dad. Dad. Dad, Patricia Laughton."

She waited, a look of grim satisfaction on her face. I didn't hear anything coming from the other end of the phone. The pause seemed interminable, and she stood stock still, jaw clenched, and I watched her eyes get brighter as they started to fill with tears. Finally she said, "I'll be home in a few days, Dad." And she hung up and put her head in her hands and cried, and I held her, confused. Finally she said, "I knew it. I *knew* it."

"Knew what?"

"She's his campaign manager."

"Oh. So . . . ?"

She looked at me.

"Oh," I said. "Oh. Oh, jeez."

Thus does Josephine blackmail her way to a brief period of freedom.

* * *

Do Austin Methune and Josephine Lindahl, teenagers in love lying together unsupervised each night in a bed in a romantic hideaway, do they, well, *do* they?

I will not lie. There are repeated incidents of both hanky and panky.

But for me, none of those activities compares with just being together, holding each other, whispering, sharing our secrets, falling asleep intertwined. If someone made a pronouncement that time would now stop and I would get this and nothing else forevermore, I would be content.

To answer your question more completely: While there has been hanky panky, there hasn't been Hanky Panky. I'm still technically in the *V* column.

But the night that Josephine blackmails her dad, when we're wrapped around each other in the bed, she says, "You never asked me if *I* was a virgin."

"I didn't think it was my business."

"Do you want to know?"

"It's okay if you're not."

"I know it's okay if I'm not."

"Well?"

"Yes."

"You *are?*"

"Yes."

"Why did *you* wait?"

"I wanted someone special too."

We lie there in the dark, and she starts to smile and I start to smile until we're both giggling.

"Okay, yes," I say.

"Yes," she says.

"But not yet," I say. "Not yet."

"When?"

"The night of the show."

"Okay. The night of the show."

We kiss and go at it and nearly break our own promise but manage not to. Because here's the thing: When you know that you're together forever, why rush it?

* * *

And Todd.

The first day I picked him up, he was waiting on the corner, drumsticks in hand.

"Hey," I said.

"Hey," he didn't say, just nodded. Then climbed on the back and we rode wordlessly to the studio.

And that's how he's been. If someone were to transcribe every word Todd has said since the day I spirited him away from the lawn crew, it wouldn't fill half a page.

In the studio you get about five phrases from him: *Okay; Yeah; Sure; You mean like this?;* and *Got it.* I think he said more to me back when we were mowing lawns and he was threatening my life. Maybe this is just how jocks do the whole interpersonal-relations thing: grunts and nods, the occasional menacing outburst, maybe the mutual removal of lice.

There was one odd exception. It was just the two of us in the studio, Shane out to smoke, Josephine in the bathroom. I was strumming one of my own songs that I'd been working on, singing a few of the lyrics softly.

"That yours?" Todd said, and I nearly jumped.

"Yes."

He paused, like he wasn't sure he was the one who had spoken. Then, "It's a good song."

"Thanks."

"Needs balls, though."

Other than that, silence. It's the same at dinner each night. Todd sits with us without really being with us, and I'd wager that if you pulled that sneaky teacher trick on him—"Mr. Malloy? Can you tell me what we've been discussing for the past ten minutes?"—he'd fail every time.

For the most part Shane has seemed content to let Todd be Todd, other than entertaining himself now and then by saying something like, "Todd, please, would you shut the hell up already?" But on our third night in our regular booth at the bowling alley I keep noticing him glancing at Todd, rolling some question around in his head. Finally he indicates the fading bruise on Todd's cheek.

"Todd, tell me something. What happened there? That some sort of summer hockey league fight?"

Todd chews a bit and says through some food, "My dad hit me."

Josephine puts her fork onto her gluten-free salad and sits back.

"Really?" she says.

Todd takes another bite, glances at me.

"Yeah, really," I say. "I saw it."

Josephine looks at me. Shane is watching Todd and has a funny half smile on his face.

"Has he done that before?" Josephine says to Todd.

Todd nods absently, sips his Coke.

"Does he—I mean, what about your mom?" says Josephine.

"Yeah, sure, he's slapped her a few times."

Josephine is aghast.

"What? You should tell someone! You should call the police! You guys should leave!"

Todd gives her a look, something akin to an eye roll, and returns his attention to his burger, done with the conversation.

Shane says, "Yeah, well, it's never quite that easy when you're living it. Right?" Looking at Todd as he says it.

Todd's chewing slows, then stops.

"Uh-huh," says Shane. "I grew up down near Odessa. Odessa, Texas. Scrub brush, oil fields, doublewides." Stretching it out to *wiiiiiiides,* his accent stronger now. "My old man—this guy's grandfather"—tilting his head once toward me—"he worked in the fields. What you call a roustabout. Used to get loaded, *pshooo.*" He mimes a punch. "I left when I was, what, sixteen, off to be a big star. Never saw him or spoke to him again."

We wait while he takes a sip of beer. Todd swallows, his burger forgotten in his hand.

"Now, I can't say as I'm a great expert at being a dad." A brief glance at me. "But I *can* tell you it ain't too late."

"Not too late for what?" says Todd.

"For you to not become like him."

*   *   *

When we leave the restaurant, Todd is somehow even more quiet than before, like he's retreated deep inside himself somewhere. Shane pulls me aside and says, "Hey—you have to go home? You want to come hang out a bit tonight?"

So there's some subterfuge with me pretending to take Josephine home—Me: "You sure it's okay?" Her: "Of course.

214

Go hang out with your dad"—and then I go around to Shane's front door where the horseshoe is mounted and ring the doorbell.

We end up lying on the roof. We talk about the show, music, nothing, me wondering if that's all he wants, just some company.

I say, "Where's the horseshoe from?"

"My granddaddy. My mom's dad. He was an honest-to-God cowboy, way back."

"Your dad," I say. "I didn't know that stuff about him."

"Yeah, why would you. Maybe growing up like that, maybe that's why I left KD. Afraid I'd turn out like him."

He lights another cigarette while I think about that.

"So you *did* know about me."

He's quiet. He exhales smoke and it briefly blurs the stars, blurs a portion of the moon before dissipating.

"Yes. Or I suspected."

"You told me you didn't know."

"Yeah. I wasn't being honest with either of us. I blocked it out for so long. Austin, I'm sorry. I'm sorry for being dishonest about it, and I'm sorry for leaving."

He's got his head turned, observing me, maybe apprehensive that we're going to have a repeat of my hysterics in the bar and this time I'll hurl myself off the roof.

"You all right?" he says.

"Yeah, I'm all right," I say. "What I said before, in the bar, I didn't mean it. I'm glad you came back. I'm glad we met."

"Me too." He gives me a pat on the shoulder, and this time I don't feel like batting it away.

"But are you gonna leave again?"

"Well, I have to."

"You don't *have* to."

"This isn't really my home, Austin."

"Could be. Could be your home. You could live up here. Lots of people make music up here. *Prince* makes music up here."

"Well, I ain't exactly Prince. Plus I don't think I'd make it through the winter. Plus, look, I'm gonna be traveling a lot. You want to make money as a musician nowadays, you have to play shows constantly. Can't just sell records like you used to. All that streaming crap wrecked it. Not that I used to sell a lot of records."

He takes another drag on his cigarette.

"So, yeah, I'll be moving on. We've got the show tomorrow, and then I was going to fly out for the show in New York next week. Then back here for a few weeks until the end of the month, then probably back to Nashville for a spell."

"To finish the album?"

"Yeah. But we can hang out till I go, you want."

"Okay," I say.

He turns his head toward me.

"Hey," he says.

"What."

"Even after I go, I'll be *around*," he says. "You know what I mean?"

"No."

He rolls onto his side and props his head on his elbow.

"I mean, I want you in my life. I want to be in your life. I want to come visit you and have you visit me and, when you're old enough, maybe you can come and hang out with me for a bit, and who knows?"

"Yeah?"

"Yeah. Meeting you, Austin, it's changed my life. I might leave, but that doesn't mean I'm *leaving*. You get it? I won't ever leave you again. You hear me, right? I won't ever leave you again."

* * *

Josephine stirs when I climb into bed with her.

"You have a good talk?" she says sleepily.

"Yeah."

"Good. You excited about tomorrow?"

"Yeah. Shane Tyler and the Children's Crusade. It's a good name."

She makes a half-asleep sound that's not quite assent.

"What?"

"Nothing."

"What?"

She yawns. "You know what happened in the children's crusade, right?"

"No."

"The Middle Ages. A bunch of kids marched off to free the Holy Land."

"And?"

She doesn't answer at first, starting to doze again.

"Hey."

"Hm?"

217

"So what happened to them?"

"The kids? They all died."

She yawns again, and pretty soon she's asleep.

I stay awake for a long time.

CHAPTER 23

I've been back and forth through midnight twice /
the first time fun / the second / not so nice

Gravity returns when I go to get the Replacements T-shirt.

It's Friday. Show day. The plan is to meet at the studio for a late-afternoon rehearsal, then food, then the show.

But I need my Replacements T-shirt for the show, because I just need it, can't visualize performing without it. Except it's at home.

When I explain to Josephine that I have to go home to get my Replacements T-shirt — "Okay. Wait. Why?" "Because. I just need it" — she says she's going to walk around the lake and let's meet later. So off I go, midmorning, knowing that my mom will be at the nail salon and Rick will be off somewhere, suing people or doing whatever he does.

I park my bike on the driveway, walk through the front door, and stop. There are balloons and flowers everywhere. Literally everywhere. Balloons mounded on the floor, flower petals, helium balloons tied to chairs and tables, gently waving in the air currents.

"What the hell?" I mutter under my breath, kicking at some of the balloons blocking my path.

"Are you home?"

Rick's voice, happy, eager, pleasantly surprised. Until he bounds into the kitchen doorway and sees that it's me. Then he's unpleasantly surprised. Like I am.

"Oh," he says.

"Oh," I say.

We regard each other. He's wearing an apron and holding a hand mixer.

"Didn't expect to see you," he says.

"Yeah. I was just stopping in to get some stuff."

I look around at the balloons and flowers. Rick watches me.

"I take it you didn't read any of the several texts I sent you," he says.

"Nope."

"Okay. And I furthermore assume you forgot."

"Furthermore assume I . . . ?"

"It's your mom's birthday."

"Oh. Oh, crap," I say, with a familiar sinking feeling. "Right. Sorry."

He shrugs. "Don't apologize to me."

"I'll get her something."

"Uh-huh."

I look around some more at all the decorations. Only now do I notice the giant sign on the wall that says HAPPY BIRTH-

DAY, KELLY!!! in thick marker. Rick has drawn hearts and smiley faces on it.

"Well, I'm glad you're okay, at least."

I don't say anything.

"I guess you quit the lawn crew."

"I'll still going to pay you back. It's just going to take a bit longer."

He nods. "Okay. Well, I have a cake to make," he says, and disappears back into the kitchen.

I stand there for a minute, expecting him to come out again, but he doesn't. So I go upstairs and start rifling through my disorganized drawers, trying to find the Replacements shirt. I can hear the whirring of the blender.

"'I have a cake to make,'" I mutter. "'I have a *cake* to make.'"

There. I grab the shirt—THE REPLACEMENTS: SORRY, MA, I FORGOT TO TAKE OUT THE TRASH, which, irony, and head down the stairs, wondering whether I'm supposed to say anything to Rick— *Well, I'm going now. See you later.* Or do I just leave? But the decision is made for me. When I get to the bottom of the stairs, Rick reemerges from the kitchen, wiping his hands on a dishcloth.

"Austin," he says, "I wasn't going to say anything, because it doesn't feel like my place to do so, but then I thought, no. I'm going to treat you with respect. I'm going to speak to you like I would any person in this situation. First off, despite everything that is going on, I think that it is inconsiderate of you not to at least spend time with your mother on her birthday."

"Do you?"

"Yes, I do."

"Okay, can we back up a bit? To the part where you said it's not your place? You were right. It's not your place."

"Fine. Then forgive me for overstepping my bounds. But you know how important birthdays are to your mother."

"'How important'—really? Ask her how important my thirteenth birthday was. That's the one she missed because she was in friggin' rehab. Was that one important?"

"Ah. Yes, that sounds awful. But how long are you going to hold on to that?"

"You a lawyer or a therapist?"

"What is it, then? You need to get revenge on your mom? That what this is?"

"Revenge? I don't want revenge. I just don't need you standing here and transmitting life wisdom to me."

"Doesn't take a huge amount of wisdom to see that it's your mother's birthday, and she loves you and she's been very concerned about you, and she *misses* you—"

"You know something? Just because you two are screwing doesn't make you my dad."

"Oh, spare me the clichés. That's also rather disrespectful toward your mother, and she doesn't deserve that."

"Really? Isn't that what she is to you? Someone to screw?"

"I'd say that's a pretty fundamental misreading of our relationship."

I don't know why that came out of my mouth, all bile and spite and venom. Rick is absolutely calm, not a trace of anger in his voice. That's what it is, he's so completely unruffled, and it makes me even angrier.

And as if he's reading my mind:

"Austin, there's not much you could say that will hurt me or upset me. I don't think you can even imagine the things people have said to me over the years."

"Probably because you're an asshole."

I think he actually smiles slightly.

"Probably. The point is, and I've said this before, you can say anything you want to me. Really. I don't like you insulting your mother, but let's put that aside. I think our relationship would benefit if you'd start being more honest with me."

"Gosh, Rick, thanks, but I don't see that we actually have a relationship," I say. "I have a dad." Which sounds absurd the instant it passes my lips.

"I know you do," says Rick. "He was also pretty adamant about that."

"What?"

Rick shakes his head. "Nothing. It doesn't matter. Austin, I have no desire to—"

"You called him? You called Shane?"

"Called him? Why would I call him? He came over here."

That makes me pause.

"No he didn't."

"Okay. Fine."

"What are you talking about?"

"He came over here."

"To talk to *you?*"

He gives me a *Don't be daft* look.

"Why do you think he's in town, Austin? He could have recorded his album anywhere."

"There's an engineer here he likes!"

"Okay. Anyway, it doesn't matter. I should not have mentioned it. Listen . . . maybe we can move beyond all of this, everything that has happened over the past few days. I think it would be wonderful if you would be here tonight for your mother's birthday party. I know she would really appreciate it. And I know you don't believe this, but I'd be happy to see you as well."

I'm not listening. "You're jealous, aren't you," I say. "That he's talking to her."

He cocks his head. "Am *I* the one who's jealous?"

"You're such an asshole," I say. "Such an asshole."

Then to show how mature I am I roughly grab the nearest helium balloon, holding it like I have it in a headlock, and jab it with my motorcycle key. Then jab it again, once, twice, three more times before it pops.

I look at Rick defiantly. He's impassive.

"Asshole," I say again, and leave.

* * *

"Asshole, asshole, asshole," I mutter the whole way back to Shane's. "Asshole!" I yell out at forty miles an hour. "Asshole!"—this time directed at another squirrel that darts in front of me at a stop sign, probably a cousin of the one I screamed at when I was mowing, and now they can compare notes, say, *Wait a second—what did the guy look like? That is so weird!*

I park near Shane's, sit for a while doing a little more Tourette-y *asshole asshole asshole,* then restart my bike and motor the rest of the way to his house.

I march up to his front door and jab my finger at his doorbell—and jerk it to a halt a quarter inch before actually pressing the button. What do I say? What am I going to ask? Do I *want* to know the answer?

So I stand there, go to press the button, stop myself, do it twice more.

I reach up and touch the horseshoe, trace my fingertips along its pitted, rusted surface. As I'm doing that the door opens suddenly and there's Shane, holding his guitar by the neck, starting in surprise to see me in front of him, then breaking out into a smile.

"Hey! What are you doing here?"

"I don't know, I just—"

"Good to see you!"

He uses his free arm to give me a quick hug.

"Everything okay?"

"Yeah, I—you going somewhere?"

"I was going to that spot—what do you call it? Whitfield's?"

"Whitmore's."

"Yeah, there. I was just gonna go sit there a bit. Come with me!"

"Okay, sure."

"You okay? You look spooked."

"No, all good."

*   *   *

In the car he's talking about the show and about our songs and he's so happy I want to let go and ride the wave with him, let it carry me along and forget the anxiety that is swirling beneath. Knowing that saying anything, asking anything, would mean paddling against that tide, breakers crashing down on me . . .

When we get to Whitmore's it's the same, the two of us

sitting against a tree, Shane playing something, the day so beautiful . . . but there's still the red-flag part of my mind telling me, *Say something, say something, you have to say something,* and just as I'm building up to it Shane says, "Man, I was thinking about our conversation the other night. I wish you could come to New York with me."

"For the show?"

"Yes. And more."

"More?"

"I wish—I mean, it's crazy—but I had this vision of going on tour with you, like Jeff Tweedy did with his son. Go around the country, the two of us, play shows together. Write songs. The two of us."

"Are you serious?"

"Hell yes. The two of us."

The two of us.

Just like that the world expands, a giant deep breath. This is the answer I was waiting for all along, the way to extend the enchantment of this week forever.

"Shane," I say, "I would love that. I would *love* that."

He laughs and pounds me on the back, and we start talking over each other about where we could go, places we'll play, people we'll meet. It's all crystal clear now: the vague Big Secret Plan of the future has just become the Big Not Secret Plan of right now, the Big Plan that's actually happening. Shane and me, traveling together, performing together, writing songs together, the two of us the missing pieces that we've both lacked. So painfully obvious all the time and I never dared to think it.

"We could be based in Nashville."

"How about New York? Josephine's gonna be in New York."

"Sure, New York! Bushwick, Greenpoint, some place like that . . ."

I can see it—touring with Shane, coming into town now and then to visit Josephine, and then when she goes to school in New York, we can live together!

"Shane, that would be so awesome . . ."

"*Will* be so awesome. *Will* be. We're doing it!"

A train is coming, and as it rumbles by and blows its horn Shane clambers to his feet and whoops along with it: "WOOOOOO!" and I jump up and join him, "WOOOOO!!", both of us raising our fists to the sky.

Back in the car, jabbering on excitedly, Shane telling me about what it's like to play in Austin, how the crowds are in New Orleans, how Tucson is better than you think it would be. It's only then that I glance up and realize we're in downtown Edina, near my house, near where my mom—

"Whoa, whoa, whoa, why are we stopping here?" I ask Shane. We're pulling up to the curb right outside the nail salon.

"Just stopping in to say a quick hello to KD," says Shane, putting the Range Rover in park. "And goodbye."

"Shane, wait—are you sure?"

"Yeah, c'mon, it's just a quick visit. Want to come?"

"Shane, no."

There she is, my mother, seated at a small table across from some rich Edina lady, concentrating hard on her nails. Shane is already opening his door and climbing out. My stomach knots and double-knots, all that joy and optimism vanishing.

"Shane, I don't know that this is such a great idea . . ."

"Nonsense. Come say hi."

"No, Shane, please, don't do this."

"What are you so upset about?"

"Shane . . ."

He's looking at himself in the sideview mirror, pretends to fix his eyebrows, gives me a wink, then strides toward the entrance.

"Shane, no, don't—"

Then he stops, turns on his heels, and comes back to the car.

"Goddammit, Shane, I thought you were serious," I say as he approaches.

"Just forgot this," he says, and opens the rear passenger door and pulls out the guitar.

"Shane, c'mon," I say. "Shane. Shane!"

I'm talking to his back, which is receding rapidly. He gets to the door of the salon, and I slump down in my seat, unable to watch— *Oh, God . . .* —and then I can't bear it and I straighten up just enough to peek over the edge of the car window.

He's inside. He's talking animatedly to the woman at the reception desk, who has a confused, cautious smile on her face, and he's indicating my mom, who just now is looking up and noticing him. I can't hear anything, but I clearly see her saying, "Shane!" Then she tilts her head back toward the ceiling and slumps her shoulders forward and I see her say, *"Auugh!"* and then she straightens and says, "What the *hell* are you *doing* here?!"

He's in profile to me, so I can see the smile on his face,

and he's holding out a hand to placate her—*Hold on, hold on,* he's saying, and I can see her saying, *Shane, no. NO. Get out of here,* but instead he starts strumming the guitar and singing to her, and I'm flashing back to a day on Cedar Lake when I got brained with a mandolin.

The people in the salon are giggling or confused or stunned, and my mom is apologizing to the woman in front of her and standing up to deal with Shane, who by now is down on one knee singing with enthusiastic abandon.

Now everyone is giggling, even the rich Edina lady—isn't this *adorable?!* It is sort of funny, it's so completely stupid and outrageous, and I'm half laughing while also gritting my teeth and clawing at the side of my head with my fingernails. It's total absurd RomCom, Shane on one knee giving it his all, the other women enjoying the entertainment, except in this particular RomCom the girl is clenching what appear to be cuticle scissors in her hand, and if I know my mom, there's a good chance she's going to stab Shane in the throat with them.

I should get out of the car. I should get out of the car and get the hell in the salon *now,* this instant, pull Shane out of there, get between the two of them before something truly awful happens. I sit up more, hand on the door handle, hesitating—*what do I do what do I do*—slump down again. Shane is still going. My mom is frozen in front of him, fists clenched at her sides. *This is the woman who would have clubbed you to death with a piece of firewood!* I want to shout at him, but the time for that was when we pulled up to the curb.

I want to flee, let whatever dreadful doom that's about to ensue do so without me. But I don't. I'm glued to my seat, then—*crap, no*—my mom is on the move, striding toward Shane, accelerating with each step, she's on top of him—and then she has passed him, marching right past the reception desk and straight-arming the door open.

When she steps out onto the sidewalk, I see that she's starting to cry but fighting it, jaw fixed, lips a compressed line. She's not ten feet from me. I sit up, hand automatically coming up in a semiwave, and I want to call out to her, but just at that instant her eyes fall on me and I see the moment when she recognizes me. Then she turns and stalks away down the sidewalk.

CHAPTER 24

I've told all of my secrets to you /
help me figure out which ones are true

"Well, *that* worked," says Shane when he gets back in the car, and he starts to laugh. I don't say anything or even look at him. I don't know what to do. For the first time, I'm afraid around him, and I'm not sure if I'm afraid for him or *of* him.

"What's wrong with you?" he asks.

"Nothing."

"Okay."

He's still unnaturally happy as he drives, overamped, singing, drumming on the steering wheel. I don't want to think about why he's so happy, I can't, I can't, terrified that he's on coke or meth—or, worse, that he's *not,* this is just *him,* and my anxiety is so sharp that it's a fight not to start hyperventilating, and suddenly there are bursts and pops of music in my head, jagged stabs of guitar and feedback, and I press my temple hard against the frame of the truck so the vibration will drown it out.

As we're driving Shane's mood starts to ebb, the glow fading like a tube in an old-fashioned amplifier. By the time we arrive back at his place he's quiet and tired, down from whatever high he'd been riding. When I climb out of the truck, he's still sitting at the wheel.

"I'll see you at rehearsal later," he says.

*   *   *

Of course he doesn't show up for rehearsal.

It's just Todd and Josephine and me, waiting, pacing, checking the time on our phones. I've texted him a few times and gotten nothing. I can feel Josephine watching me. I didn't tell her anything about what happened, barely said a word to her when I snuck back into the granny apartment and we left together on the bike.

"Are you all right?" she says to me now, probably the fifth time.

"I'm fine."

Todd says, "Screw this. It's nearly showtime. Maybe he's at the venue."

*   *   *

Of course he's not at the venue.

I see some people I recognize from the party and ask them all if they've seen Shane. We find the bar manager. He hasn't seen him. "I mean, c'mon, he's supposed to go on in ten minutes," he adds, miffed.

Go outside, wait. Go back inside, look around, the way you rummage in your pocket for the fifth time for the key

232

that you already know isn't there. Reconvene with Todd and Josephine, Josephine saying, "No one has seen him."

Then: "Austin!"

It's Amy. A rushed greeting, hugs, Amy telling me she came back a day early to surprise Shane, both of us saying at the same time, "Have you seen him?"

A quick hug to Josephine, an intro to Todd.

"I've been calling and emailing and texting, but he's totally off the grid," says Amy. While we're in a tight huddle, Amy asking whether we should call the police or check the emergency rooms, I hear a familiar voice.

"Yo, dude, wassup?!"

Patrick, sauntering over, arms open for hugs from everyone.

"Patrick," says Amy, "have you seen Shane?"

"He ain't here?"

"No."

"Oh. Uh-oh." The face of a kid who knows that something valuable got broken.

"Patrick, what?" says Amy.

"No, I was just thinking . . ."

Amy grabs him by the wrist and marches him away from us, and we watch the two of them converse, Patrick still looking like a guilty, defensive kid, Amy getting more and more agitated and doing a face palm.

"This can't be good," says Josephine.

Amy marches back to us. "I'm going to get Shane," she says.

"What's going on?" I say to Amy. "Everything okay?"

"No. I don't know. Shane went to some party," she says.

"He did? Why'd he do that? Is that bad?" One look at her and I can see the answer. "It's bad, isn't it."

"It's all fine. I just have to go."

"Okay, pretty obvious that it's not all fine. I'm going with you."

"No, you're not."

"Yes I am."

"Yo, let's get a move on," says Patrick, standing near the exit.

"If you're going, so am I," says Josephine.

*   *   *

There's more arguing about whether or not we're coming along, but we all end up in Patrick's beat-up Camry, Amy in the passenger seat, Josephine and me crammed in the back along with Todd. He had followed us out of the bar.

"You're coming?" I said, and he kind of nodded and shrugged at the same time.

Patrick is thinking out loud as he drives. "I *think* it's this way."

"You *think* it is, or it *is?*" says Amy.

"C'mon now, I'm trying to be helpful."

"Yeah, you sure helped Shane."

"He asked me, I told him about the party. I didn't make him go," says Patrick.

Josephine leans close against me in the back seat, and we hold hands tightly.

Patrick takes us to some neighborhood in North Minneapolis, the kind that scares you when you drive through it, old houses with collapsing decks and peeling paint and bars

234

or plywood on the doors and windows. We get lost, every decaying block more or less identical — "It's here. No, wait, that ain't it . . ." — until we get to a street that has cars parked along the curb and we slow, inching along until Amy says, "There. There's the Rover."

Patrick points out one of the crumbling houses, the first-floor lights on. "That's it, I think."

We park at the foot of the drive.

"All right, I'm going in," says Amy, the music emanating from the house growing louder as she opens the car door. "Patrick, you going to help out here?"

"Yyyyeah," says Patrick. "So here's the thing. I kind of have this beef? With some folks at this party . . . ?"

"Christ. Fine. Stay here," says Amy. "You too!" she says, leaning in to point at all of us in the back seat.

As soon as she's through the front door, I say, "I'm going in."

"Austin . . ." says Josephine.

"Don't worry. I'll be right back."

I climb out of the car and start walking toward the house, my sense of foreboding growing as I near the battered screen door. Behind me, I hear a car door open and close.

"Austin, wait."

When Josephine catches up to me, I say, "I don't think you should go in there."

"I don't think either of us should go in there."

I reach out for her hand. She grabs mine and we walk the rest of the way to the entrance.

The front door delivers us right into what I think is supposed to be the living room. It's packed with people, no furniture on the ratty carpet, the air smoky. The Rolling Stones cranked way up loud. I once went to a frat party that felt a little like this—like there were no actual grownups maintaining the house, that it was just a rotting shell to hide bad activities from prying eyes. But this is that times ten. We pause just inside, Josephine scrunching up her nose. "You okay?" I say.

"I'm okay. Let's find Shane."

I spot Amy up ahead and we squeeze through, Josephine following close behind me, not letting go of my hand. "I'm a little scared of these people," she whispers to me, and I don't want to admit it, but so am I. I find myself picking people out of the crowd who look normal and trying to take comfort in that. *See? That guy over there looks okay, that woman there looks like she could teach school. Doesn't he sort of look like the guy who manages the grocery store?* But there are also people who look hard, like they've maybe seen prison bars from the wrong side.

Amy is finishing a conversation with a guy who looks like a stoned Rastafarian Viking, dreads in his blond hair, his scraggly beard bound into braids by little rubber bands.

"Dunno, man, try downstairs," he's saying, raising his eyebrows when he spots Josephine.

"I told you—" starts Amy when she sees me.

"Let's just find Shane," I say.

We file down the narrow, unlit stairway, picking our way past people leaning against the drywall. The basement is dim and smells like mold and cigarette smoke and weed. Josephine is coughing.

As my eyes adjust to the low light I start to discern shadowy figures standing in the center of the room, then a sofa with three people slouched in it against the wall. There's a flare of light, someone lighting a cigarette or a joint or *something,* and Amy says, "There he is."

He's slumped in a chair in the corner, head lolled backwards. Amy goes to him first. I can hear her saying, "Shane. Shane. Shane!" as I move toward her, Josephine close behind me. Amy is shaking him. "Shane!" she repeats, but he doesn't respond.

"He's drunk," I say, hoping he's just drunk, not something worse.

"Oh, God," says Josephine.

Another light flares and she whispers to me, "What are those people smoking over there?"

"Smoking?" says Amy, straightening up, furious. "They're not smoking. They're cooking heroin."

"Oh, Jesus," I hear myself say.

Amy swears, shaking her head. "He promised," she says. "He *promised.*"

"Hey, pretty lady, you need something?"

Some man with stringy long hair and a goatee approaching, talking at Amy, a smile that's really a threat. I feel the adrenaline start, the weak-kneed prefight sick feel, Josephine squeezing my upper arm, hard. Everything is so awful right now, and it's about to get so much worse. I step forward to put myself between Stringy Hair and our group, but then someone pushes me roughly aside, and it's Todd, moving in front of me, fists ready. "We don't want nothing from you," he says. "We gonna have a problem, buddy?"

"Whoa, easy now," says stringy hair, still smiling, like he's amused, but he backs away, hands up, and suddenly I'm deeply appreciative of Todd and his pit-bull jock aggression.

"We've got to get Shane out of here," Josephine whispers to me, just as Todd says in a low voice, "Methune, what the hell is this?!"

"Shane," says Amy, shaking him, but he doesn't respond. She leans close and half shouts, "Shane! Wake up! Wake! Up!"

Shane groans and makes a noise like, *MMmmmrrrr.*

Amy winds up and slaps him across the face, hard, Josephine taking in a quick startled breath. "Shane, *wake the hell up!*"

Beyond Todd, I can see Stringy Hair talking to another guy who has a shaved head and looks mean, Stringy Hair gesturing toward us.

"Todd," I say, "we have to get him out of here."

"Yeah, no kidding."

"Wake up, Shane!" Amy again. Choked-up angry tears in her voice.

Shane groans again. I can see Stringy Hair and Shaved Head sniggering.

"Screw this," says Todd. "Methune, help me get him up."

"What's your plan?"

"Plan? I'm gonna friggin' carry him."

In the end it takes all of us yanking on Shane's arms to get him upright enough for Todd to squat down and hoist him up into a fireman's carry.

As Todd starts staggering toward the stairs, Stringy Hair moves into his path, once again displaying his hyena grin. Shaved Head is behind him. Josephine's nails are digging into my upper arm.

"Get out of my way," says Todd quietly, teeth gritted.

"What's your rush?" says Stringy. "Whyn't you leave the girls?"

"Buddy," says Todd, the same quiet tone but an even harder edge, "I have to put this guy down, it's gonna be a rough friggin' night for you."

Delivering it not to Stringy but to Shaved Head, the real danger. He and Todd are staring each other down. Shaved Head massive, growing larger with every moment, looks like he could eat Todd as a snack. But if Todd feels any fear, I can't detect it, just the violence inside him barely kept in check.

An eternity of them staring at each other, of my heart pounding. Then Shaved Head just shrugs, bored, and turns away, pulling Stringy along with him.

Todd staggers and grunts and wheezes his way up the stairs, the three of us following, our hands out toward him like we're spotting a gymnast, me twisting to make sure that Baldy and Stringy aren't coming up behind us.

When we reach the ground floor, Todd pushes his way through to the front door, gasping, "Get the hell out the way!" to the people in his path. As soon as he's outside he drops Shane on the patchy grass, none too gently, and sits, knees up, gulping air. Amy goes to kneel next to Shane, holding his hand and stroking his face. Josephine starts retching in the bushes.

"Awesome!" says Patrick, who is standing on the lawn by the curb. "You found him!"

* * *

"I knew I shouldn't have left. I *knew* I *shouldn't* have *left*."

Amy, driving the car, smacking the steering wheel each

time she says *knew*. Shane between me and Todd in the back seat, occasionally moaning. Josephine directly in front of me in the passenger seat, her face greenish white, the window rolled down in case she has to retch again.

When Patrick helped us load Shane into the Rover, he said, "So, I guess you guys ain't doing the show tonight?"

"Yeah, you think?" said Amy.

"I *knew* I *shouldn't* have *LEFT!*" she says again now.

Next to me, Shane manages a "Whuz goin' on?"

I reach out my hand and place it on Josephine's shoulder. She doesn't brush it away or stiffen, but she doesn't react to it either. I give her shoulder a gentle squeeze. *Hello?* After a moment, she reaches up and pats my hand politely, twice, then drops her hand back to her lap. I let my own hand drop too.

"I thought I'd come back early and give him a nice surprise," Amy is saying. "Well, there was certainly a surprise, that's for sure."

Josephine hunches forward suddenly, then leans her head out the window and dry heaves.

When she sits back in her seat, I put my hand on her shoulder again. Amy glances at her, says, "How are you doing, sweetie?"

"I just want to go home."

"Of course. Austin, once we get Shane back to the house, you have got to get this poor girl home. He's going to get you home, okay, sweetie?"

"Okay."

I lean forward.

"Josephine, wait. *Home* home?"

She just nods miserably.

"Josephine, no. You can't go home!" I say, just a little too loud.

"What do you mean, no?" asks Amy. "What are you talking about? Where else is she going to stay?"

Which leads to me spilling the beans and Amy saying, "WHAT?!" and "I knew I shouldn't have left!"

"Shane has been letting you stay there? Is he *crazy*?"

"No, Amy, listen, he didn't know we were there."

"What?!"

"Amy . . ."

"I cannot believe this. I knew I shouldn't have left. I *knew* I *should not have left*."

"Hey, babe," slurs Shane from the back seat. "That you?"

"Oh, shut up, Shane."

* * *

When we get to his house, Shane is conscious enough that Todd and I can flank him, his arms over our shoulders, and do the wounded-comrade stumble from the Rover to the front door and awkwardly, groaningly, up the stairs to the bedroom.

"Put him on his side so he doesn't choke on his own sick," says Amy. "Although at this point, he deserves it."

"Hey, babe?" says Shane is that gloopy voice. "I don' thing I'm gonna do tha' show in New Yorg."

Amy shakes her head like she's trying not to scream. Then she shoves the keys at me and says, "Get that girl home."

Josephine is downstairs. Todd pretends to be interested in the bookshelves while I go over to her and hug her. She doesn't respond for a moment, just rests a hand on my hip, then suddenly puts her arms around me and pulls me close, almost desperate.

241

"Hey," I say. "Hey."

"Austin," she says, "I'm sorry."

"Sorry why?"

"I just have to go home."

"I know. I know. But maybe if you stayed . . ."

"I still love you. I love you. But I just want to go home."
Starting to cry now.

"Okay. I'll take you. I'll take you now."

But even as I'm saying that there's a horn honk from out
front. I look at Josephine.

"My mom. I texted my mom. Austin, I'm so sorry . . ."

"Josephine, I'm really—"

"I just need to go. Please let me go. I love you."

"Please don't. Not after everything—"

"I have to. I'm sorry. I have to."

The horn honks again. She releases me and steps back,
wipes her eyes, tries to smile.

"Song's not over, right?" I say.

"It's not over."

"Okay," I say.

"Okay," she says.

She wipes her eyes again. "Todd," she says, "you live on
Benson, right?"

"Yeah, Benson."

"You want a ride?"

Shrug. "Yeah, sure."

"We'll talk tomorrow? We'll talk?" I say, moving with
Josephine to open the door for her.

"Of course," she says.

"Should I call you tomorrow?"

"Yes."

"What time?"

"I don't know. I'll call you."

"Make sure you do."

"I will," she says, moving past me, then hesitating as I lean forward for another hug, the embrace awkward and stiff, the kiss brief. There's a Cadillac idling at the curb, the dome light on, her mother visible inside, watching us, glaring at me.

"We'll talk tomorrow, right?" I say as Josephine walks down the path toward the car.

"Yes."

"Don't forget to call."

She holds a hand up over her shoulder without looking back at me. She climbs into the passenger seat, Todd gets in back, and I watch as she sits back heavily, her hands coming up to cover her face, then the dome light goes off and the car pulls away.

CHAPTER 25

Last night I dreamed I had a hole in my head /
thirteen angels and demons dancing on the bed /
I was six times alive / and I was seven times dead

I wake from bad, sweaty dreams, squinting in the brightness of the room. Sunlight is blooming through the translucent fabric of the shades. There are birds chirping outside. It takes me a moment to figure out why I'm in Shane's kitchen and why the perspective is so weird and why I'm so stiff and achy.

After Josephine and Todd left last night, I didn't know what to do. I couldn't go upstairs to talk with Amy, couldn't go home, couldn't go to the granny apartment and sleep in the bed without Josephine, so I just sat at the kitchen table and put my head down and cried and must have fallen asleep like that.

Ding dong.

The front doorbell. Someone is ringing the front bell. That's what woke me up.

Maybe it's Josephine, I think, and raise my head, then realize that doesn't make any sense and lay my head down again.

The bell rings again, then again, then it just becomes an insistent string of *ding-dong ding-dong ding-dong.*

I should get up and get it, but I just sit there.

Thump thump thump as someone comes downstairs. I hear the door open and Amy say, "What on earth is—"

"Where is he?!"

Oh. God.

I'm instantly up out of the chair and out of the kitchen and into the living room, right into an ongoing firefight.

"Who the hell are you, girly?" says the new arrival.

"Who am I? What are you talking about! You're the one just walked in here!"

"Mom," I say, "what are you doing here?!"

"Well, well, well," says my mom. "Of course you're here. Of *course.* Hope I didn't wake you up."

"Mom!"

"What's going on?" says Amy, still half asleep. She's wearing pajama bottoms and one of Shane's T-shirts.

"You the latest girlfriend?" says my mom.

"Mom—"

"'Cuz if you're the latest girlfriend, honey, I wish you the best of luck."

"Amy, this is my mom."

"Uh . . . hi?" says Amy.

"Hi yourself. What are you, eighteen?"

"Mom . . ."

"You know," says Amy, "I don't mean to be rude, but since *you* are . . ."

245

"Oh, shut it. Where is he? And don't say 'who.'"

"Mom, what are you doing here?"

"You're asking me what *I'm* doing here? I thought you were playing runaway at Devon's. Where is Shane?!"

"Shane's upstairs sleeping," says Amy.

"Upstairs drunk, you mean. Get him."

"Austin, what is going on?" says Amy. "I'm up there dead asleep—"

"Amy, I'm so sorry about this," I say. "Mom—"

"I'm not talking to you right now," she says. "I will deal with you later." She jabs a finger at Amy. "Now you go get Shane, or I swear to the Lord I will take his granddaddy's horseshoe off that front door and go upstairs and beat him to death with it."

"Okay, first, you don't walk in here and order me around. Second, I don't imagine he particularly wants to see you," says Amy.

"Oh, really? Is that why he keeps calling me and dropping by the house and showing up at my place of work like some goddamn clown and nearly getting me fired?"

"You're lying," says Amy.

"Oh, for Christ's sake, little girl. Wake up. I was lying, I wouldn't friggin' be here. How you think I knew where to find him? He texted me the friggin' address five times and invited me over!"

"Okay, and now it's time for you to go."

Instead my mom turns to me. "How was all y'all's little show last night?" she says, holding up her hand, and I realize she's clutching a rumpled sheet of paper. "Y'all have fun?" She crumples the paper into a ball and backhands it at me. It rebounds off my chest and I reach for it reflexively, bobbling it around before catching it.

"Listen, lady," Amy says.

"Don't you 'listen' me!"

"Don't you tell me what to—"

As they tell each other what not to do I uncrumple the paper. A flyer, printed in old-timey medicine show letters. YOU ARE CORDIALLY INVITED TO A BIRTHDAY PERFORMANCE FOR YOU BY SHANE TYLER AND THE CHILDREN'S CRUSADE, FEATURING THE VERY TALENTED AUSTIN METHUNE

"Would you please leave already?" Amy is saying.

"Shane!" shouts my mother, directing her voice upstairs, her southern coming out full. "Shane Tyler, I know you're up there!"

"Lady—"

"Shut yer yap. Shane! Shane Tyler! You get your ass down here right now!"

Amy has her hands clapped to the sides of her head. "I cannot believe this is happening," she says.

"Oh, it's happening. Shane!" bellows my mom. "Shane Tyler! Shane Tyler, you get out of bed and come down here right now, or . . ."

Shane has appeared at the top of the stairs.

We all watch as he descends, slowly, grimacing, holding the banister like an old man, like his whole body pains him. At the bottom of the stairs he passes Amy, resting a hand on her shoulder, and then he walks stiffly toward my mom and comes to a halt a short pace in front of her, and the two of them just stand there looking at each other, arms at their sides, not saying a word.

I haven't breathed since he first appeared.

No one moves. Their faces looked carved from stone, facing each other in a silent tableau. I'm steeling myself for the inevitable, when my mom will wind up and smack him or open her mouth and start screaming.

Instead I realize that her eyes are starting to brim with tears. So are Shane's. They're both fixed in place, tears starting to overflow. Then he takes a step closer to her and opens his arms and she responds, moving to him and gently embracing him, the both of them swaying and rocking, tears streaming down my mom's cheeks from her closed eyes. Shane is the same. She wipes at her nose and her eyes with her wrist and leans her head against his shoulder.

"Oh, Shane," says my mom. "Shane, Shane, Shane. Why do you have to be so dumb?"

"I don't know," says Shane.

In the background Amy is watching, hugging herself, shoulders high as if she were sheltering from the cold.

"I still love you," says Shane. "All these years, I always loved you."

My mom wipes more tears. "I love you too, Shane. I loved you more than I ever loved anyone, and I always will. But, Shane, I don't want to see you ever again. Ever."

"Yeah," says Shane. "Yeah."

She stands on her toes to give him a kiss on the forehead, and then a final hug, and then she steps back from him. He's watching her with helpless longing and sadness, the way you might look when someone you desperately love has died.

My mother turns to me. "Come on," she says.

I don't move.

"Austin," says my mom. Then again: "Austin."

"It was all a lie."

My voice sounds flat. Shane doesn't meet my gaze, stares at the carpet.

"All this," I say quietly, gesturing with the flyer without raising my arm, because even that would require more energy than I can summon. "It was all for her. The show, all that, you were just using me. I was just bait." My fingers open. The paper falls. "You never sent that track to Barry, did you."

Now he looks up. "Kid . . ." he says. Shaking his head in apology, or helplessness.

I nod.

"Let's go," says my mom.

I follow her out to her car and we drive away.

* * *

"Just give me a little more time," says Josephine.

"You said a week. It's been a week."

"Austin, it's been three days."

"It feels like a week. It feels like a month."

"Austin . . ."

Dusk. I'm at a playground, the one where I broke my arm for Martha Meinke's benefit. One hand holding the phone to my ear, the other anchoring me to the tetherball pole, my body leaning away from it as I circle around and around and around. Trampling five cigarette butts farther into the ring of dirt with each revolution. Thinking of lighting up again.

"There's some party tonight at Jason Goodman's house," I say.

"Austin, don't you think that's enough parties for a bit?"

"So come hang out. We can just hang out."

"I can't. Not tonight."

"Fine. Tomorrow. What about tomorrow?"

"No. I promised to help my dad out at the mall, hand out flyers."

"What?!"

"Look, it's complicated. I'm trying to play nice. Don't judge."

We're quiet.

"It all feels like a dream," she says.

"Yes."

"I didn't want it to end."

"No."

"Have you heard from Shane?"

"No."

"You angry at him?"

"I don't know."

"You and your mom talking yet?"

"No."

"You should try."

All my mom said when she retrieved me from Shane's was "I have to go to work." When she got home that night, she made dinner and took hers upstairs. It's been that way since, both of us spending our evenings in our rooms, avoiding each other, my mom leaving for work before I'm up. Roommates who don't speak the same language. Roommates whose countries are at war with each other.

Rick was there the first night, but now he's in Milwaukee

on some important Rick business. Which, thank God. Because if I had to talk to him right now I'd say, *Pardon me for a moment*, and then I'd go and ingest every single household cleaner in the broom closet.

I was irritable and itchy tonight, restless restless restless, couldn't write a song, couldn't watch TV, couldn't make it past two panels of Calvin and Hobbes. I paced around the house. On my mom's desk I saw the application to Marymount Academy, a pen resting on it. I left the house and got on my bike and ended up here, calling Josephine for the hundredth time.

"I miss you," I say, also for the hundredth time.

"I miss you, too," she says.

"So why not come to the party?"

"Austin, no. And you shouldn't go either."

"Josephine, just say it. Just say it. Are you breaking up with me?"

"No! It's just that I'm scared," she says. "I'm scared and I need time away to think, so that I can come back."

"But you'll come back."

"Austin, what did I tell you before?"

"What."

"On the beach. I told you that I'm true. And I meant it. Remember that," she says. "I'm true. Are you?"

"Yes."

"So give me some time."

I stay in the park until the sun sets, smoking that sixth cigarette, and then one more for good measure. I compose another text to Shane that I know I won't send.

Am I angry at him? I don't know. The whole concert, this whole magic week, what was it? Shane's pathetic effort to get my mom to come to the show.

She must have told him no, Josephine said, *the morning of the concert.*

Which makes sense, with everything that happened that day. What was it he said before the flameout? *Just stopping in to say a quick hello to KD. And goodbye.*

I *should* be angry. He lied to me, used me. But I guess I sort of used him, too. And there's something else. The way he would look at me, like he cared. Like he was proud of me.

So instead of being angry I'm . . . what? Empty. Empty and confused.

Which is how I end up on my bike again, heading to his house. Going there to ask Shane the question Josephine put to me: *Who are you?*

I park my bike at the curb. If he's not home, I'll wait until he is. *Who are you, Shane Tyler?* I follow the walkway toward his front door. Then halfway there slow nearly to a stop.

"No."

Then pick up the pace again and reach the front door and stand there staring at it, like staring at it hard enough will make what's missing reappear.

The horseshoe. The horseshoe is gone.

"No!"

In its place, thumbtacked to the door, is an envelope. *Austin,* it says in Shane's handwriting.

I don't need to peer through the window or go around back to see if the Rover is there to know. He's gone. Gone for good.

That's who he is.

Then I do feel angry.

Blowtorch fury, rage, ambushing me like it did in the booth at the bar, and now the music in my head joins the fray, all discord and noise and jagged edges, and I stagger back and close my eyes and clutch at my head like I'm trying to hold my skull together.

* * *

Drinking hard, drinking with a destination in mind, one beer, two, pushing to the keg for my third, people saying, *Austin! Good to see you! Yo, you okay? You look kinda intense . . .*

Too-loud music, shouted conversations, everything smelling beer-sour, weed-sweet, cigarette-foul. Kids making out in the corners, lines at the bathrooms, kegs out back, rumors of the act of intercourse taking place between so-and-so in the basement bathroom or *in the parents' room on the parents' bed!*

On Shane's doorstep when my hearing returned and I could focus my eyes, I tore that note off the door and crumpled it and threw it down and stomped on it, screaming and swearing at it, like I was killing it. Not needing to read it, already knowing the goodbye BS that would be written there: *Dear Austin, I'm so sorry but hope you'll understand that it's better this way . . .*

Then I texted Josephine, *you have to call me,* then called her and left a babbled, crazy message as I paced on Shane's front lawn — "He *left!* He said he wouldn't leave — he promised . . ."— then texted her again to *callmecallmecallme,* and then just wrote, *I'm going to the party.* Stomped to my bike, turned around, stomped back, snatched up the flattened envelope and jammed it in my pocket. Then red-lined it to the party, blowing lights and stop signs.

I won't ever leave you again.

The final lie. Who Shane is.

Well, here's to Shane! I say, on the first round of shots. *To Shane!* on the second. *Bottomsh up for Shane!* on the third. The alcohol finally delivering me to where I want to be, everything a pleasant blurry glow, silly conversations, dancing, sweaty hugs, *Hey, dude! Whassup! High five!* Getting my party on.

Then, "Austin!"

My goodness, does Alison look nice.

* * *

Alison and I are kissing.

It started when she came over and said, "Austin! It's so good to see you!"

Huge hug.

"Aw, this is so good," I said, "No, don't let go. Never let me go." She giggled and squeezed me back, and whispered in my ear, "I'm *so* glad you're here." Then, "Are you here with someone . . . ?"

"Nope." That someone didn't even care enough to answer my texts. So forget that someone.

And she smiled and said, "Good."

I said, "Wait—are you still broken up with Todd?"

"Yes."

"You sure?"

"Very sure."

"Like, completely, totally—"

"How can I get you to shut up?"

"Well," I said, "you could try kissing me."

So she did. She tried that, and it worked really, really well.

Part of me is saying, *Don't, don't, don't, don't, don't,* but the rest of my brain is a thousand pinball machines hitting tilt at the same time, against a backdrop of fireworks, with a side of supernova.

When we resurface, I goggle at her and say, "Why?"

She smiles her naughty smile again and says, "You're not the only one with a playlist, you know."

Alison and I are kissing, hands everywhere, nothing stopping us anymore. Now she's pulling away, pulling me by my wrist, and we're heading upstairs, squeezing past people, Alison leading me down the hallway and through an open door which she shuts and locks, and *we are the people in the parents' room,* clawing at each other, clothes coming off, leaping onto the bed, Alison whispering, "I have a condom . . ."

And so I go and do something that I wanted to be special with someone who is special, but instead I do it with Alison. And when we stumble out afterward, flushed and sweaty and straightening our clothes, there's Josephine at the top of the stairs. Freezing in place when she spots us, one foot still on the next-to-top step, hand on the banister. Incomprehension turning to shock turning to devastation, and before I can say, "No, Jo—" she's spinning and pushing her way back down the crowded stairs, knocking drinks aside, people pressing themselves against the walls and the banister, watching her go.

CHAPTER 26

The sum of us / is all there is of me / take the you from this two /
and there's no math that I can do / to even get me back to zero

The air in the mall is overchilled, overaroma'd with fast
food smells and cloying perfumes wafting out of candle and
cosmetics shops. I dodge past families and old people with
those wheeled walkers and herdlets of fourteen-year-old
girls. There's a central crossroads up ahead, and I spot Gerald
Lindahl, big smile, sleeves of his flannel work shirt rolled up.
He's shaking hands, distributing campaign literature.

Then I see Josephine, her back to me, about ten yards
beyond where her father is, listlessly offering pamphlets to
bored, incurious shoppers. To get to her I have to pass right by
her father, and he very nearly clotheslines me with a pamphlet
in the face, saying, "Here you go, young man!"

I grab it automatically just as I hear Jacqueline say, "Don't
give him one!" and there she is in my way blocking my path to
Josephine, moving left and right as I try to maneuver around

her. "What are you doing here?!" she snarls, and snatches the flyer from my hand.

Gerald Lindahl is watching us, still with his big politician's smile, like he wants to show that he's in on the big joke and in control of the situation.

"Everything all right?" he says.

"No! This is the guy who—hey! Get back here!"

I duck around Jacqueline and start quick-stepping it toward Josephine, who is still facing the other direction, talking with an elderly woman who is examining the campaign materials.

When Josephine fled the party, I chased her, but the party closed around me and she was gone. Only then did I see all the texts from her, the missed calls: *I was at dinner, I couldn't answer. Are you all right? I'm so worried about you . . .*

"Josey!" yells Jacqueline, and Josephine turns, her expression questioning, and then she spots me and I see her curse and she spins and walks rapidly away, the old woman looking up in surprise.

"Josephine!" I say, breaking into a half trot. "Hold up! Wait!"

Josephine is still stalking away, and then she abruptly stops and turns just as I'm about to reach her, and I nearly run into her and skewer my right eyeball on the index finger that she's jabbing at me.

"Get out of here!" she says.

"Josephine, please, I—"

"I don't want to hear it!"

"Please, please just listen to me."

Instead she pushes past me to march back in the direction we came from.

"Josephine!" I grab her by the elbow and she spins again, yanking her arm out of my grasp, and then she gives me a jarring two-handed push in the chest.

"You proud of yourself?" she says. "I trusted you and I thought I loved you and you screwed that girl Alison. How could you do that? How could you!"

We're right next to one of those pushcart kiosks that sells makeup and perfume, and the girl is watching us with absolute undisguised fascination, chewing her gum in slow motion.

Josephine's father is conferring with a mall guard, Jacqueline gesturing emphatically at us. The mall guard is nodding, adjusting his utility belt, starting to amble in my direction.

"Josephine, could we please just talk about this?"

"That's what we're doing. We're talking about it. You know how that girl Alison treats people like me? The things she's said to me in the hall? Do you know? And you screwed her. She told *everyone*. You chose her over me. You chose *her!* I told you I was true. I told you I was *true,* and you said you'd wait for me, and you just . . ."

She starts sobbing before she can finish the sentence.

"I'm so sorry, Josephine. I'm so, so sorry." Holding my arms out to her to comfort her. "I love you. I've never loved anyone like you. I haven't slept all night. I feel like my soul is burning, Josephine, like all the lights in the universe have gone dark, like—"

"Oh, Jesus Christ. Save it, Austin. Song's over. This is real life."

"Josephine—"

"I never want to speak to you again. Ever. *Ever.*"

258

She pushes past me. I turn to follow and run right into the security guard, arms wide like he's guarding the path to a basketball net.

"Whoa, youngster," he says. "Hold on now."

"Josephine!" I shout after her. "Josephine! *Josephine!*"

But she's moving away, her fast walk becoming a run, and she sprints past her sister and her father and keeps going and disappears around a corner.

"C'mon, buddy, let's go," the security guard says. "Get up, let's go," because I'm squatting down, hands over my head, crying. He pulls me to my feet and I don't resist, the perfume girl shaking her head at me in disgust.

"You *suck*," she says.

* * *

WOOOOOOOOOOOOOOOOO!

The rail is vibrating so hard it hurts the back of my head, distorts my vision of the clouds into a jaggedy, jumpy blur. The train blasts its horn again. I'm happy for the noise and the shaking because they're drowning out any music that might dare intrude. And I'm so tired of everything.

The train whistles again. I don't even bother turning my head to look at it. This time there's no Devon and Alex to pull me off. They're gone. Josephine's gone. My mother is there, but she's gone. Shane is gone.

I told you I was true.

I won't ever leave you again.

And he did. He left me again. There will be a stage empty in New York tomorrow night, because he won't go there. I know it in my bones, know it like I knew when I saw that note that he was gone forever.

HOOOOOOOOWOOOOOOOOOOO!!!!

In a few moments I'll be gone forever too. Because I can't think of a single reason to get up.

I close my eyes. Josephine, lying in my arms. Shane, smiling at me as I joined him onstage. Josephine when we sang together, our eyes meeting. An empty stage, Shane running away, running for eternity, running in some cloudy half existence.

An empty stage, no one there to fill it.

An empty stage.

Actually, you know what?

* * *

Farms. Communities. Woods. Farms. Slow traffic. Smooth traffic. Families in SUVs. People who look like they're driving to business meetings. People picking noses and singing to music and talking into cell phones.

The GPS in Rick's Audi telling me I have fourteen hours of driving left to New York, just enough time to make it to a venue where an empty stage awaits.

The extra key to Rick's Audi was in the kitchen drawer where he always leaves it. I doubt my mother will check the garage and notice the car is gone.

I have a duffle bag full of clothes in the trunk, along with all the cans of soup I could find, a loaf of bread, some peanut butter, some jelly. The guitar—Shane's old guitar—is across the back seat.

Before I shut off my cell phone, so I can't be contacted or tracked, I send Josephine one single text:

I'm going to New York. I'm sorry. I love you forever.

Her voice says to me now, *What are you doing?*

I say, *I have a show to do.*
And then? she says.
I turn up the radio.

* * *

I stay in the right-hand lane the whole time, driving the speed limit, holding my breath each time I see a highway patrol car. I watch the distance to empty fuel indicator, the number dropping, dropping. I don't stop for gas until it's at fourteen miles and my bladder is about to rupture. When I fill up, I think the couple at the next pump are whispering about me — what is that kid doing driving that car? I pay in cash, buy a bunch of energy drinks and candy bars and beef jerky, get out of there as quickly as possible.

I drive until the sun sets, drive until it's dark, stopping two more times to fill up. I drive until it's agony to keep my eyes open, until I start thinking, the road is straight here, I'll just close my lids for a little while . . .

Juddering buzz as the car tires plow onto the safety bumps on the shoulder. Heart-thumping panic as I'm jarred awake, jerking the wheel to get the car back into the proper lane. Still breathing hard as I take the next exit and drive on an anonymous, empty stretch of country road. The GPS map says I'm somewhere in western Pennsylvania. It's after two a.m. I'm so tired it's wretched misery, but I don't know what to do. I can't go to a motel. I'm afraid of parking the car in plain view. I find a gas station that looks like it's been closed for a decade and pull behind the building, near a rusted Dumpster, and close my eyes just for a few minutes to figure things out.

It's way past dawn when I wake up, first a few moments of blurry confusion and then more heart-thumping panic, expecting to be surrounded by a SWAT team. There is no SWAT team. There's a decaying gas station on a pitted asphalt lot that's crumbling into a woods, off a lonely stretch of nowhere road.

I pee behind a tree, do some half-assed stretching, get back in the car and back on the highway, and keep going.

I drive for hours and hours more, stopping once in a roadside diner, again feeling paranoid that people are talking about me. Signs starting to appear indicating that New York City is somewhere ahead. By early evening the traffic is tightening, the surroundings becoming less and less rural and open. More signs for the city. What I'm driving through becomes weird and industrial and gnarled, tangles of rusting girder bridges and highway overpasses marring wetlands, my first transactions with toll booths. Then in the failing light I see it in the distance: Manhattan spiked across the horizon.

* * *

I drive through the Holland Tunnel into Manhattan, overwhelmed, exhilarated, the traffic like a video game generated by someone with a meth issue, a thousand potential accidents gnashing their teeth at me on every block. Over the Williamsburg bridge into Brooklyn, the clock ticking, the gig supposed to start in thirty minutes. The GPS voice leads me to the venue and I drive by it slowly, then circle the blocks for another twenty minutes looking for a parking spot, starting to sweat, swearing.

I finally see someone pull out and do my best to parallel park, *ee rr ee rr* back and forth in the space while people behind me honk and curse.

I'm already late as I sprint back toward the venue, dodging

the bearded clones in flannel and tight jeans who crowd the sidewalk, spilling out of all the bars to smoke. My lungs are burning, my arm burning as I try to hold the guitar case away from my body so it's not thumping against me, trying to find the right cadence so it's not swinging wildly with each step.

The doorman bars my way with a massive hand. "I'm playing tonight I'm playing tonight I'm playing!" I gasp.

"Where's your ID?" he says.

"I'm supposed to be"—gulp of air—"onstage right now!"

I point to the small chalkboard mounted next to the door with the evening's lineup, SHANE TYLER 9:00 P.M. scribbled on it.

Beetled brow, frowny face.

"Please," I say.

He twists and shouts inside: "Ben. Ben!"

Ben appears, the king of the hipsters: epic ZZ Top beard, thick horn-rimmed glasses, flannel.

"What's up?"

"This kid says he's Shane Tyler."

"You are *not* Shane Tyler."

"No, I'm his son," I say.

He stares at me.

"What?"

"His son. I'm his son."

"Well, whoop-dee-doo for you. Where's Shane? He's supposed to playing at"—he checks his watch—"five minutes ago, and he's not here. And I called his label rep, and *they* don't know where he is, and I called *him,* and *he's* not answering. You're his kid—how come you don't know where he is?"

"He's not coming. But *I* can play."

Ben stares at me. Before he can answer, I hear, "Ben! What's up!"

Ben nods gruffly at someone behind me. "Shefford," he says, and then he's doing the soul shake and half hug with a tall guy with a shaved head and goofy cheerful grin and T-shirt that says TRIPPY on it.

"What's up!" says Shefford to the bouncer, and they knock fists, and Shefford says, "What's up!" to me like I count, and I knock fists automatically.

"Your guys all here?" Ben asks Shefford. He has dismissed me.

"Now?" says Shefford. "I thought we didn't go on until ten. I wanted to see Shane Tyler. He started yet?"

"Jerkoff bailed," says Ben.

"Aw, that sucks."

"Yeah, I got a bunch of people here thinking he's about to go on."

"I could play," I say.

"How fast could you get everyone here?" Ben says to Shefford.

"I could play," I say again.

"You think you could get your people here in, like, twenty minutes?" Ben says.

"C'mon, seriously?" says Shefford. "You know how everyone rolls."

"Now I have to friggin' refund all these people."

"I could play."

"So? Get the label to pay you back."

"Yeah. You go deal with those turds."

264

"I could play."

"I'll just keep the house music on. You guys get going as early as you can," says Ben.

"I'm telling you, they're not going to be here for an hour."

"I could—"

"I *heard* you," says Ben to me. Now to Shefford: "He says he's Shane Tyler's kid."

"What?!" says Shefford. "Badass!" He jabs his hand out to me for a handshake. "Your dad is awesome."

"His dad's an asshole," says Ben.

"Whoa," says Shefford.

"No, he's right," I say. "He's an asshole."

Shefford laughs. "Why don't you let him play?"

"Why don't you . . ." says Ben, suggesting something physically improbable.

"I just drove here from Minneapolis. I drove straight through."

"That is so. Rock. And. Roll," says Shefford. "You hear how rock 'n' roll that is? He drove here from Minneapolis. Let him play."

Ben glares at me, shakes his head. "Fine. But I'm not paying you," he says, and goes inside.

* * *

As soon as he says I can play, I don't want to play.

I don't look at the crowd as I tune up and do a quick sound check, struggling to adjust the height of the mic.

Then I look. It's a pretty big room, crowded, everyone standing. The house music shuts off. It's time. Faces turn toward me, curious, expectant. Prickly sweat. Heart racing.

Here it is, what I came all this way to do, what I've always dreamed of doing.

"Um," I say. "Hi. Shane couldn't make it tonight. I'm his son, Austin."

If there's a murmur of surprise or any reaction at all, I don't register it, because I immediately start playing the opening chords to "Good Fun," my eyes closed.

When I start singing the first verse, my voice is timid and shaky, my hands greasy with sweat. I keep my eyes closed as I sing, or keep my sightline fixed above the crowd. About halfway into the song, my voice starts to even out and settle, my confidence growing a bit. I can do this. I can *do* this.

Then I let my gaze drop lower, and it falls upon some guy in the front row, a guy in his thirties in a leather jacket and T-shirt. Catching the precise instant when he turns and looks at his friend, the two of them sharing eye rolls and snarky smiles. *What did we expect?* that look says. And it's like a drop of ink in a pool of clear water, diffusing outward, darkening and polluting everything, and I see others in the crowd trading similar glances, everyone coming to the same conclusion at once, their interest fading, people starting to talk to each other instead of listen. It's not even hostility. It's worse. It's boredom and indifference.

When I played with Shane, it was like a dream where you're flying. This is every nightmare you've ever had where you forgot about the test or didn't learn your lines or you're naked onstage.

Going into the third verse, I play the wrong chord and have to readjust. I'm looking forward in my mind to the upcoming parts of the song, but it's like a road vanishing into

266

the mist. I'm going to run out of words any moment—here it comes, here it comes, I can't remember, it's gone—and my voice falters and I stop singing and just strum the guitar, and then I stop that, too.

I restart from the beginning of the verse and stop again.

Start again. Stop.

Everyone's attention is back on me, but for the wrong reason. Now people are turning away, embarrassed for me, embarrassed for this child onstage, too painful to watch, one guy actually half covering his eyes with his hand, a car wreck playing out in front of him.

A dreadful moment when I just stand there, not moving, not playing, exposed. My darkest fear of the worst thing that could ever happen onstage.

"Sorry," I say, too far from the mic for it to pick me up properly. I unstrap the guitar and grab it by the neck and jump off the stage, not bothering with the case, who cares, and I shame-trudge my way through the crowd as fast as I can, head down, ignoring Shefford saying "Kid! Kid!" I'm gasping for breath as I stagger outside, and suddenly I'm so angry it feels like all my cells are exploding, and *SMASH* I slam Shane's guitar on the sidewalk *SMASH SMASH SMASH* until the body shatters and breaks off *SMASH* and all I have is the neck, the strings still connected to the bridge and a ruined remnant of guitar, and then I hurl the whole mess away from me and stand there panting and wild-eyed.

"Okay, that one? You can't blame that on me."

I spin around.

It's Todd Malloy.

CHAPTER 27

Stay an angry young man / as long as you can /
the trick is knowing how and when / to come back down to land

I want to flee. I want to sit on the ground and sob. I want to start gibbering and giggling and tear my hair out. I want to run into his arms.

Instead I just stand there, stupefied, slack-jawed.

The first thing that comes out of my mouth: "I swear I thought you guys broke up."

When he just cocks his head and looks at me, confused, I say, "Todd, what the hell are you *doing* here?"

"I stole my dad's credit card and got a plane ticket."

"Nice!" says Shefford, who must have followed me out of the bar.

"Are you *nuts?*" I say.

"Dude, you stole a friggin' *car* and *drove* here."

"This is *fantastic*," says Shefford.

"Who is this?" says Todd, jerking his thumb at Shefford.

"I'm Shefford," says Shefford, sticking out his hand.

"Could you give us a minute?" says Todd.

"Yeah, yeah, sure," Shefford says, and retires to a spot approximately three feet farther away.

"How did you even know I was here?"

"Josephine called me, asked if I'd seen you, told me what happened. I thought, damn, if he's going, I'm going."

It's taken me this long to process that Todd has an impressive new shiner under his left eye.

"Yeah," he says, noting my gaze. "That helped. And now I'm here, and *you* have to get back in *there*."

"What?!"

"Not my business, but he's right," says Shefford.

"Would you please?"

"Sorry."

"Todd, I'm not going back in there."

"Oh, you're going back in there, and you're getting on that stage."

"I can't!"

"You're going to. You're gonna get on that stage, and I'm gonna play drums, and you're gonna strum your guitar and sing."

"I don't have a guitar," I say, pointing to the wreckage on the sidewalk.

"You can use my electric," volunteers Shefford.

"You can use his electric," seconds Todd.

"You don't have a drum set."

"There's a house kit all set up," says Shefford.

"Todd, I was a complete disaster in there!"

"Uh, *yeah*. I saw. I got in there just as you were crapping

269

your pants. Look, I was in a game once, and this guy hit me with—"

"Oh, God, don't give me a sports metaphor."

"You *can't pussy out*. You can't."

"I can. I did. I'm done."

When I start to walk away, Todd runs around in front of me and blocks my path.

"Todd, don't. Please let me go."

"Methune, you remember that party with your dad? Down in that basement?"

"Yes. What."

"That guy? He would have kicked my ass. He would have kicked. My. Ass. But there's two things I can do well. I can play drums, and I can stand my ground. I won't back down. You can't back down now. Don't you get it? You're so . . . you're so goddamn *good,* Methune. You can't back down in front of these assholes."

"Are you complimenting me?"

"Yes. Don't make me do it again."

I try to push past again. He stops me with a hand on my chest.

"Todd, you can't make me do this."

"No. But *you* can. Methune, you *got* this."

"I do?"

"Yes, you do. *We* got this."

* * *

As Shefford and Todd are frog marching me back into the venue, Shefford says, "Look, just play loud."

"What if I screw up again?" I say.

"Play louder."

270

* * *

Hasty last-minute planning as Shefford steers us through the crowd to the stage, Todd going through the set list. "And no namby-pamby Simon and Garfunkel crap. We're going hard, straight-up Jack White, Black Keys, whatever. Got it?"

Everything moving very quickly. Shefford playing roadie, plugging in his guitar for me and fiddling briefly with the amp settings; Todd thumping on the bass pedal and rearranging some things; me adjusting the guitar strap and not looking at the crowd, and just as I say to Shefford, "I don't think I can—" he grabs the mic and bellows into it, "What's up, mofos! Please welcome to the stage *Austin Methune!*" And everyone's turning toward us and there's an explosion behind me as Todd assaults the drums, and screw it, I hit the opening chord, the amp erupting like a volcano, and as Shefford goes airborne, diving from the stage, I hear a howl come out of my throat I've never heard before and oh, it is *on*.

* * *

TAP TAP TAP.

Here's another really bad way to be woken up: Lawyer Rick rapping a key on the driver-side window of the car in which you're sleeping. The car that belongs to him that you stole and drove to another state.

TAP TAP TAP.

The driver's seat is leaned all the way back, and I prop myself up on my elbows to goggle at Rick. He's standing right outside the door, hands on hips, bent at the waist, peering into the car like a traffic cop. His expression like a cop's too: unreadable, blank.

Oh, crap.

271

* * *

The show.

The show is a distorted white-hot blur. I only remember snippets: yowling through the songs, the gunshot reports of Todd firing off accent notes, glimpses of faces looking at me in surprise. Looking at me with respect.

Jumping off the stage afterward, Shefford saying, "Yeah, mofos!", beers shoved in our hands, drinking, more drinking, Shefford's band playing an ear-crushing set.

When Todd and I stumbled out of the bar, I said, "That was awesome! You were awesome! *We* were *awesome!*"

"No," said Todd. "We *sucked*. But who gives a crap? You got up there, Methune," and he punched me in the shoulder, ow, and I LOVE TODD MALLOY.

Plans were made: Todd's got a return flight at nine a.m. We're gonna stay out all night. We're in Brooklyn, right? We're gonna PARTY! But first, let's just head back to the car for a quick disco napzzzzzz . . .

* * *

TAP. TAP. TAP.

"Okay . . . sorry, wait a . . . second . . ."

I start fumbling with the door, too sleep clumsy and muddled to figure out if I'm supposed to be rolling down the window or opening the door, or how to do either of those operations. Rick observes me for a few seconds, then concentrates briefly on something in his hand, and—*bleepBLOOP*—the door unlocks. I guess he has his copy of the key fob.

I open the door about six inches, just so I don't have to let reality come flooding in all at once. Rick rests his left hand on the top of the door and his right on the roof and leans forward and we contemplate each other, Rick going in and out of focus.

"Car's got a LoJack on it," he says finally. "Vehicle locator."

"Oh," I say.

"Whuzzah? What's going on?"

Todd, sitting up in the passenger seat, doing some drool control with a forearm dragged across his mouth.

"Oh, crap," he says. Then, "Who are you?"

"I'm the guy who owns the car," says Rick.

"Oh, crap."

"Yes," says Rick. "Oh, crap."

We all ponder the *Oh, crap*ness of the situation.

"Cool car, though," says Todd.

* * *

"Out," says Rick to me. "You too," he says to Todd.

We both comply, standing awkwardly on the sidewalk. Rick does a circle around the car, checking it for damage in the illumination provided by the streetlight overhead, then nods to himself, apparently satisfied. Then he walks directly up to Todd, hands on hips, regards him impassively for a moment, then proceeds to prosecuting-attorney the living hell out of him.

"State your full name."

"Todd Patrick Malloy."

"Place of residence?"

And so on, a rapid-fire line of interrogation that Todd answers without a hint of attitude or resistance, obediently spilling every last detail as if he were under oath. I have to hand it to Rick. It's . . . impressive.

"Please tell me you're eighteen," says Rick.

"I'm eighteen."

"You're not, are you."

"Uh . . . no. No, sir."

"I imagine your parents have no idea you're here."

"I've stayed out all night before."

"But not, presumably, in an entirely different state, without permission."

Todd doesn't say anything.

"Right," says Rick.

He sighs and rubs his eyes, no doubt envisioning potential legal liabilities.

"What I should be doing," he says to Todd, "is informing both the authorities and your parents of your presence here."

"Yes, sir."

Todd waits. I wait.

"Ah, screw it," says Rick. "Both of you, in the car."

*   *   *

What is Rick feeling as he pilots the car through the late-night traffic over the Williamsburg Bridge to Manhattan? I haven't the foggiest. He's silent until we reach a stoplight and he fiddles with his phone, then hands it to me. "Tell them we're in suite 442 and we want to order room service. Get what you want. I want a burger and fries. Medium on the burger."

I take the phone, moving like I'm underwater, and tell the voice on the other end that we're in 442 and would like to order room service.

*   *   *

So now it's two a.m. and Rick and I are sitting at a table in a suite in a fancy Manhattan hotel eating burgers and fries.

Todd's food is sitting untouched on the tray under its metal cover, Todd already out cold on the sofa after saying he was just gonna close his eyes for a second. Rick still hasn't said anything. He seems content to sit and eat like there's nothing particularly unusual about, well, everything.

"Um . . . my mom . . ." I finally say.

"Yeah, your mom. She's very relieved that I found you, although she didn't express it exactly in those terms. By the way, I met your friend Josephine."

"What?"

"Around the time I got back and realized the car was gone, she came by the house and told us what happened."

"She hates me."

"Cared enough about you to try and help. Anyway, I told your mom I'd go fetch you and went to the airport."

"I stole your car."

"No kidding."

"It's a crime."

"Yes. It's grand theft auto, which is a felony. Plus you transported it across state lines, which makes it a *federal* crime. That's the kind where the DOJ, the Department of Justice, gets involved, and you get a visit from folks who refer to themselves as special agents. By which I mean they're FBI."

He pauses to dip a french fry in ketchup.

"That," he says, "would be unpleasant."

He goes back to his french fries, sips some water. I'm not sure if he has anything else to say.

"Rick, I'm really sorry."

He nods absently.

"Yeah, whatever."

275

"You're not gonna . . . ?"

"What, have you arrested? That what you want? You think I'm going to put you through the criminal justice system? I'm pretty familiar with that side of things. I have a fair sense of what the outcome would be."

"My mom's gonna send me to that military academy."

"Doubt it. For my part I told her it was about the worst idea imaginable. I'm sure she'll figure out some punishment for you, but"—he shrugs—"what's the point? You'll either learn or you won't. You'll keep doing stupid crap, sabotage yourself, or you won't. Doesn't matter much what I do or your mom does. But here's how it works: Very soon you'll get to be a real grownup and comprehend that the world doesn't revolve around you. That you, and only you, are responsible for you. No one else."

He wipes his hands and mouth with his napkin, stands up.

"Okay. I'm going to take a shower and go to sleep." He glances at Todd on the sofa. "Looks like you get the floor."

CHAPTER 28

Last verse / same as the worst thing I've ever done

Rick is snoring in the bedroom as I gather my things quietly in the darkness. Todd doesn't stir. I slip silently out of the room, easing the door closed. It's four a.m.

The hallway is empty. The elevator is empty. The *bong* it makes when it arrives is loud and lonely in the deserted hallway. There's no one else in the lobby except a single night clerk behind the reception desk.

"Checking out, sir?" he says, eyeing my bag.

"No, I'm just . . ." I say, pointing to the exit, then walk through the double doors out into the Manhattan night.

* * *

When I wake up, the sun is bright in my eyes. There are people talking. I close my eyes against the glare and listen to the conversation. It takes a moment for me to figure out it's the TV, tuned to CNN.

"Get up," says Rick. "We have to take Todd to the airport."

* * *

When I walked out of the hotel, I stood for a moment on the sidewalk, listening to the sounds of the city at night, trying to decide which way to go.

As I shifted my weight back and forth, standing there, I became aware that I had something in my back pocket. The note from Shane.

I dug it out and looked at it without opening it. Ten yards from me was a trash can. Well, at least that was a direction. I walked to the can and held the envelope over it, preparing to drop it in.

Then didn't. Instead I opened the letter.

It wasn't a long note, the *Dear Austin* note I'd been expecting. It simply said,

It's not too late for you, either.

I'm not sure how long I stood there, reading and rereading those seven words. Then I folded up the note and returned it to my pocket.

"Welcome back, sir," said the night clerk without expression when I came in. I didn't say anything to him as I trudged to the elevator bank and went upstairs.

* * *

When we get to LaGuardia Airport Todd says, "You can just drop me off at the curb."

Rick says, "Yeah . . . no."

We park and go in with Todd, Rick helping him print out his boarding pass from the kiosk and then escorting him to the security line.

278

Before Todd joins the line, he looks at me and nods. I nod back. He sticks out a hand and we shake.

"You did good, Methune."

"You too, Malloy."

Then Rick squares himself up with Todd, like he did last night, and says, "Todd? At some point I assume your parents are going to see their credit card bill and have some difficult questions for you. But as for me being here? It never happened."

"Yes, sir."

"Did any of this happen?"

"No, sir."

"Did you see me here?"

"No, sir."

"You have a good flight."

"Yes, sir. Thank you, sir."

We wait until Todd has made it through the metal detectors.

"All right," says Rick. "We've got a long drive ahead."

* * *

A long drive with no words. West through the ugly industrial tangle that rings the city, west into Pennsylvania. We eat lunch at a rest-stop McDonald's. We stay that night in a nondescript Holiday Inn just off a cloverleaf. Rick pays for two adjoining rooms.

Before closing his door for the night, he says, "If you run out like you did last night, I'm leaving you here."

* * *

When I come down for breakfast the next morning, he's already at a table, eating. He glances up briefly from his paper and says, "I paid for the buffet breakfast," so I go and fill up a plate and join him.

I sit there for a bit, my eggs getting colder and rubbery-er. There are only a few other people in the restaurant. Rick reads his paper, sipping his coffee.

"Rick," I say.

Still reading, he says, "Yes?"

"Why?"

"Why what?"

"Why this? Why'd you come for me?"

"Wanted to make sure my car was okay."

I don't say anything.

He sighs and puts down the paper. "Austin . . . first off, you're a thoughtless little asshole. I mean, you do some absolutely ridiculous, inconsiderate things. I don't think you have an ounce of malice in you—and believe me, in the D.A.'s office I dealt with some pretty malignant young men. But still, your behavior's hard to forgive, especially because you end up hurting your mother so much."

He sips his coffee while my face burns.

"But of *course* I came. You're Kelly's son. I love her, and she loves you. Of *course* I came. I *had* to. I may not be your father, but I had a responsibility to come for you."

He picks up his paper, and I think he's done. Then he puts it down again.

"And you know, there's something else. I'm aware that my opinion doesn't carry much weight with you. But, Austin, I think you have a real light in you. I'm hoping that you can bring that light, bring *Austin,* to the world, because the world could use it. I don't know *how* you're going to do it, whether it's through music or art or being the world's best lawyer— that's a joke, by the way—but whatever it is, it's going to take hard work and effort on your part, not just gliding by on talent. But I have faith, Austin, that you can make it through, that you can find your way. And the world will be better because of it. That's why I came for you, Austin." He picks up the paper. "Eat your eggs."

* * *

We both go up to our rooms to get our bags. When we reconvene in the parking lot, I say, "Rick . . ."

"Yeah?"

"Thanks."

"Yep." He tosses me the keys. "You drive."

So I do. Rick even falls asleep for a bit, then wakes up, and we listen to music on satellite radio, settling on an alternative station, Rick asking now and then about who we're listening to. Other than that, we go long stretches without talking. We stop at a gas station, and Rick takes over driving.

At one point, guess what comes on the radio: "Good Fun."

I change the station.

After a minute, Rick says, "This may sound weird to you."

"What?"

"Don't take it the wrong way."

"Um . . . can I make that decision after you say it?"

"Sure. You can reserve that right. The thing is, I actually really enjoy your father's music."

"Excuse me?"

"I have both his albums. I used to listen to them all the time. I saw him play live once."

I absorb that.

"What are you thinking?" he says.

"I'm thinking, yeah, that is really weird."

"Agreed. But it's true. I think your dad is, well, he's sort of a genius. *Is* a genius."

He checks the mirror and changes lanes.

"I'm about the least creative person I've ever met," says Rick. "So maybe I have more respect for it, I'm more awed by it, than other people. I sometimes think that real artists—like your dad—their job is to go to the edge and sort of report back to the rest of us. But you know what Nietzsche said about the abyss."

"I do?"

"He said something like, You stare long enough into it, and pretty soon it stares back at you."

I think about what Shane said about being on good terms with the devil without being his friend.

"So, yes, I think your father is a genius."

"I'm sorry I ever met him," I say quietly.

Rick doesn't answer.

A hundred miles later he says, "I'm not sure exactly how you regard my relationship with your mother." Sounding more like his old stiff self. "You said some rather harsh things about it, but I assumed it was because you were upset."

"Sorry. I was being an asshole."

"You sure were. But again, I understand. You know that we plan to get married."

"You asking for permission?"

"No. But I'm hoping that even if it doesn't make you happy, it's something you can at least accept."

A mile goes by before I say anything.

"Yeah, it's all right. I think it's good."

He nods, then sticks his hand out. I shake it.

And that's pretty much all the talking we do until we get home, my mother running out of the house to greet us as we crunch into the driveway.

CHAPTER 29

I can see us better now that it's all in the past tense /
it was all good fun / from a safe distance

I made it into twelfth grade. Squeaked in. A 67 on my final math exam. Rick helped me study, strings were pulled, tests retaken.

Josephine refused to speak with me for the rest of the summer. I called her, I texted her, I emailed her, I stopped by her house. Her sister answered the door and told me to go away, using language you'd never believe could come out of that beautiful face.

"I just want to talk to her."

"She doesn't want to talk to you. Go away."

"No. Can you please just go get her?"

She pulls out her phone.

"If you don't leave, I'm going to video you, and I'm going to put it online."

I left.

I did more calling, texting, emailing. No response. I'm more or less friends with Devon again, and I showed him all the drafts of my emails to get his advice. Finally he said, "Austin, face facts. She's gone. You're not going to pathetic your way back to her."

Josephine and I finally ran into each other in the hall about two weeks after school started—okay, I did a little recon and figured out her schedule and planted myself at a spot where I knew I'd see her—and we talked.

Hey.

Hey.

You good?

Yeah.

Good.

Yeah.

Shuffle shuffle throat clearing.

Then she said, "I'm still so angry at you."

"I'm so sorry," I said. "I'm just . . . I'd like to be friends, at least."

"Nope," she said. "Not yet. Maybe never."

"Because of that one time?"

"One time's plenty."

"Yeah."

More shuffling.

"I think about you every day," I said.

She sighed. "That still doesn't fix it for me."

She walked away and I watched her go.

A few weeks later, I started seeing her in the hall with Gary Eichten, who wears collared shirts and nice sweaters and is probably Ivy League bound. Sometimes we'd see each other and she'd smile at me or give a little wave, but whatever happened between us had been wrapped up and packed away somewhere very deep.

I'll think about that, and about her, and about everything that happened, for the rest of my life. Sometimes I'll be feeling good, and I'll wonder why, and I'll realize that it's because I'd forgotten about her for a bit. Then I remember and feel bad again.

I told you I was true, she said. She did say it, and I said it too, and then . . . It's the lowest thing I've ever done. I blamed it on drinking. I blamed it on Shane. I blamed it on Josephine. But it was me. Whenever I think of what I did, and the pain in her eyes when she found out, it stops me dead in my tracks like I've run smack into a wall of shame.

Alison: dating a new guy, football player, someone even larger than Todd. She winks at me sometimes in the hall. No thank you.

My mom didn't punish me for the whole New York thing. It's like she knew—better than I did, really—that whatever Austin had run away, a different one had come back. All she said was, "I'm so glad you're safe."

She and Rick got married in late September at the Lake Harriet Rose Garden. A tiny ceremony, a few of her friends, a few of his. I didn't bring a date. Devon lent me a guitar, and I played and sang "The Book of Love" for them and my mom bawled. I didn't do a much better job of keeping it together. It's hard to sing while there's snot streaming down your upper lip.

The mandolin: When I told Rick again that I would definitely pay him back, he shrugged and said, "I'm really not that concerned about it. But you will need a job."

And so Rick's Downtown Grill gained a very dedicated new dishwasher. There are team meetings. I've never missed one.

I've stopped smoking weed. Well, not stopped. It's a special-occasion thing, now, once a month. Haven't really been drinking, either. Whenever Devon's around, he won't let me: "Austin, think about it. Between your mom and your dad, you pretty much hit the genetic lottery for addiction. Give whatever brain cells you have left a break." I've been smoking a lot, though. Those burning-stick things are hard to put down.

And the music.

After a break, I started hearing it again. I still can't catch up to it. But sometimes I can get ahead of it. Because I've been writing songs, whole songs that have a beginning, middle, and end. Mostly about having your heart mushed, or having someone you love hate you. And be justified in hating you because it's your fault. Most of the songs *suuuuck*. But now sometimes at night when I hear the music, I recognize it, because I wrote it, and I say, *Aha! I got you, I got here first!*

Maybe the weirdest thing is Todd. It's sort of like we're friends now, as much as you can be friends with someone who doesn't talk much. He bought himself a cheap drum set, which he set up in my basement. He comes over a lot and we play stuff together. Sometimes he drops by when I'm not here to pound on the drums by himself. I figure he's just getting away from whatever awfulness is going on at home. Also, I think he lost a lot of friends when he up and quit the hockey team.

"Why'd you quit?"

"Piss off my dad."

We rarely discuss what happened in New York, or mention Shane. Once when his name came up I muttered something about what an asshole he turned out to be.

"Yeah, well, there's worse," said Todd.

As for the thing with Alison and me, I didn't think Todd knew about it, seeing as how I still have all my teeth. But then one day out of nowhere he stopped in the middle of a song and said, "You know what I don't get?"

"What?"

"You had Josephine. Why would you ever bother with someone like Alison?"

Which was sort of worse than him punching me.

* * *

If you watched the Grammys, you probably saw Amy perform. And if you search "Amy Adler boyfriend" you'll see pictures of her with a well-known singer who is not Shane Tyler. She sent me a nice email—*Let's not lose touch,* all that, said she'll always appreciate Shane. *But he's like the song, isn't he,* she wrote. *He's good fun from a safe distance.*

* * *

As for Shane, I've never heard anything from him.

Nothing.

No email, text, call, letter, nothing.

What did you expect? says my mom.

* * *

Shane's new album came out in early December.

I saw references to it on Pitchfork and in *Rolling Stone, Rolling Stone* giving it five out of five stars. The label released it online but also did an old-school version for the audio hipsters and elderly snobs, a vinyl version like they used to do decades ago, liner notes and all that. Other than glancing at the headlines—seeing them took me by surprise, gave me a stomachache—I made sure to ignore everything else about the album.

A few days after it comes out, I'm down in the basement, going to the edge of the abyss and creating mediocre music out of the experience. I hear a polite *ahem.*

"Sorry to interrupt," says Rick, standing in the doorway. "I thought . . . I thought perhaps you should see this."

The vinyl version of Shane's record. The cover is a moody, high-contrast concert shot of Shane, blue lighting.

"Why'd you bring that?"

"I was at the record store, poking around"—Rick being one of the elderly snobs with a turntable—"and saw it, and—well, you should take a look."

"I'd rather not."

"Okay," he says. He doesn't move.

I sigh. "Oh, all right."

He brings it to me. "Don't tell your mother I got it."

I take it from him, give it a quick once-over, and try to hand it back to him.

"No, read the other side," he says.

I flip it over. It's got the normal stuff, the track listings, credits, fine print. I don't absorb any of it.

"Congratulations," he says.

"What?"

He points to the track listings.

Among the song titles is "Rosalie."

Cowritten with Austin Methune.

I'm quiet for a second.

"Oh," I say.

"Yes," he says. "Also, look here." He points.

In small type at the lower right-hand corner of the album it says, *Dedicated to Austin Methune, my son, who helped me more than he can ever know.*

"Oh," I say.

"Yes."

* * *

The album did pretty well, and "Rosalie" was the single. It's not the version we recorded with him that day—someone else is singing the harmony, and there's more production on it. You've probably heard it a few times if you listen to any podcasts or radio that's actually worth listening to. You might also have seen him on NPR, doing one of their Tiny Desk Concerts. Or maybe you heard the interview where he talks about his confessional new album and about kicking heroin and being clean for the first time since he was fourteen and all the people he hurt who will probably never speak to him again. I think I know some of them.

In January I received a check in the mail with a printed note from the record label, explaining that the figure represented a mixture of royalties from radio and online play, as well as live performances. Not a huge amount, but an amount. Certainly far more than the zero I had earned from music before.

I got checks in February, March, April. So when Rick's birthday came around, I pooled the money with some from my mom, and we bought him a 1919 Gibson A2 mandolin, a real thing of beauty.

When he opened it, he nodded gravely and thanked me, and then said, "I'm going to give you custodial responsibility for this. That means taking care of it and playing it a lot. Do you accept?"

I accepted.

CODA

I had an ocean of words to say to you /
but they've drained away / and now I'm through

I'm neither lazy nor a coward.

Okay, fine, that's not entirely true. I'm still a bit of both, although now I'd say they have much smaller roles in the clown orchestra that is Austin Methune. The third bassoon and, I don't know, the triangle, for example.

I will, however, still do pretty much anything if a girl is watching.

But that's not why I'm doing what I'm doing now, riding my motorcycle with a mandolin strapped to my back, a mandolin that technically belongs to Rick the Lawyer. There are no girls watching. Although I *am* on my way to another encounter with Todd Malloy.

I graduated today. Another squeaker, but I did it, stood up there and got my hand shaken by the principal, and I waved at the crowd, my mom going nuts and embarrassing me. Also,

I got into a real college, the University of Minnesota, with a music scholarship, a recommendation written for me by well-respected music producer Ed Verna.

After the graduation ceremony, when everyone was milling about, I saw Josephine with her family, including first-term state senator Gerald Lindahl. Josephine got into Yale, and I heard she was leaving in a few days for a summer program in Paris, and I'd never see her again.

When we spotted each other, she came running over and gave me a big hug.

"I knew you could do it," she said.

And I said, "I still love you and I'll always love you and this makes me so sad."

And she said, "Oh," in the way you say that about something that is adorable but painful, and she gave me another hug. Then she squeezed my arm and smiled at me, the heartbreak smile, the smile you give someone when you're okay and they're not, and said, "Will you promise to keep in touch?"

I murmured something—yes, sure, of course—and she said, "Great," and gave me a third hug, and then she was gone, her receding figure getting blurrier as my eyes welled up.

I saw Mrs. Jensen. She gave me a literal pat on the head and said, "Good job, SmartTard."

There was Alex, with his parents—"We're so proud of you, Austin!"—and Devon with his—"We're so proud of you, Austin!"—who were chatting with my mom and Rick—"We're so proud of you, Austin!"—and yes, okay, I *get* it, no one expected this particular special-needs student to graduate please stop already.

And there was Todd, with . . . no one.

I don't know exactly what had been going on at Todd's place, but I do know that he was coming over more and more frequently to beat the hell out of the drums. And after a school year full of increasingly horrible crap, his dad finally left, or got kicked out. *Yesterday.* The *day before graduation.* And who knows why, but his mom didn't come to the ceremony either. So there he was, everyone hugging and celebrating, and he was glum and alone, and before I could ask him if he was coming to the big party at Devon's tonight, he had disappeared.

I called and texted him a few times and got nothing. So after dinner, when I should have been heading over to Devon's, I instead found myself grabbing the mandolin and heading over to Todd's, and here I am.

No one answers the door until the third ring. It opens, and I see Todd's mom for the first time. She looks haunted. Like she's been crying, maybe for years.

"Hi there. I'm Austin Methune. Todd's friend. Is Todd home?"

She stares at me a moment. "He's in his room." She steps back and I enter, and as she walks away she listlessly points down the hallway.

I take a gamble that his door is the one with the giant Wayne Gretzky poster on it. I knock.

"Todd? It's Austin."

Nothing.

"Todd?"

"What do you want?"

"You all right?"

"Yep."

"Want to talk or something?"

294

"Nope."

"You sure?"

"Yep."

Mr. Gretzky and I regard each other. I take the mandolin out of the case.

"Come on, Todd, come on out, don't sit in your room and pout," I sing.

Neither Wayne nor Todd responds.

"The evening's warm, the sky is clear, come on out of your room already and let's you and me go drink a nonalcoholic beeeeeer. . . ."

"Methune, get the hell out of here."

"Don't be mad, don't be sad, come hang out and you'll be glad."

Stomping footsteps. Todd violently jerks the door open and glares at me.

"Methune, if you don't get out of here with your frigging mandolin, I'll . . ."

"What?"

Todd hesitates. Then the legendary bully and one-time scourge of the Edina public school system sighs, shoulders sagging. He shakes his head. "Screw it. Nothing." He looks like he's been doing some crying of his own.

"Come on. Let's go to the party."

"I don't want to."

"You can't just sit in your room."

"Why not?"

"Because we graduated, and there's a party, and there's girls and all that."

"I told you — I don't want to go to the party."

He starts to close the door.

"Wait."

"What."

"Don't just sit here alone. Come hang out."

"And do what."

"I don't know. I've got, like, five really bad new songs we can work on."

He considers that.

"Yeah?" he says.

"Yeah," I say. "Come on, Todd. Let's go play some music."